Billionaire
Unforgettable

THE BILLIONAIRE'S OBSESSION
Tanner

J. S. SCOTT

Billionaire Unforgettable

Proof editing by Virginia Tesi Carey
Cover photo by Wander Aguiar Photography
Cover designed by Sarah Kil Creative Studio

ISBN: 979-8-343588-91-0 (Print)
ISBN: 978-1-959932-17-8 (E-Book)

Contents

Chapter 1

Hannah

"Good morning, Silas," I called out as I entered The Mug And Jug with an armful of cinnamon rolls.

It was early in the morning, but the door had been unlocked because Silas was always expecting his morning delivery.

The elderly man stepped up to the counter of the establishment that served as both a coffee shop in the morning and the local bar in the evening with a welcoming smile. "Morning, Hannah," he said. "Where's Joy today?"

I grinned back at him at the mention of my mother's name as I plopped the trays on the bar. "She said she's a little tired today," I answered. "After she finished baking, I told her I'd take the shift at Sweet Mornings."

My mom had been operating the local donut shop for decades, a little takeout store right across from The Mug And Jug on Main Street in Crystal Fork, Montana.

Delivering her cinnamon rolls to Silas to sell with his gourmet coffees in the morning had been a routine she'd followed for as long as I could remember.

Silas frowned. "Is she okay? Didn't she finish her cardiac rehab? I thought she was doing good."

My heart warmed because he looked so concerned. "She says she's fine. She told me that she got into a good movie last night and stayed up too late."

Personally, I thought that my mother deserved to retire so she could do whatever she wanted, but she said she'd be bored if she didn't spend her mornings baking and chatting with everyone at Sweet Mornings.

I worried about her a lot, especially since she'd had a heart attack that had required emergency cardiac surgery several months ago.

She *was* doing well, but I'd decided that I never wanted to be in Seattle when my mother was in Montana having emergency surgery ever again.

The time it had taken for me to get to her here in Montana had been agonizing.

Relocating back to Crystal Fork after my mom's heart attack and surgery hadn't been easy for me, but it was better than me living in Seattle and worrying about her all the time.

"Got time for a coffee and a little chat?" Silas asked with a grin.

"Always," I answered and plopped my ass on a stool at the bar. "I'll have the usual, and I'd appreciate the chat since you're about the only person who's nice to me in this town these days."

The older man shot me a questioning glance as he started making me a latte. "That can't possibly be true. You're one of the sweetest and prettiest girls in this town."

I rolled my eyes.

I wasn't a girl. I was thirty-four years old, but maybe I seemed young to a man who had already seen his eightieth birthday in the rearview mirror.

I adored Silas, but I was also immune to his flirtatious compliments, no matter how well-meaning they were.

I finally shrugged. "Everyone seems to think that I dumped one of Crystal Fork's heroes and ran off with another man to Seattle. There aren't very many people who like me here anymore."

"Do you want my advice?" Silas queried.

I tried not to smile because I knew that however I answered his question, I was going to get that advice, whether I wanted it…or not.

I'd known Silas all my life, and he was known for giving advice to anyone who would listen.

"Sure," I shot back and was rewarded with an approving smile.

"Ignore them," he advised. "People in this town think they know the truth about everyone's business, but they don't know squat. Honestly, what happened between you and Tanner is old news. It was a long time ago. They'll get over it when they see that you haven't changed a bit."

Honestly, I *had* changed. I wasn't the same woman who had been engaged to Tanner Remington years ago.

I sighed as Silas slid the coffee across the bar to me. "Nobody really wants to give me that chance of becoming reacquainted, unfortunately."

Tanner and I had both grown up here in Crystal Fork. He was almost five years older than me, so we'd never really known each other when we were younger. He'd gone off to college, and I'd moved to New York City to go to cosmetology school right after high school. We'd pretty much been strangers when we'd met up in New York as adults.

Tanner had finished college, relocated to New York, and had started a new job on Wall Street.

I'd just started my first job as a cosmetologist at the time.

Since my mother and his mother were close friends, they suggested that we meet up so I could introduce Tanner to more of New York City.

That casual coffee meetup between Tanner and me in New York had turned into a seven year relationship for the two of us.

I'd spent the majority of my twenties with Tanner.

He and his two brothers had built their own business during our time in New York, and I'd advanced my career in cosmetology by learning as many extra skills as possible.

We'd gotten engaged before the two of us moved back to Crystal Fork together after Tanner's older brother, Kaleb, had relocated the KTD Remington headquarters back to Montana.

Our relationship had ended badly, but I wasn't exactly a villain because I'd left Tanner, and I definitely hadn't left him for another man.

The people in this town assumed what they wanted to assume.

I'd grown up with a lot of the people in this town, and they were good people, but they lived in a small world. Gossiping and speculating was a ritual in Crystal Fork.

"Have you talked to Tanner at all since you moved back home?" Silas questioned.

I curled my hands around the warm mug. "No," I said flatly. "I think it's better if we don't. He goes out of his way to avoid me most of the time, and I really have nothing to say to him. We've both moved on. Like you said, it's been a long time."

If Tanner had something to say, he could have contacted me in Seattle, but he hadn't. He still spoke to my mother when he saw her, but he'd never once asked her about me. She'd known exactly where I was, and knowing my mom, she would have given Tanner any information he'd wanted.

"It wouldn't hurt for the two of you to talk about it if it's really water under the bridge, Hannah. Maybe you can get some kind of closure."

My stomach twisted at the thought of actually discussing my heartbreak with Tanner Remington.

Breaking up with him had nearly destroyed me, and I wanted to leave that pain in the past.

"Why?" I asked right before I took a sip of the coffee.

I let the taste of a good coffee roll over my tastebuds, closing my eyes for a moment because Silas's coffee was *that good*.

I'd lived in Seattle for seven years, but I'd never had a cup of coffee as good as The Mug And Jug could brew up, and that was saying something since Seattle was known for their coffee.

"Why?" Silas repeated. "Maybe I think he owes it to you to set the record straight in this town. If people knew you were on good terms with each other, maybe they'd stop ignoring you like you were at fault."

Silas was one of the few people in town who knew my side of the story, and I loved him for defending me, but I didn't want to renew my acquaintance with Tanner Remington.

"It doesn't matter," I said softly. "I'll probably move to Billings once I convince myself that Mom is really okay. I'll still be close enough to her that we can still see each other often."

"Wouldn't you rather be able to see her almost every day?" Silas asked.

I fiddled with the handle of the mug. "You know I do. Her heart attack scared me to death, and she's all I have. I guess that really woke me up to the fact that I wasn't spending enough time with her, and that she was getting older. I think sometimes we get so involved with work and life that we forget what's really important."

My mother and I had always been close, and she'd been so happy when I'd moved back to Cystal Fork the first time with Tanner.

However, she'd been the first one to encourage me to take a great opportunity in Seattle when Tanner and I had broken up, even though she'd rather have me closer.

She'd wanted me to be happy, even if that meant that I'd be moving eight hundred miles away from her.

My only parent had always wanted what was best for *me* first.

Now it was time for me to think about what was best for *her.*

I was her only child, a daughter she thought she'd never have until she finally got pregnant in her thirties.

She'd raised me well, and she'd done it alone because we'd lost my dad when I was an infant.

Mom had just celebrated her seventieth birthday.

Granted, she was extremely independent and capable, but after that scare with her heart attack and her cardiac surgery, I wanted to spend as much time with her as I possibly could.

Even if that meant that I'd have to deal with the life and the heart-ache I'd left behind in Crystal Fork years ago.

"The older you get, the faster time seems to pass by," Silas pondered. "Joy will love having you closer to her, but she doesn't want to see you miserable in a place where you're not comfortable."

I swallowed more of my coffee before I answered, "That's just it. I've always loved it here. I missed Crystal Fork and the people here. I guess I didn't expect to be treated like a pariah. Everyone adores the Remingtons, and I'm basically an outsider now."

"I'm not defending the way that people are treating you, Hannah, but he was pretty heartbroken. He wasn't himself after it happened, but he never wanted to talk about it," Silas mentioned. "I still think you should talk to him. He could set the record straight."

"I'm not sure *he* knows what happened," I confessed reluctantly.

"Then maybe you can set him straight on the whole thing," Silas suggested. "He broke your heart, and he still thinks you left him for someone else."

"I got over it," I informed Silas. "And I'm not the same woman that I was seven years ago, Silas."

He shook his head. "I think you're exactly the same woman you were seven years ago. You just hide that soft heart of yours better than you used to."

Ha! I didn't just hide it. I'd shoved that part of myself that had loved Tanner more than life itself so deep that it would never see the light of day again.

Our relationship was part of my past, and I'd probably never let myself be that vulnerable to anyone again.

"I grew up," I told Silas before I swallowed the last of my coffee.

I'd left Crystal Fork devastated, but I'd found success in Seattle beyond my wildest dreams.

I'd gone to Seattle to start a business with two cosmetologists that I'd known in New York, and we'd built that business into something special and lucrative.

Giving up my partnership in that business had been one of the hardest things I'd ever done, but I'd had to do it to make the move back to Crystal Fork.

I'd lost that identity and reputation that I'd worked so hard for in Seattle, but the experience and confidence it had given me was still incredibly valuable to me.

"If it means anything, I think you grew up way quicker than Tanner," Silas mumbled. "But he seems to have his priorities straight and his head more together now."

I took a quick look at the clock over the bar before I leaned forward and gave Silas a quick kiss on the cheek. "I have to go. I need to open the store soon."

Sweet Mornings opened early and usually closed by early afternoon because my mother ran out of donuts.

"You call me if you need anything," Silas insisted. "I'm right across the street."

My heart warmed because of the sincerity in his gaze.

"Thanks for the advice and the coffee," I told him with a smile.

"I've got more of the same whenever you want it."

I wanted to kiss the older man again for being so kind to me.

Probably because kindness from the people in Crystal Fork was in very short supply for me right now.

Chapter 2

Tanner

"Anything else I can get for you boys?" Charlie asked as I pushed my empty plate away from me so she could collect it easier.

I shook my head, and then looked at my two brothers, Kaleb and Devon.

I was stuffed full of the best biscuits and gravy in Montana.

"I'm full," my older brother Kaleb said as he handed his own empty plate to Charlie. "It was an amazing breakfast as usual, Charlie."

"Agreed," my younger brother Devon said as Charlie took his plate. "Thanks, Charlie."

"No need to thank me. Breakfast is the least I can do for you three since you're headed out to my farm to work on my chicken coop," she said gratefully.

My brothers and I had stopped at Charlie's restaurant for breakfast before we headed out to her farm. It was Saturday, and my brothers and I had stopped going to our offices in Billings on the weekends unless it was an emergency a long time ago.

❧ ∂ ❧

The older woman had a very large flock of chickens to keep her restaurant stocked with fresh eggs, and she had a large chicken coop that needed repairs before winter set in.

One of the things I liked about Crystal Fork was the way everyone stepped up to help each other when something needed to get done. There would be more people out on the farm to help, all of them willing to work until that chicken coop was like new again.

Granted, living in a small town meant that everyone knew your business, but if work needed to get done, they'd all step up to help.

Charlie was beloved by everyone in Crystal Fork. She owned the only great place to eat in town, and she treated her customers like family.

Unfortunately, she'd lost her husband to a stroke years ago, and her son lived out of state, so when Charlie needed something, she never even had to ask.

I actually enjoyed working outside after spending the week in my office, so I was always up for helping people with outside work on the weekends.

I grinned at Charlie. "You really didn't need to bribe us with breakfast to get us to go out and work on your chicken coop."

"Speak for yourself," Devon quipped. "I'm never going to turn down a good breakfast here."

Charlie beamed at my younger brother. "Like I already told you, breakfast is on the house."

Kaleb looked like he was going to argue, but stopped himself from saying something at the last minute.

Arguing with Charlie was pointless, and we all knew it. She was sweet, but she could be as stubborn as a mule when she wanted to be. It didn't matter to her that we were all billionaires and could definitely afford to pay for our own breakfast.

"We'll leave a large tip," I told Kaleb quietly as Charlie wandered away with our empty plates.

"That's the plan," Kaleb agreed before he took a slug of his coffee.

"What is Anna doing today while you're working out at Charlie's farm?" Devon asked Kaleb curiously.

Kaleb had recently married Annelise Kendrick, one of the most famous pop stars on the planet. It was probably more difficult for him to be away from home on a Saturday than it was for Devon and me because my older brother was the only one of us who was now married.

Kaleb was living in wedded bliss, and he liked being home with Anna on the weekends.

"She didn't seem particularly disappointed that I'd be gone," Kaleb grumbled unhappily. "She's going to Billings with Mom later to do some shopping."

I smirked because my brother sounded offended that his wife was making the best of her time away from him.

Truthfully, Anna was as in love with Kaleb as he was with her, but she was an independent, highly successful woman who was used to spending time on her own.

Anna had lost her own parents, and she had grown exceptionally close to our mother.

"You'll survive for one day without her," Devon said unsympathetically. "You two were together constantly on your honeymoon. The disgustingly sweet pictures of you two are almost nauseating. That much togetherness would drive me crazy."

Kaleb and Anna had just returned from that honeymoon. They'd escaped to a secluded villa in Italy to maintain some of their privacy. People here were getting used to having a celebrity like Anna in their town, and they adored Anna as a person.

However, she was generally mobbed in other places in the US if she was recognized.

I didn't agree with my cynical younger brother about the pictures of their honeymoon.

Kaleb and Anna had looked joyful in those pictures, and I was glad he'd found the woman who could make him *that* happy.

I'd experienced a love like that at one time.

Devon hadn't, so he had no idea how the right woman in a man's life could be everything to him.

My relationship hadn't worked out, but I didn't resent the fact that my older brother's had.

As weird as the pairing of a pop star and a billionaire from Montana might seem, Kaleb and Anna were perfect for each other.

"You're just jealous because no woman wants to put up with your crabby ass," Kaleb joked.

"I don't want a woman glued to my hip every day," Devon argued. "Being with the same woman day in and day out would make me completely insane. I happen to like my freedom."

I wasn't quite sure that was true.

The truth was that Devon had never found a woman who made him so obsessed that he didn't *want* to be away from her.

Hell, I'd felt that way once, and having it end badly had nearly killed me.

Like Devon, I was perfectly all right with being alone now.

"We'd better head out," Kaleb said before he drained the last of his coffee, totally ignoring Devon's comment about women. "That chicken coop isn't going to repair itself."

I nodded, and then felt my phone vibrate in the pocket of my jeans.

I pulled it out of my pocket and stared at the text for a moment in surprise.

"Something wrong?" Devon asked.

"It's Mom," I grumbled.

"She okay?" Kaleb asked, his voice concerned.

"Yeah," I said distractedly. "She asked me to pick her up some apple fritters from Sweet Mornings before I head out to the farm."

It was a weird request.

Number one...my mother was best friends with Joy Griffin, the woman who owned the donut shop. If she wanted donuts, she'd hop into her vehicle and get them so she could chat with Joy.

Number two...Mom loved to bake, and she always had more muffins and cookies around the house than she could eat herself.

And number three...she rarely asked one of her sons for help with anything. She was an independent woman who did whatever she wanted when she wanted to do it.

"Since when does our mother have cravings for apple fritters?" Devon questioned with a frown.

I shrugged. "It's not a big deal. I'll grab them, drop them off at the ranch, and meet you two out at Charlie's farm. It's basically on the way. Maybe that's why she asked."

Mom's ranch was outside of town, essentially on the same back highway we had to take to get to Charlie's place.

Joy Griffin was my ex-fiancée's mother, but there had never been any hard feelings between the two of us.

Kaleb shook his head as he stood. "I still think her request *is* a little odd. When is the last time Mom asked us to get donuts for her from Sweet Mornings?"

Um…the answer to that question would be…never.

"She never asks for anything," Devon affirmed as he slid out of the booth and stood. "She's stubborn. She does everything herself."

I quickly texted my mother, stood up, and shoved my cell back into my pocket.

All of us dropped a hefty tip that would cover the cost of the breakfast and a large tip on the table before we headed outside.

Charlie's was busy on Saturday morning, and there were people waiting for a table who would be more than happy that we were vacating the booth.

"I don't mind," I told my brothers. "She doesn't ask for much. It's not a problem."

Honestly, I'd be happy if my mother would let us do more for her.

After my father had passed away four years ago, she'd decided to lease a lot of the ranch's land to other farmers and ranchers, but there was still plenty for her to do alone around the property.

She insisted that caring for her home and a few horses wasn't a burden, but she wasn't getting any younger, and we didn't see it that way.

"She's up to something," Devon warned.

I shrugged. "She wants me to drop off some donuts. I don't know how something like that can have some kind of ulterior motive."

Devon shot me a dubious glance as we walked out of the restaurant. "If Mom is doing something out of the ordinary, there has to be something behind it."

"It is unusual for her," Kaleb said thoughtfully as he unlocked his vehicle. "But I have to agree with Tanner. Getting her donuts isn't exactly a nefarious request. You're being paranoid, Devon."

"Don't say that I didn't warn you," Devon grumbled as he walked to his vehicle parked next to Kaleb's. "Bring us some donuts."

"We just ate breakfast," I reminded him.

"I'll be hungry in a few hours," he answered.

Kaleb grinned. "I like the chocolate bars, cream filled."

"I'll get enough for the whole crew," I said as I left, walking toward Main Street.

Sweet Mornings was just down the street. There was no point in taking my SUV.

After the huge breakfast I'd just consumed, and considering the donuts I was going to eat later, I probably needed the exercise.

The small town was bustling because it was a weekend.

It was after nine, so all of the shops were open, and small groups of people were gathered on the sidewalks to trade gossip and news.

It was fall in Montana, but we'd been blessed with an incredibly warm fall this year, and everyone liked being able to be outside for extended periods of time when the weather was decent.

Crystal Fork was a typical small town. I didn't know everyone personally, but I was familiar with a lot of the faces because I'd grown up here.

I'd said "good morning" to a lot of people by the time I reached Sweet Mornings.

The folks around here might be into everyone's business, but most of them were welcoming and polite.

I stopped short as the glass door to Sweet Mornings came into view.

"Fuck!" I cursed under my breath as I saw who was manning the counter this morning.

Hannah.

My ex had been back in town since her mother had suffered a heart attack several months ago.

We'd managed to avoid running into each other directly for months now.

Devon's ominous warning floated through my head as I stared at the beautiful, dark haired woman at the counter of Sweet Mornings.

Now I was skeptical, too.

Had my mother somehow known that Hannah would be here?

That theory made sense because she was so close to Hannah's mother, Joy.

I can't just stand outside like an idiot.

People around me were starting to stare and put the pieces together as to why I was hesitant to enter the bakery.

Hannah Griffin had been out of my life for over seven years.

We meant nothing to each other anymore.

It's not like we can avoid each other forever.

From what I'd heard, she was back in Montana for good, and I wasn't going anywhere.

It would be helpful if seeing her didn't faze me anymore, but I'd be lying to myself if I tried to say that some of the memories of us didn't still haunt me just a little.

I gritted my teeth and headed toward the door of Sweet Mornings, determined not to let the fact that Hannah was here completely ruin my day.

Chapter 3

Hannah

My heart sank to my feet when I saw Tanner enter Sweet Mornings.

Shit! Shit! Shit!

He stood in line behind the family I was currently serving, and it didn't look like he was about to leave because I was the one working the counter this morning.

What in the hell was Tanner Remington doing here?

He'd never frequented the donut shop.

He was more likely to go to The Mug And Jug for coffee and a cinnamon roll, or to Charlie's for breakfast.

I tried to keep my composure as I checked out the customers in front of him, keeping a smile plastered on my face as I gave them their change.

Don't panic, Hannah. This isn't a big deal.

I could serve him just like I took care of other customers.

Unfortunately, as the previous customers left and Tanner stepped forward, it *felt* like a very big deal.

Sweet Mornings was essentially a small storefront with bakery cases and a small baking kitchen in the back room.

The place was way too small for the likes of Tanner Remington.

It felt like his huge presence sucked all of the oxygen from the small space.

My heart literally ached as I turned my fixed smile toward him.

Dammit! I hated the way that Tanner's muscular body and gorgeous face could still get to me.

"Tanner," I acknowledged because doing anything else would be ridiculous. "What can I get for you?"

I could hardly pretend that he was a stranger.

The two of us had a past that spanned over seven years together.

"I need some donuts," he said in that deep baritone that made my female hormones stand at attention.

I froze for a moment, transfixed because it had been so many years since I'd actually heard that sexy voice of his.

He was dressed casually in jeans and a long-sleeved T-shirt just like I was, and he looked so good to me that my heart tripped.

Stop it, Hannah! You're acting like a fool.

I wasn't going to moon over a guy who had nearly destroyed me years ago.

"I figured that was why you were here," I said, forcing a cool tone from my lips even though my heart was racing.

"Mom sent me here for apple fritters, which is something she'd never normally ask me to do," he said huskily. "Why are you here today?"

"My mother was tired," I replied politely. "I told her I'd work the counter today."

"Do you think this was a set-up?" he asked with a rueful smile.

Surprise rolled over me as I realized what he was asking.

My mother never complained of tiredness, and his mother had probably never asked for apple fritters.

Millie had never been particularly fond of donuts.

"You think the two of them conspired to get us to talk to each other?" I asked.

He shrugged his broad shoulders. "It wouldn't exactly surprise me. They are best friends."

Crap! Now that he mentioned it, I had to agree that it wasn't impossible.

Like Silas, Mom had encouraged me to face Tanner and deal with our past to stop the gossip about the two of us.

Tanner explained what he wanted for his mother and the crew of people that were going to be working on Charlie's farm today. I started to box up his order, happy to have something to look at other than his handsome self.

"People think I'm still heartbroken," Tanner said conversationally.

"And they think I'm a bitch," I shot back as I loaded donuts into a box. "Everyone hates me around here because they think I broke your heart."

"Didn't you?" he asked smoothly. "You did leave me, Hannah."

God, I really hadn't wanted to get into our past, but his comment made me so irritated that I retorted, "For a very good reason."

Luckily, there was no one else in the store to hear us bickering.

"What reason?" Tanner demanded. "I was on a business trip in Tokyo. When I got back, you were gone. You left for Seattle the day before I got back."

"I told you on the phone that I was leaving. You told me to do whatever made me happy," I said icily as I put an apple fritter in a box with more force than was necessary.

"Not possible," he answered in an annoyed tone. "If you had said you were leaving, I would have done everything possible to make sure that didn't happen."

My anger started to fizzle away.

Like I'd suspected, he had no idea what I'd said that day. His answer had been automatic because he hadn't been listening to what I'd said.

"You didn't hear what I was saying, Tanner," I said in a calmer voice. "It had been that way with us for a while. Your company was everything to you and your brothers. You were so distracted with world domination after Kaleb set up your headquarters in Billings that you never noticed that I wasn't happy. I tried to talk to you. You just weren't listening."

I'd loved being back in Crystal Fork, but there was very little opportunity for my profession here. I ended up working with Tina at her shop in Crystal Fork doing old style perms and haircuts.

Maybe that would have been enough for me if my relationship with Tanner hadn't gotten so broken. Maybe I would have eventually sought out something else in Billings if Tanner hadn't completely changed once we'd moved back to Montana.

The last time we'd talked when he was in Tokyo, I'd told him that if things didn't improve between the two of us, I had to go.

When he'd told me to do whatever made me happy, I suspected he hadn't been listening.

He hadn't been listening to me for a very long time, and I'd gotten to the point where I couldn't take it anymore.

I'd felt disregarded and unloved, and feeling that way had been slowly killing me.

"Maybe I was a little distracted," he admitted reluctantly. "But I would have heard you if you'd told me how you felt."

I rolled my eyes.

The man was still in total denial about what had happened.

"You didn't," I said flatly as I sealed one of the boxes. "I'd been trying to get you to hear me for a long time. You were completely obsessed with KTD Remington. I got that. You, Kaleb, and Devon had built that company from nothing. You wanted to succeed. I waited on the sidelines and supported you, but I finally realized that I was never going to come first with you anymore, no matter how successful you became."

"You always came first, Hannah," Tanner said gruffly.

"Did I?" I asked, shooting him a pointed stare. "Do you realize that the last time I talked to you was my birthday? I didn't want a gift. You'd given me so many material things, and we were building our home. Maybe I just wanted you to acknowledge the fact that you remembered."

It hadn't always been that way with Tanner.

We'd spent a lot of blissful, meaningful years together before his intense obsession with KTD's success.

Once KTD had started its rapid rise to success, everything had gone downhill from there.

I didn't mind that he had to travel.

I didn't mind that he was a little distracted sometimes.

What I did mind was the complete and utter disregard that he showed me once he became successful.

It had slowly and painfully ripped my heart out.

I tried to be patient and give him some time to adjust to his success.

I'd hoped that he'd go back to appreciating what we'd had.

Unfortunately, that had never happened.

"Did I really forget your birthday?" Tanner asked hesitantly.

"Yes," I answered simply. "Just like you forgot a lot of other personal things. We were building a home together. You couldn't even be bothered to give me any input. We were also planning a wedding, but you never wanted to discuss an actual date."

"I wanted you to do whatever you wanted," he protested.

"And now you're probably living in a home that I planned and decorated," I answered drily.

Tanner and I had never lived in his home together. It was close to completion when I'd left, but we'd still had another few months before it would be ready.

Our wedding had also been planned, but those plans were never really executed since he'd put off setting a date.

"I always thought there was someone else," Tanner told me.

My head shot up and I met his earnest gaze. "Seriously?" I said in a disappointed voice.

I'd been so crazy in love with Tanner Remington that I'd never looked at another man after we'd met.

He'd been my everything for over seven years after that.

"Yes," he answered grumpily. "You didn't even leave a note or any explanation. I overheard your mother mention to someone that she thought you'd be happy in Seattle. I assumed that meant that you'd be happy with someone else."

Obviously, Tanner had never asked my mother for specifics or he would have found out the truth.

"I wasn't," I said as I pushed the boxes of donuts toward him. "I mean, I was happy, but not with another man. A woman doesn't just get over a very long relationship to skip off with another guy. Well, maybe some women can, but you should have known me better than that."

"I wasn't exactly thinking rationally at the time," he confessed in a graveled voice.

I shook my head as I took the credit card he offered me for the donuts. "It's over, Tanner. It was over a long time ago. Sometimes priorities change. People change. We were young when we got together. I was barely twenty, and you hadn't been out of college for long. Maybe I just wasn't what you needed anymore."

God, it was still hard to say those words, but it was probably the truth.

"That's not true," Tanner said irritably.

I held up a hand. "This happened a long time ago. We're different people now. It doesn't matter. I think we've both moved on."

"Is that really how you feel?" he questioned.

"Yes," I lied. "We don't mean anything to each other anymore, but I'm glad you know now that I wasn't fleeing with another guy."

At that point, I'd do or say almost anything not to have to talk about our old life anymore.

Leaving Tanner had been the hardest thing I'd ever done, and as much as I wanted to deny it, talking about that time in my life did still hurt.

He picked up the boxes looking like he had more to say, but another customer walked through the door before he could say another word.

"Have a good day, Tanner," I said, just like I'd say to any other customer.

He ran a hand through his wavy brown hair, his gorgeous blue eyes swirling with some kind of emotion I couldn't completely decipher.

"You, too, Hannah," he finally said politely. "It was good to see you again."

Without another word, he turned and left.

I let out a sigh of relief, and it took me a moment to pull myself together enough to greet the next customer.

Well, at least we'd broken the ice between the two of us.

We probably wouldn't have to go out of our way to avoid each other anymore.

Maybe I should be happy about that, but seeing Tanner again, hearing his voice, and talking to him had shaken me up more than I'd thought it would.

Tanner

"I can't believe you just set me up like that," I grumbled to my mother as I sat her damn apple fritters on her kitchen counter.

Her eyes widened as she answered, "I have no idea what you're talking about."

She knew exactly what I was talking about, and her innocent expression wasn't fooling me. "You sent me to Sweet Mornings knowing full well that Hannah was helping her mom out today."

I loved and respected my mother, but this stunt was way out of line.

"Oh, Hannah was there?" she asked, trying to keep up her pretense.

I turned to face her, but she wouldn't quite look me in the eyes.

I glared at her. "You knew she was there. Cut the innocent act, Mother. You and Joy planned this. You wanted the two of us to meet face-to-face. The question is...why? What was the point?"

I was still mulling over Hannah's statements, and I wasn't sure what to think.

I'd spent the last seven years assuming she'd taken off with another man.

It was the only explanation I could think of for her quickly leaving town like that without a word.

Fuck! Had I really been ignorant about her motivations all those years ago?

The Hannah I'd known wasn't a liar, but then again, from the moment she'd up and left like that, I'd assumed I hadn't ever known the *real* Hannah.

My mother finally met my gaze, and she looked irritated as she dropped the pretense. "It was time, Tanner. The people in this town have treated Hannah poorly since she came back to Crystal Fork. They're assuming that *she* broke *your* heart."

"She did," I informed her.

Mom rolled her eyes. "No one would know that judging from your behavior after she left. You never discussed it. Even mentioning Hannah's name after she left was off-limits. I love you, son, but you're an idiot sometimes."

I frowned at her. I was thirty-nine years old, and in all of those years, my mother had never called me an idiot. "I didn't want to talk about it."

It had taken me years to even open up to my brothers about my suspicions that Hannah had left me for another man, and my broken heart wasn't something I'd really wanted to discuss with my mother.

I was bitter and angry right after Hannah had left. Anything I would have said back then wasn't something for my mother's ears.

"You didn't want to talk about much of anything except business," she told me. "Hannah was supportive of you and patient. But there's only so much a woman can handle before she's just…done. I won't claim that I know everything that went on between you and Hannah, but I was here, Tanner. I saw the obsession you and your brothers had with KTD Remington. There was no room for anyone or anything that would distract you three from your goals. There was no room for Hannah in your life anymore."

"That's not true," I said angrily. "I loved her. I was going to marry her. We were building a life here in Crystal Fork."

"Hannah was trying to build a life here," my mother said, disgusted. "You were never here, and when you were here physically, your mind was someplace else. You can't take a woman for granted for that long and not expect her to feel unappreciated and unwanted. She moved back here for you, Tanner. Because *you* needed to move here when Kaleb established the headquarters here. Her career opportunities were limited, but she loved you."

I raked a frustrated hand through my hair. "I know she had a thriving career in New York. I told her I'd make that up to her somehow."

Hannah had built a huge clientele at a salon in Manhattan. She was well known there for her creativity and her variety of skills. She'd had her own ambitions, and she'd worked her ass off to get trained in every up and coming trend in the market.

"And how did that 'making it up to her' thing go for you?" she questioned drily.

I leaned back against the kitchen counter and tried to remember what exactly I had done to make it up to her.

Honestly, I didn't remember talking about it with Hannah after we'd moved to Montana.

"I don't recall," I said truthfully. "She was working at our salon here."

"And she hated it," Mom informed me. "Hannah was up on all of the latest techniques and skills, and Tina was, and still is, old school. If Hannah suggested anything, her ideas were shot down immediately. You know this town doesn't really like change. People who want services that are more creative go to Billings."

"She should have talked to me about it," I said thoughtfully.

"She did," my mother answered. "I think your favorite response was to tell Hannah to do whatever made her happy. You were never listening to her, Tanner, and that went on for a very long time. Can you really blame her for finally giving up? Plants and flowers need some kind of attention to thrive. Relationships are no different. Your father and I were married for decades, but we never forgot to be available to listen to each other without distractions. If you don't, a relationship will wither and die."

I pulled out one of the kitchen chairs and sat at the table. "Shit!" I cursed. "Is that really what happened? I thought that Hannah had found someone else. She just…left. Without a single word."

For once, my mother didn't bother to scold me for cursing.

She sat down across from me with a somber expression. "She was withering and dying, Tanner. She had to do something to save herself. There was never anyone else. She was crazy in love with you."

I wanted to stay pissed off, but none of this was Mom's fault. "I wish I would have known this seven years ago."

She shook her head. "You weren't ready to listen, and I'm not sure it would have made a difference back then. Your head was somewhere else."

"I loved Hannah," I protested.

"But you didn't learn to appreciate what you had," she shot back. "I'm sure you thought you'd have plenty of time to spoil her and listen to her in the future, after you'd built KTD into a mega holding company. But putting love on hold indefinitely wasn't fair to her, Tanner. Now, she's back in Crystal Fork and being treated horribly for something that wasn't her mistake." She let out a long sigh. "Maybe I shouldn't have set you up, but I guess I was hoping that if you two started being friendly, people would treat her better. Forgive me?"

I let out a long breath as I nodded. "I understand why you did it. But next time, just talk to me first."

I couldn't stay angry at my mother for something I'd done.

To be truthful, I probably was a major dick to Hannah, and I hated myself for that.

For years, she'd been my rock, and I'd taken that for granted.

She'd always been there for me while KTD was growing in New York.

There had been times when she'd come home from a long shift at work, and then get dressed up to go wherever I needed her to be as my date while I was climbing the ladder on Wall Street.

She'd made *my* career her priority, but when had I been there to support her hopes and dreams?

Hannah and I had been together for so long that I hadn't appreciated all of the things she'd done to build my career.

"When Dad died," I said slowly. "I realized how much I'd always taken for granted."

It had never occurred to me that he could suddenly die one day from a heart attack and not be there anymore.

My father's death had been a punch to the gut for me and for my brothers.

Since then, we'd all learned a huge lesson about letting our company rule our lives.

Mom reached out and gently touched my forearm. "You've all changed, and I'm grateful for that. I'm proud of all of you, and I know you have good hearts. You just got lost in your phenomenal success for a while. Everyone makes mistakes, Tanner. Don't beat yourself up forever for that."

"I lost track of the fact that Hannah was my entire life," I drawled. "I'd say that was a pretty huge mistake."

"It's not about the mistakes we make in life, Tanner. It's what we do about them after that mistake is made that matters."

She was right, and I was going to fix this situation as soon as possible.

Hannah needed to be treated right in this town, and I was going to make damn sure that happened.

"Has she gotten a job yet?" I asked my mother. Obviously, she knew far more about Hannah's life than I did.

That was another thing I was going to resolve as soon as possible.

"Tina has been treating her like dirt," my mother answered sadly. "But I'm not sure she'd go back there anyway. Joy said that she's doing freelance jobs right now. Most of them are out of the area since she isn't highly regarded here in Crystal Fork. She had a very successful business in Seattle. A partnership with two other cosmetologists. They went to the clients for events, most of them large weddings for some very important people. Those three girls built up quite a reputation. Joy said they were so busy that they took on contractors to do different events across the state. Hannah sold her third of the partnership to move back here to Crystal Fork, so I don't think she's hurting financially. I'm sure that wasn't an easy decision for her, but being close to her mother was her priority after Joy's heart attack."

I wasn't surprised that she'd made that choice. The Hannah I'd known had always put other people first.

I also wasn't shocked that she'd been incredibly successful in Seattle.

Hannah was highly intelligent and hardworking. One of her biggest assets was her ability to connect with people.

She was also very capable of being a savvy businesswoman.

Unfortunately, I'd never put as much faith in her as she'd always put in me.

But obviously she'd thrived just fine without my support.

"I know that look, Tanner," my mother said in a teasing voice. "What are you thinking?"

I grinned at her. "I'm thinking it's time for Hannah and me to become friends. I hate the fact that people in this town need my approval to treat her right, but if that's what it takes, I'll happily do it."

Mom sent me a doubtful look. "That might not be as easy as you think. She's going to be wary."

I shrugged. "Then I guess I'll just have to prove to her that I've changed."

Truthfully, I *had* changed.

I knew what my priorities were now.

Yeah, I still worked hard at our offices in Billings every day, but I knew when to stop working and pay attention to what was really important.

My brothers and I owned one of the biggest holding companies in the world, and we were all billionaires.

When our father had died, we'd all realized what we'd sacrificed for that kind of success.

We'd all decided to get a damn life and spend more time doing what was important to us.

We usually didn't let much time go by without talking to Mom and spending time with the people we cared about.

I wished that I had learned that lesson before Hannah had been forced to leave.

"Do you think she'll believe that you've changed?" Mom questioned.

"She'll believe it," I said gruffly.

I was going to put my single-minded stubbornness toward something important this time, and I didn't plan on failing.

Chapter 5

Hannah

I closed my laptop and rose from the small kitchen table in my apartment after I'd finished answering my email.

I had put up a basic website for my freelancing, and I checked my email often, hoping I'd start to get more bookings.

Work was slow for me, which was a huge change from what I was used to in Seattle.

My lifestyle had been almost hectic there, and my business had been so crazy that I rarely had any free time with nothing to do in Seattle.

Now, I didn't know what to do with myself when I didn't have a freelance gig here.

I got an occasional event here in Montana because of my reputation in Seattle, which usually meant I had to travel somewhere within the state.

I was used to traveling. Our business had taken us everywhere in Washington before we'd hired contractors in various cities so we could expand.

What I *wasn't* used to was being idle for any length of time.

Mom didn't really need me to take care of her anymore, and having so much free time was making me completely insane.

My small apartment was so clean I could eat off the floors if I wanted to, and my cupboards were so organized it was ridiculous. There was only so much I could do in a small, one bedroom apartment.

I really missed my friends and my partners in Seattle.

We'd always made time at least once or twice a week for dinner together or a night out.

I had my mother here in Crystal Fork, which was my priority, but I was still lonely. I missed having things to do and places to go all the time.

Things in Crystal Fork moved at a much slower pace, and there wasn't much to do for a single woman without friends on a Saturday evening.

I sighed as I opened the fridge and pulled out a bottle of white wine that I'd picked up at the store.

I'd had a discussion with Mom about the way she'd set me up to meet with Tanner in person this morning.

Honestly, she'd been pretty unremorseful about the whole thing.

In the end, it was hard for me to stay mad at her because she'd been trying to help me. And that meeting with Tanner had been inevitable since we lived in the same small town.

It wasn't like I would have been able to avoid meeting up with him at some point.

I just wished I'd been a little more prepared for that encounter.

I also wished that I'd handled it a little better.

In Seattle, I'd convinced myself that Tanner meant nothing to me anymore.

He *should* mean nothing to me since it had been over seven years since we'd broken up.

Unfortunately, I guessed that I was still carrying some baggage from that relationship.

Maybe that wasn't so unusual since Tanner Remington had been such a huge part of my life for so long.

I was still trying to wrap my head around the fact that he'd thought I'd left him for another guy.

Maybe I should have left a note or some kind of explanation, but trying to communicate with Tanner back then had seemed pretty useless.

I poured myself a glass of wine and reached for one of the donuts that my mother had convinced me to take home from Sweet Mornings earlier in the day.

Mom didn't eat her own donuts anymore. She was on a heart healthy diet now, so she made sure any leftovers at the store went to someone else after the store closed.

I'd already demolished one of those huge donuts earlier, and if I kept eating leftovers from Sweet Mornings, my butt wouldn't fit into my jeans anymore.

I was one of those women who wasn't blessed with a fast metabolism.

I'd been overweight when I was younger, until the beginning of my senior year in high school. I'd gotten a used mountain bike with the money I'd saved from an after-school job. I'd ridden almost every day, and I'd fallen in love with that hobby.

Over time, that extra weight had slowly melted off from frequent exercise and less time spent indoors eating.

To stay fit, I had to be active, and I had to watch my carbs.

Today, I was watching my carbs…right before I ate them.

Unfortunately, I could be a stress eater sometimes.

Things will get better. I'll get more work eventually, and I'll be busier than I am right now.

I just hoped that happened before I ate an entire store full of donuts.

I startled a little when a text came in on my phone because the apartment was so quiet and the phone was right next to me on the counter.

My eyes widened when I opened the text.

Tanner: *Hi, Hannah. It's Tanner. Meet me at The Mug And Jug around eight?*

What in the hell? Tanner didn't have my current number, so he must have gotten it from my mother.

Um...no. Not just *no*, but *hell no.*

Things had been awkward between me and Tanner this morning, and the last thing I wanted was a repeat of that experience.

Me: *Sorry. I'm busy.*

Okay, I was lying, but what else was I supposed to say?

Tanner: *Doing what? This is Crystal Fork, not Seattle.*

He was right. There wasn't much to do on a Saturday night here except go to The Mug And Jug or hang out with friends.

He probably already knew that I definitely didn't have any friends here in Crystal Fork anymore.

I'd only been to The Mug And Jug once when the bar was open at night since I'd returned to Crystal Fork, and it hadn't been a pleasant experience since most people didn't want to talk to me.

I'd had one drink and left.

It had been a humbling experience for a woman who loved people.

That had also been about the time I'd started to hear the rumors about me leaving Tanner for another guy.

Me: *I've been there once. It was enough for me. People weren't exactly friendly.*

Tanner: *I'll be there. I'll be friendly. I'll save us a table. Or do you want me to pick you up?*

I let out a frustrated breath. If there was one thing I knew about Tanner Remington, it was that he could be very stubborn when he wanted something.

Me: *Why?*

It made absolutely no sense that he suddenly wanted to hang out with me on a Saturday night.

Tanner: *I think I owe you an apology, and I like to do my groveling in person.*

A startled laugh escaped from my lips before I could stop it.

Tanner didn't have a clue how to grovel, and apologies were rare for him.

He'd obviously thought about what I'd said this morning, and apparently, he'd believed me.

God, it still made me crazy that he'd actually believed that I'd leave him for another man.

Me: *No apologies necessary. It was a long time ago.*

Tanner: *Which means the apology is long overdue. Meet me. Please. I'll make sure everyone knows that there are no hard feelings between the two of us.*

Okay, when he put it that way, the offer was…tempting.

I *was* really tired of being treated like an outcast because everyone thought I'd hurt one of their billionaire golden boys.

Really, I couldn't blame the people in this town. Crystal Fork protected their own, and Tanner Remington had done a lot for people in this town. All of the Remingtons did.

It irked me a little that I couldn't just be accepted back into the town because I was a good person, but I'd grown up here. I knew how things worked here.

If Tanner accepted me, everyone else would do the same when they realized that I hadn't crushed his heart.

I'd been gone for a long time, so right now, no one considered me one of their own.

My thumbs hovered over the text keyboard.

I shouldn't.

I really, really shouldn't.

But against my better judgement, I was going to meet him anyway.

It seemed that loneliness was an intense motivation to fix my situation.

Me: *One drink. I can't stay long. I'll meet you at eight.*

Tanner: *Did you eat dinner?*

I looked at the half eaten donut I'd set on the counter.

I decided to lie. My dinner plans were none of his business. I'd make a sandwich or something before I left.

Me: *Yes.*

Tanner: *I'll head out early so I can get a table. See you soon.*

I took a deep breath.

I wasn't sure what had motivated him to help me, but he certainly didn't need to do it.

The whole thing was confusing. Tanner Remington rarely thought about anything else except his obsession with KTD Remington.

Me: *Tanner?*

Tanner: *Yeah?*

Me: *Thanks for doing this. It means a lot to me.*

I was fairly certain this one drink would help change my situation in Crystal Fork, and since my mother was here and I wanted to be in the area, it would make my life a lot easier.

Yeah, Tanner had been a major asshole, but that had happened years ago.

The man was a billionaire and people adored him and his family in Crystal Fork.

There was really no benefit to him for helping me.

My chest squeezed from a brief moment of nostalgia.

At one time, Tanner had been a good man with a very good heart.

Maybe some of that kindness still existed.

Or maybe I just wanted to believe that it did.

Tanner: *Don't thank me, Hannah. I was an asshole. Maybe it was a long time ago, but I'd like to make things right.*

Me: *You don't have to.*

Tanner: *No, I don't. I want to. I'm heading out to get a table. See you at eight.*

I looked at the time on my phone and set it back on the counter.

It was already after seven, but my apartment was in town, and I could walk to The Mug And Jug.

I polished off my donut and called it dinner before I took my glass of wine into the bedroom.

I was dressed in a pair of old jeans and a ratty shirt that had seen better days.

I'd showered after I'd gotten home from my shift at Sweet Mornings, and I'd dressed like I was going to be a couch potato for the evening. That was, after all, how things had been for me for a while now.

I don't need to get dressed up for Tanner.

The Mug And Jug was extremely casual, and Tanner Remington had seen me at my worst and my best over the years that we were together.

However, I enjoyed doing my makeup and my hair since it was part of my business to look good.

And at the moment, I needed a little confidence booster.

I didn't want to look like I was trying too hard or overdressed, so I put on a decent pair of straight jeans and a cute, ruby red sweater. The top was fitted, but the neckline wasn't exactly sexy.

I added a pair of casual ankle boots, some bangle bracelets, and some earrings that matched my top.

I stood in front of the mirror in the bathroom and did my makeup and hair.

I used makeup shades and colors that made my brown eyes pop, and then added a little curl to my shoulder length, dark brown hair.

I was a makeup and hair expert, so I was done in record time.

I put on a light, floral perfume, which was my favorite.

Heavy scents made my eyes water, so I stuck with something that fit my personal style.

When I was finished, I surveyed myself in the mirror.

Mission accomplished.

I looked nice, but not like I was trying to impress anyone.

I slipped on a birthstone ring that I had bought myself in Seattle.

When I'd left Tanner, I'd left my engagement ring and any other jewelry he'd given me at our apartment.

My finger had felt so bare that I'd bought an inexpensive ring for myself to replace the diamond I'd left behind.

"I'm ready," I said aloud as I turned away from the mirror to get my purse and a fleece jacket in case I needed it.

I wasn't sure I was ready to sit across from Tanner at a bar, but I was trying to be optimistic.

Something in my belly fluttered as I thought about looking at him and hearing his sexy voice earlier in the day.

I hated that there was still some lingering attraction there for me.

Then again, why wouldn't there be?

There were very few women who could meet a guy like Tanner and *not* be physically attracted to him.

With his stunning blue eyes and his very large, hot body, he was a hard man not to notice.

The chemistry between the two of us was always off the charts, even if our communication did suck at the end of our relationship.

It was probably perfectly normal that he didn't leave me completely unmoved now.

"You can do this, Hannah," I said to myself encouragingly. "It's just a drink. Things ended with Tanner a long time ago."

So many years had passed.

I'd made a new life for myself in Seattle. A very successful and fulfilling life.

I was a much different woman than I'd been when Tanner and I were together.

I wasn't as young or as naïve as I had been back then.

I also wasn't afraid of standing up for myself anymore.

I'd found myself in Seattle, and I'd never be afraid to speak my mind or put up with giving everything and getting very little back ever again.

I grabbed my phone from the kitchen and noticed that it was nearly eight.

I might be a little late because I was walking to The Mug And Jug.

As I left my apartment, I didn't feel guilty about being behind schedule.

I'd waited for Tanner Remington to look up and see me for a long time.

He could wait a few minutes for me.

Chapter 6

Tanner

"Are you worried that Hannah isn't going to show?" Devon asked as we sat at a small table at The Mug And Jug.

Hell, maybe I'd glanced at my watch one too many times. My younger brother might be a cynic, but he was one of the most observant people I knew.

He could also be supportive when he wanted to be, and it was obvious that he was lending me some moral support by plopping his ass down in the chair meant for Hannah.

Devon had been here with friends, but had strolled over to talk when he'd seen me snagging a table.

I'd told Kaleb and Devon about what had happened with Hannah when we were out at Charlie's farm.

"I think she'll show," I answered confidently, but it was after eight, and I could hardly blame her lateness on traffic.

A few cars moving in the same direction was considered our traffic in Crystal Fork.

"She'll be here," Devon said in an unusually sympathetic tone. "Hannah isn't the type to stand someone up."

I shot him a questioning glance. "You say that like you respect her."

He shrugged. "I always liked and respected Hannah. I only disliked her when I thought that she dumped you. Now that I know that you were the idiot, I like and respect her again."

"Unfortunately, I think I probably deserved to get dumped," I admitted. I'd thought a lot about the things my mother and Hannah had said to me earlier. "What in the hell happened to us during those years, Devon? It's one thing to work hard to achieve a goal, but it's another when nothing else matters except reaching that goal."

Devon didn't throw out excuses for either of us as he replied candidly, "KTD became so successful so fast that I think all of us lost our minds. I don't think any of us expected to become billionaires, but I don't think it was just the money. It was the challenge to become one of the best. We wanted to prove ourselves so much that we got lost in the game."

He was probably right.

Besting our competitors was our main goal, and our success had put us on a high that had become addictive.

Looking back now on what had happened with Hannah, I knew I'd neglected her to the point that she couldn't deal with that kind of disrespect anymore. And fuck knew she had deserved better than that from me.

Hannah had helped me build that company I'd been obsessed with, and her support had gotten me through some rough patches.

It was funny how the mind worked sometimes. I'd convinced myself that I was working for us, for my future with Hannah. In reality, I'd become a man that I'd never wanted to be during those years. A guy I hadn't wanted to acknowledge after I'd come to my senses.

"I can't change what happened," I said regretfully. "But I can make sure people don't treat her like the villain in our story anymore."

"What can I do to help?" Devon asked.

I shot him a surprised glance.

"What?" he asked. "I told you that I liked Hannah. Hell, I thought she was going to be my sister-in-law, and she was like family."

"Be nice to her," I suggested.

"That's not hard to do," he replied. "She's always been nice to me. I'm not sure that one drink with you tonight is going to change the whole town's opinion overnight, but I'll do what I can."

Some people might be warmer to Hannah after they saw us together, but Devon was right. That was why I was on a mission to make sure that Hannah and I were seen together *a lot* in the future.

I looked at my watch again, and started to sweat just a little.

"She's never late," I muttered.

"Maybe she's changed," Devon said. "It's been years since you two have seen each other."

It was hard for me to believe that Hannah had changed *that* much.

A moment later, the woman we'd been talking about finally sauntered through the door.

Christ! How was I supposed to treat Hannah Griffin like a friend? It would help if she wasn't just as beautiful as she'd always been to me.

She was dressed casually, but she looked more sophisticated and more confident than she'd ever been before.

Hannah lit up the bar just by walking through the door, and my cock reacted instinctively, an instantaneous reaction I hadn't had in a very long time.

That wasn't exactly comfortable for me since she wasn't now and hadn't been my woman in a long time.

But it was a spontaneous reaction that I couldn't exactly control.

Maybe my brain had been in denial and misinformed about our breakup, but my primitive instincts toward Hannah had definitely never gone away.

"She's here," I said, unable to stop myself from staring at Hannah as she looked around the bar.

Seeing Hannah in *anything* red brought back memories.

Red had always been her color, and it was sexy as fuck on her.

"Relax," Devon said quietly. "She's not going anywhere. She's here to have a drink with you."

Hell, did I really look that uptight?

Hannah's gaze finally connected with mine, and when she smiled at me, my gut actually clenched because it reminded me of the way she used to look at me.

Fuck! I needed to get a grip.

Those days were in the past, but it was hard not to remember the times when things had been good with Hannah.

Really good.

Devon and I both stood as Hannah approached the table.

She nodded at me and looked at Devon in surprise.

"Hey, Devon," she said in a wary voice, the look on her face uncertain, like she wasn't sure what kind of reception she'd get from him.

"Hannah," he said in a deep baritone and opened his arms to her.

She hesitated for a brief moment before she threw herself into my younger brother's arms.

Everyone in my family had been close to Hannah, and she'd always adored both of my brothers like they were her own siblings.

At one time, she'd wholeheartedly jumped into my brothers' arms without hesitation and hugged them until they could barely breathe.

Showing affection to the people she cared about had been as natural as breathing to her.

Devon wrapped his arms around Hannah's waist and twirled her around the same way he'd done years ago. "You look good," he said as he set her back on her feet. "Seattle was obviously good to you."

She nodded as she let Devon go and shot him a sweet smile.

Fuck!

It was hell watching my brother cuddle up to Hannah when I knew I'd never get that same reaction from her again.

I wasn't sure why that irritated me after all these years, but it did.

"Seattle was good," Hannah told Devon. "But I'm back in Montana for good now."

Devon winked at her a little flirtatiously. "Then I guess we got lucky."

Okay, I *had* told Devon to be nice to Hannah, but he didn't need to be *that* nice.

Hannah isn't your woman anymore, asshole. Suck it up.

"I'm here with some friends," Devon informed Hannah. "But I'm sure we'll bump into each other again. We'll catch up next time."

I gritted my teeth as the two said goodbye to each other, and Devon wandered back to his table.

I knew my younger brother, and part of me wondered if he'd winked at Hannah just to annoy me.

Hannah settled herself into the chair that Devon had vacated.

"No live music tonight," she observed.

The Mug And Jug had some local bands that played at the bar on weekends sometimes.

"Not tonight," I answered. "Silas can't always find local people to play."

The place was quieter than usual without a live band, but the night was young. It would get rowdier as more and more people started coming in and drinking too much.

The waitress stopped at our table, and I asked for another beer on tap.

Without thinking, I asked for a strawberry daiquiri for Hannah.

"Wait," I said to the waitress as I looked at Hannah. "Sorry. Old habit. Do you want something else?"

She shook her head. "Nope. That's still my go-to cocktail, but thanks for asking."

The waitress nodded and walked away to get our drinks.

"Some people are staring," Hannah observed as she reached for a pretzel from the basket between us.

I grinned at her. "Isn't that what we want them to do? Smile, Hannah. Look like you want to be here."

She looked a little pensive and uncomfortable, and I hated it.

She did smile at me, and I suddenly forgot why we were really here.

Fuck! I'd missed that smile.

"You're right," she said as her gaze met mine. "But you know I hate being the center of attention."

That was true. Hannah preferred to be in the background cheering other people on.

The thing was, people *did* notice Hannah, but she'd never really recognized that people were drawn to her.

Right now, it was impossible to ignore since some people were blatantly staring.

"Ignore them," I insisted. "Listen to me grovel instead."

She laughed, and the sound was like another gut punch to me. "I haven't heard any groveling yet."

"I'm sorry," I said sincerely, leaning forward so she could hear every word I said. "I got so caught up in the success of KTD that I lost track of us. It wasn't because I didn't love you at the time, or that I needed something different. I was just an asshole."

She held up a hand. "That's enough. I think I just realized that groveling doesn't suit you. I got way too used to your cocky, bossy attitude."

I smirked. "It wouldn't kill me to continue."

Hell, I hadn't even gotten started with all of the apologies I wanted to make to her.

"Nah," she said. "You wouldn't be the Tanner Remington I knew if you did. I think there was a small part of me that almost expected you to come storming into Seattle to get me back. You can be really hardheaded."

I wondered if that was really what she had wanted. Had she left me to wake my ass up?

Had she hoped that I'd come after her?

"I thought you were with someone else. If I'd known that you weren't with someone else, and that *I'd* been the reason you left, that's probably exactly what would have happened. Or at least, that's what I'd like to think would have happened. At that point, I wasn't able to pull my head out of my ass. I'm not that guy anymore, Hannah. My brothers and I rarely travel anymore, and as you can see, we don't work weekends. After we lost Dad, I think we all realized how short life can be, and that we needed to pay attention to the real priorities in our lives."

She reached out and put her hand on my forearm. "I'm so sorry about your father. He was a good man."

"He was," I agreed. "He was full of life until the day we lost him. If we would have known, we would have spent more time with him. He was healthy, working the ranch like a man half his age one day and gone the next. I think that sudden loss jolted all of us back to reality."

She shook her head. "I know you thought you had plenty of time. I went through the same thing with my mother when I nearly lost her. I felt like I should have been a better daughter. I could have come home to see her instead of her coming to Seattle once in a while. I should have been here for her. Things like that will eat you alive. You couldn't have known, Tanner, and he was so proud of all of you."

"It's been well over four years now," I said grimly. "I'm done beating myself up about it. I decided I just need to do better because that's what he would have told me to do. That's why we're home more often and spending more time with Mom. If we have to travel, one of us goes instead of all three of us."

"You're a good son," Hannah said with a wistful smile.

"But a really bad fiancé," I joked.

"It wasn't all bad," she reminded me. "But I think we had more fun when you didn't have a lot of money."

She removed her hand from my arm, and I missed her gentle touch almost immediately.

"Speaking of those days," I said. "Are you still riding your bike?"

Hannah loved mountain biking, and she'd introduced me to the sport when we were in New York.

Some of my best memories with Hannah were when the two of us had escaped from the city to find remote trails to bike.

In the beginning, neither of us were flush with cash.

She was still establishing her career, and my entry level job hadn't paid me a lot of money compared to the expenses of living in New York.

Yes, my parents had money, but I'd always worked in college, and I'd been determined to make it on my own once I'd graduated from college.

I'd gotten a used mountain bike after Hannah and I had started dating, and we'd spent a lot of time on the trails exploring together.

She shook her head. "Not here. I sold my bike in Seattle before I moved. I need to find another one. But I spent as much time as I possibly could on the trails in Washington."

The waitress dropped our drinks off at the table, and Hannah took a sip of her cocktail before she continued, "The trails in Washington were amazing."

"I created a trail system across my property that spans Devon and Kaleb's property, too. They use it for horse trails and hiking, but it works well for mountain bikes, too."

My land and my brothers' were all connected, so it was a pretty impressive trail system with a plethora of different routes through different areas.

"Considering how much land you all own, I'm sure it's amazing," she said enthusiastically.

"I have extra bikes. I think you should come explore those trails with me tomorrow. The weather looks good. I'd like to be friends, Hannah."

I wasn't sure whether to be insulted or amused by the startled and stunned look on her gorgeous face, but this was a battle that was important to me, and one that I didn't plan on losing.

Chapter 7

Hannah

I took the dainty straw out of my drink and took a large slug of
my cocktail.

Surely he wasn't serious.

I took a second long gulp of my drink before I met his gaze.

"You're kidding, right?" I asked after I'd swallowed.

His eyes never wavered from mine. "I'm deadly serious. We need
to be seen together for a while so we can convince people that we're
friends. We might as well enjoy that time together. Do you want
another drink? It looks like you killed that one off in a hurry."

God, he *wasn't* joking.

"You can't just become friends with your ex-fiancée," I said as I
dropped the straw back into my drink.

He shrugged and polished off his beer. "Why not? Our relationship
started off as a friendship."

"And we slept together after dating for only a month or two. We
moved in together six months later. That's not exactly a convincing
argument."

Yes, Tanner and I had planned on being friends in the very beginning, but we'd been so attracted to each other that we'd given up on that plan in a hurry.

He lifted a brow. "Are you worried the same thing will happen again?"

I shook my head adamantly. "No!"

Getting involved with Tanner Remington in any way would be completely insane.

Like it or not, I *was* still physically attracted to him. So much so that I wanted to tear my clothes off and beg him to fuck me on this tiny little table right now.

Messing with that kind of attraction was dangerous.

Tanner was dangerous.

I couldn't and wouldn't dive into that kind of insanity again.

"There's no reason that we *can't* be friends," he said stubbornly.

There were a lot of reasons we couldn't be friends, but I wasn't about to tell him about them since every one of them involved my rampant attraction to him.

"Not happening," I said before I swilled the last of my drink through the tiny little useless straw.

"Are you done?" he asked as he nodded at my drink.

"Yes."

"Let's get out of here," he suggested as he rose to his feet and dropped some money on the table. "It's getting a little noisy in here."

As I rose, I realized that The Mug And Jug was packed, and some people were hooting and hollering from too much alcohol.

Since it was a typical Saturday night at The Mug And Jug, I hadn't really noticed that the place was filling up and getting rowdier.

People came here to blow off steam after a long week.

He motioned for me to lead the way, and I dodged the crowd until we got outside of the bar.

"Did you drive?" he asked as we stood on the sidewalk.

"No," I told him as I donned my fleece jacket and started walking toward my place. "My apartment is a ten minute walk from here, and I needed the exercise. Thanks for doing this tonight."

I desperately needed some space from Tanner, and we absolutely were not going to be spending time together in the future.

I just…couldn't.

Being this close to him again elicited so many emotions from me that it was…confusing.

"Then I'll walk you home," he offered as he fell into step next to me.

He didn't have a jacket on, but he was wearing what looked like a very warm, navy sweater that looked amazing on him because it contrasted those gorgeous blue eyes of his.

Dammit! I'd thought that my attraction to Tanner would be gone by now.

Not only was my physical attraction still alive and well when it came to him, but there was also something different about Tanner that intrigued me.

I do not need to explore why Tanner seems…different.

The man was trouble for me, wrapped in one gorgeous, gigantic package.

"That's not necessary, Tanner," I protested.

Crystal Fork wasn't exactly a high crime area, and I'd gotten around in Seattle by myself just fine for a long time.

"It is necessary," he said huskily. "It will give me time to convince you that we really do need to be friends for a while. You know how slow this town is to come around."

"I don't want to be friends," I said bluntly. "Look, I appreciate what you did tonight. If the town still wants to snub me, I can't change that."

Once we'd left the light of the bar, the streets were dark except for an occasional streetlight.

I sped up my pace, but Tanner had long legs, and he didn't really need to make any big adjustments to keep up with me.

"Of course you can change it," Tanner protested. "Hang out with me for a while."

"I can't," I said stubbornly. "I don't want to spend time with you."

Be strong, Hannah. You can do this.

"Do you hate me that much?" Tanner asked solemnly.

"Yes. No. Dammit! I don't hate you, Tanner. I just don't want to spend time with you," I said breathlessly.

"We had some really good times together, Hannah," he reminded me as he took my arm gently and pulled me to a stop. "At one time, we were best friends."

Tears welled up in my eyes, and I finally snapped. "You hurt me, Tanner," I said as I punched him in the chest. "Yes, it's been over seven years, but you hurt me so badly I wasn't sure that I would ever be able to pick up the pieces of myself and put myself together again. I can't just forget that. I was a mess when I first got to Seattle. I couldn't eat. I couldn't sleep. I could barely get out of bed in the morning because I was so damn broken. I will never, ever, go through that again, and being with you brings all of those bad memories back every damn time I see you."

I punched him again before he gently took my wrist to stop me, and wrapped his arms around me so tightly that I could barely breathe.

"I'm so fucking sorry, Hannah," he rasped against my hair. "I know I was a total dick. I was hurting, too. Maybe I had no right to feel that way since I drove you away, but it killed me to think of you being with anyone else but me back then."

All of the pain that was still locked inside me suddenly burst free, and I instinctively wrapped my arms around his neck and sobbed against his shoulder like my entire life was ending.

It was all of the old baggage I'd probably carried for years that I didn't realize was still there.

The anger.

The sorrow.

The longing.

The broken dreams.

I wasn't sure how long we stayed that way in the middle of the sidewalk in the dark, but when I was done, the panic I'd felt about being close to Tanner had subsided a little.

I reminded myself that it was *old* pain, probably some things I had unintentionally buried years ago.

"I'm sorry," I said, a little embarrassed as I pulled away from him and swiped the tears from my face. "I thought I was over it, but I went to a pretty dark place for a while after I left. I'm afraid of ever going back to that place again."

"Don't be sorry," he said roughly. "Tell me about what happened in Seattle. Talk to me, Hannah. Tell me anything you want to tell me."

He took my hand as I resumed walking at a slower pace.

I didn't have the energy or the will to pull away from him.

I'd obviously needed to get those feelings out, and I'd already completely melted down in front of him.

I wasn't going to save my dignity at this point.

In some ways, it had helped to learn that he'd cared enough about me back then to feel hurt about the breakup, too.

"It was brutal at first," I confessed. "We were together for a long time, Tanner, and I'm not sure I knew how to be alone."

I'd just turned twenty when we'd gotten together, so I'd spent most of my adult life with Tanner.

I hadn't been a virgin when we'd met, but I'd only been with one other man in my life, and that relationship had ended fairly quickly.

I continued, "I just kept putting one foot in front of the other, I guess. I survived, but I never wanted to hurt that way again. It helped when our business took off, and I was constantly busy. I made a lot of friends in Seattle, and I built a life there that I really loved."

"And now you're here in Crystal Fork again," he commented.

"It wasn't a difficult choice," I told him. "Mom is here, and she's at that age when she needs me to be here. She'd never admit that to me, but I knew it was time for me to come home. I need to be here to make sure she's okay. After her heart attack, I'd be worried about her all the time if I stayed in Seattle."

"But you miss your life in Seattle," he guessed.

"I do," I said softly. "I'm getting some occasional jobs here, but it's nothing like the success I had in Seattle. I don't think I miss the location as much as I miss having my business and my friends there."

"It will take time, Hannah," he said soothingly. "You can't just rebuild a business that quickly."

"I realized that," I agreed. "I knew it was going to take time, and I was okay with that. I guess I just feel so isolated here, which is weird because I grew up here. I guess I don't feel like I belong here anymore."

"Then let me be your friend, Hannah. Not a pretend friend. A real friend."

"I'm not sure I can do that, Tanner. It's not that I don't appreciate the offer, but our relationship was over a long time ago. We can't start over, and we can't go back."

"We can start over as friends. You've changed. I've changed. We're different people than we were years ago, Hannah. I know what's important in my life now."

"It wasn't completely your fault," I confessed. "I was insecure. I should have made you listen to me somehow. But the more you brushed me off, the more insecure I became. I wasn't doing what I wanted to do with my life in Crystal Fork, and that was my fault. I wasn't making myself happy, and your circumstances had changed so much. You were becoming incredibly successful, and I was an unhappy hairdresser in a small town. I let my self-esteem revolve around you for a long time. At some point, I think I let myself believe that I wasn't good enough for you anymore."

"I hope to hell that you eventually realized *that* wasn't true," he said gruffly.

"I did. Maybe I needed to step outside the situation and realize who I was as an individual. We'd been a couple for most of my adult life. If we were together now, I'd probably knock some sense into your head because I know I'm worth listening to. I've grown up a lot in the last seven years, and I've made my mental health a priority. That's probably why my common sense is screaming at me to stay away from you."

"But you want to come riding tomorrow on my trail system, don't you?" he teased.

"More than anything," I said with a sigh. "I've missed being on my bike, and I'm bored to tears without enough work to keep me busy."

"Then do it, Hannah. I bought a bike for Lauren to use, but mountain biking isn't really her thing. She'd rather be on a horse."

"How is she?" I asked curiously.

Lauren Collier was like an adopted sister to Tanner. She was the little sister of his best friend, who had died when Lauren had just finished with high school.

Tanner had been watching out for Lauren ever since her brother had died, and they were close.

"She's good," he said in a more upbeat voice. "She moved back to Montana, and she just moved into a house in Crystal Fork. She's working remotely on her own business now."

"She finished her doctorate degree?" I asked.

"And worked for a great company in Boston to get her experience," he informed me.

"That's fantastic," I replied as I stopped near the door of my small apartment building. "This is me."

I hadn't known Lauren well, but I'd seen her occasionally when she visited Tanner. I'd always liked her, and I was so happy that she'd reached her life goals.

"So what time are you coming to the house tomorrow?" he asked like the visit was a done deal. "If you come early, we can ride while it's warm enough, and I'll throw some food on the grill afterward. I still suck at cooking, but I can grill."

I knew that meeting with Tanner again could be disastrous.

We had too much history to start over again as friends.

But I also dreaded spending the day alone after a morning visit with my mom.

My mother had a more active social life than I did, and she had an event to attend at noon.

"I'll never hurt you again, Hannah, and you're perfectly capable of smacking me in the head if I do something stupid."

I laughed. "Okay. I'll be at Mom's for breakfast. I'll head over to your place about eleven."

I might end up regretting it, but I was a much wiser woman than I'd been seven years ago.

If being around him started to screw with my head, I'd leave and not look back.

But as of now, it did seem like he'd changed, and I didn't want to dwell on our past forever.

I wasn't sure if Tanner Remington and I could really be friends, but it would be kind of nice to have something to do on a Sunday in Crystal Fork.

I was still physically attracted to him, but I was a thirty-four year old woman. I could learn to control my hormones, right?

I finally let go of his hand as I dug out my keys for my ground floor apartment.

"I'll see you tomorrow," Tanner said in a satisfied voice.

"Tanner?" I said as he started to leave.

"Yeah?"

"Thanks for listening and letting me cry on your shoulder. I think I needed that."

"My shoulder should have always been there for you whenever you needed it," he answered regretfully. "But it will always be there if you need it in the future."

I smiled as I stood at the open door of my apartment. "I think I'm done crying over that time in my life now. I think we've both moved on."

"That's good," he rumbled as he turned to walk back to the bar to get his vehicle. "I'd much rather make you smile in the future."

I smiled wider.

Tanner had always hated to see me cry.

I closed the door and leaned my forehead against it, feeling a lot lighter and more optimistic than I had since I'd returned to Crystal Fork.

Chapter 8

Hannah

"I got a call on my way here today," I told my mother as we were eating breakfast at her house the next morning. "From Annelise Kendrick. She said she's desperate to get her hair cut and her nails done for an appearance in New York. She wants to fly in and out the same day, so she won't have a lot of time to get anything done in New York. She asked me to come to her place tomorrow."

I'd nearly choked when I'd answered the phone.

I was used to having influential clients, but not someone as uber famous as Annelise Kendrick. *The* Annelise Kendrick.

To be honest, she'd sounded...nice. And she'd actually introduced herself as Anna Remington.

My mother smiled broadly as she stirred berries into her oatmeal. "That's wonderful, Hannah. You'll like Kaleb's wife. I've met Anna several times. She's a sweet girl, and Millie treats her daughter-in-law like she's an adopted daughter to her. Were you able to take the appointment?"

That sounded like something Tanner's mother would do.

I'd always adored the woman myself.

"Of course I took it," I assured her. "I can't think of anyone who would turn down an appointment with someone like her. I'll be there for a while. Lauren Collier is going to be there, too, and Anna asked if I could squeeze Lauren in at the same time."

I didn't exactly have to juggle clients to get them on my schedule. I didn't have much on the books for the next week.

Luckily, I had the money to afford being slow for a while.

I'd anticipated it, and my partners had paid me well for my part of our business.

Still, that money wouldn't last forever, so building my business was becoming a priority now that my mother was well.

"You'll love Anna," my mother told me. "And you already know Lauren."

I had a sneaking suspicion that Tanner had something to do with this sudden appointment, but I wasn't about to complain because he or Kaleb had suggested that she use my services.

I took a bite of my whole grain bagel as I watched my mother eat her oatmeal.

No one would ever know that she'd just recovered from heart surgery.

She was in great shape because she exercised every day, and I'd just colored her hair to a pretty silver blonde color, and cut it into a stylish, shorter cut that suited her face.

"Why is it that you never really dated after you lost Dad?" I asked her curiously. "You were still a young woman when he died."

She'd always been an attractive woman, and still was at the age of seventy.

She shrugged. "Probably for the same reason you didn't date much in Seattle. I never found another man that I wanted to share my life with. I had you and Sweet Mornings to keep me busy. Your father was my soulmate. If I couldn't have the same kind of relationship again, I didn't want to settle for something mediocre. I've always preferred to be alone. I'm content with my life as it is."

That was true. Her life was full of activities and friends, and she'd never really seemed lonely.

"I dated in Seattle," I informed her.

She sent me a glance that only a mother could give to her daughter. "Once or twice in seven years. You call that dating?"

"I tried," I said with a sigh. "My heart just wasn't into it. I think I needed time to get over Tanner."

Ultimately, every man I'd tried to date got compared to what I'd had with Tanner. Not intentionally, but that spark had just never been there with anyone else.

I hadn't slept with another man since Tanner, but I wasn't about to discuss my sex life with my mother.

"Are you sure you ever really got over Tanner?" my mother asked, concerned. "I heard that you two were at The Mug And Jug last night together."

I rolled my eyes. I'd forgotten how fast the gossip could spread in this town.

"He wants to be friends," I confessed.

"That would help your business here," she said thoughtfully.

"I'm not sure I can be his friend," I confided. "We have too much history. I'm not brokenhearted anymore, but I'm not sure I can get that close to Tanner."

"Then let him be *your* friend," she suggested. "The Remington boys have changed a lot over the years, but you don't have to give him your trust right away. He needs to work to earn it after the way he treated you."

"He didn't always treat me that way," I said wistfully.

"Which is the only reason I'm telling you to let him prove himself," she answered. "He was good to you for a long time, until he lost his head over his company. He has his head on straight now. All of those boys have been there for Millie since their father died, and they do a lot for the people in this town. It took a while, but they all grew up. How did it go when you saw Tanner last night?"

"He acted like the old Tanner, sort of," I admitted. "In fact, he was probably more thoughtful than he's ever been, but it's impossible for me to forget what happened, Mom. The breakup wasn't entirely his fault. I needed to grow up, too. But it was a really painful time in my life that I'd like to just forget."

"I don't think you'll ever completely forget it," my mother mused. "But better memories with him now might help drown out the old stuff. Tanner hasn't dated another woman since you two broke up, Hannah. Maybe he never really showed it, but I think he was probably heartbroken, too."

I looked at her in surprise. "He hasn't been with anyone?"

I hated myself for asking for that clarification, but I wanted to know.

Tanner had a very healthy sexual appetite, and it was hard to believe that he hadn't been with another woman for that damn long.

She shook her head. "Not that I know of, and Millie would know. She's itching for grandchildren. She's hopeful now that Kaleb is married, but I think she's given up on Tanner and Devon."

"It's not like he hasn't dated because he's been pining over me," I said drily. "It's been over seven years, Mom."

She raised a brow. "Are you sure about that?"

"Yes," I said emphatically. "He just wants to be my friend. He's trying to help set the record straight in this town."

"And do you plan on letting him be your friend?" she probed.

"I'm going to ride bikes with him today. He has extra bikes at his house," I said reluctantly because I knew she'd misinterpret the outing as something more than what it was. "But that's it. I miss my bike, and I'd rather not be twiddling my thumbs in my apartment."

"You still think he's hot, baby girl," my mother informed me.

"Mom," I groaned. This was *not* the kind of conversation that I wanted to have with my mother.

"Don't deny it," she insisted.

"There isn't a single woman in the world who wouldn't think that Tanner Remington is attractive," I argued. "But that doesn't mean that I want to jump in bed with him again. It just means that I'm not blind."

"I think that's why you're afraid of being friends with him," she said. "I think you've forgiven him for being a jerk, but you'd rather avoid that lingering attraction. Honestly, I don't blame you for being cautious."

"Don't you think it's wiser to avoid him?" I asked curiously.

"Not necessarily," she disagreed. "Always doing the safe thing can make you miss out on opportunities in life."

"What does that mean?" I asked her, perplexed.

She reached out and took my hand. "That means that you need to figure out for yourself how much risk you're willing to take in your personal life, baby girl. I don't want to see you get hurt again, but I want to see you happy. That's a tough spot for a mother to be in. There's a big part of me that wants you to stay safe, but there's also part of me that wants you to be fearless so you get everything you deserve in life."

I squeezed her hand. "Well, I don't want Tanner Remington. He's my past, not my future."

She smiled at me. "Then let him be your friend. Have fun with him. You haven't done anything for yourself since you left Seattle. You've been too busy taking care of me. I feel guilty about that."

"Don't," I told my mother adamantly. "You've taken care of me for my entire life. And you're so stubborn that you didn't let me do very much when I was staying here with you after your surgery. You also had a lot of friends who were eager to take care of anything you needed."

Mom sighed. "Living in a small town can be exhausting sometimes. All of the gossip and everyone knowing your business. But it also has advantages. People help each other in Crystal Fork. It's not like that in the big cities."

Crystal Fork was an interesting town.

The people here were loyal to each other when one of their own needed help.

On the other hand, they had no problem gossiping about each other.

"There isn't a lot to do in this town except trade news about each other," I said jokingly.

My mother rose and picked up her dishes to take them to the kitchen. "I suppose that's true, but I've always liked the security of knowing my neighbors."

There were good things and bad things about Crystal Fork, but overall, the heart of this town was good.

There were a lot of people like Silas and Charlie here.

I just wished those other people were always as openminded and as observant as they were most of the time.

"I'd better get going," I told her as I took my dishes to the dishwasher and loaded them. "You have to get ready to go out, and I told Tanner that I'd head out to his place around eleven."

Mom turned to me. "Have fun, and don't overthink this whole situation with Tanner. I know this move from Seattle back to Crystal Fork hasn't been easy for you, Hannah. I want you to have friends. I want you to have fun. I just want you to be happy."

I wrapped my arms around her and hugged her, grateful that this woman was my mother.

I leaned back and kissed her cheek. "I'm happy," I told her honestly. "I have you here. It's just taking some time for me to adjust."

Mom patted my cheek gently. "You need more than just your mother. Try to be nice to Tanner and give him a chance. I'm not defending what he did or how he acted, but we all make some stupid mistakes sometimes."

I stepped back and scooped up my keys and my purse from the kitchen counter. "Are you saying I should forgive him?"

"Maybe not yet," she mused. "But maybe you could give him a shot at proving himself. It seems like he's trying awfully hard to make things up to you."

My mother had always adored Tanner, so her suggestion didn't really surprise me.

"It's just a bike ride and a day in each other's company," I reminded her. "I'm not saying we can actually be friends."

"You won't know unless you try it out," she said softly. "Just… be careful."

"I'm always careful," I said with a smile. "I'll stop into Sweet Mornings before I go to my appointment tomorrow. Call me if you need help. And no more trying to set me up to see Tanner again."

"No need," she said saucily as she headed for her bedroom. "That plan already worked out extremely well. You and Tanner have been seen together, and people will realize that the two of you have no hard feelings. That gossip will spread fast."

I let out an exasperated breath, but I was smiling as I headed out the door.

Chapter 9

Tanner

"Are you sure you don't want me to do something?" Hannah asked as she lazed on a lounger on the patio. "I feel a little guilty that you're doing all of the work." She had a cocktail in her hand, and she looked more relaxed than she had earlier during our ride on the trails.

Hell, no, I didn't want her to get up and start working.

She was a gorgeous sight right now in a pair of ass hugging jeans and a fall sweater crop top that molded to her curves, basking in the sun on my patio.

It had been a nice, sunny day, and ridiculously warm for this time of year in Montana.

I wasn't complaining. Some years, we'd already had our first snow here by this time already, but this area of Montana was always full of surprises when it came to the weather.

We could have a blizzard one day and Chinook winds that thawed some of that snow the following day.

But for now, we could enjoy the outdoors.

I was ready to put the steaks on the grill, and I'd taken the easy way out and bought some side dishes from the deli at the grocery store.

There was nothing else that needed to be done for dinner, and watching Hannah was quickly becoming my favorite hobby.

It was probably going to turn my balls blue, but I was willing to endure that small discomfort just to see her here in this house.

It did feel a little strange that this was the place where she was always meant to live, but she was simply a visitor today.

Fuck! I'd made so many mistakes with Hannah, and I couldn't help but feel every emotion that knowledge brought from a place I hadn't realized existed inside me.

How had I ever thought that she'd simply sailed out of my life to hook up with another guy?

Maybe that had been the only explanation I'd been able to produce at the time, but it had been an idiotic theory.

When Hannah had left, it was like I'd shoved all of that pain away about the breakup.

Refused to talk about it.

Refused to acknowledge that she wasn't ever coming back.

It was an odd defensive mechanism, but I'd compartmentalized everything that had happened in a place that I didn't acknowledge.

Yeah, part of me had been angry and hurt in the beginning, but I'd locked that shit away in a hurry.

I'd put the whole situation on hold because I hadn't truly been able to deal with the fact that she was really gone.

Now that I'd seen her again, I felt like the breakup had just happened a short time ago because I'd finally acknowledged exactly what had happened.

I felt everything I should have felt years ago because I knew the truth now.

Regret.

Remorse.

Heartache.

Disgust with myself because of the way I'd treated the most important person in my life.

I felt all of the shit that Hannah had probably dealt with years ago. Maybe *she'd* moved on, but I definitely hadn't.

She'd loved and trusted me back then, and I'd tossed those things away like they weren't important or a priority for me.

Now, I wanted another chance to at least regain her trust.

I was determined to fix at least a little of the damage I'd done.

The trail ride today had been fun, one of the best times I'd had in recent history.

But I was able to sense that Hannah was wary, trying to figure out exactly what my motives were and whether or not I was going to suddenly morph into the man she'd known before she left me.

That wasn't going to happen, but I didn't blame her for thinking that was a possibility.

After a few hours together, she seemed a little more at ease with me.

"Nothing to do for dinner," I finally assured her. "Everything else is ready."

"You went to the deli?" she questioned, amused.

I grinned at her. "How did you know?"

"Because that's what you always do when you're forced to figure out the food situation. On your nights to cook, we ate a lot of deli food."

"I'm not a good cook," I grumbled. "But I can use a microwave."

"Or go to your mom's place for dinner?" she teased.

"I'm not the only Remington who does that occasionally," I said defensively. "Okay, so Kaleb isn't really guilty of that anymore, but Devon frequents my mother's kitchen more than I do. I've learned to get creative with the microwave, the grill, and heating things up."

"What happens in the winter on nasty days when you can't grill?" she asked.

I shrugged. "I have an indoor grill."

She laughed. "You're pathetic."

Since I knew she meant that in a teasing kind of way, I didn't take offense.

She used to accuse me of that all the time when I didn't cook, and then I'd remind her that I had other talents to make up for my lack of culinary skills.

I had to force myself not to make my usual response to her comment.

Instead, I put the steaks on the grill.

"The house looks amazing," Hannah commented casually. "But I didn't see any of your paintings on the wall."

"I guess I'm like my mother in that way," I answered her honestly. "I'd rather look at someone else's work than my own."

Painting was a hobby for me.

My mother was the famous artist in the family.

She was a renowned artist for her western landscapes, but she'd retired from doing commissions or work to sell a while ago.

I hadn't inherited all of her talent, but I could turn out a reasonably good landscape.

"Your work is incredible, Tanner. It should be hanging in your home."

"I see enough of my work in my mother and brothers' homes," I told her. "I don't keep many of my paintings. I give most of them away. The only ones I kept were your favorites. You didn't take them with you."

Just like she hadn't taken a single piece of jewelry I'd given her or her engagement ring.

I'd kept everything she'd left behind in places where I wouldn't see them, but I had put them away for safekeeping.

Christ! Had I actually thought she'd be back one day?

I couldn't explain those actions any more than I could explain why I'd never dealt with our breakup.

"I couldn't take them," she said quietly.

Hell, I guess I understood that. All of those things would be a reminder of the man that had treated her like she was nothing.

Her voice was so melancholy that I decided to change the subject. "I think you should take the bike I bought for Lauren to use. She'll never use it again."

"Absolutely not," she said, sounding horrified. "That bike is top of the line. It's a dream to ride, but I was a little nervous about breaking something."

"Mountain bikes are made sturdy," I protested. "They get damaged all the time. It's all fixable. Or I'd just buy a new one."

She snorted. "I'm not used to riding a bike that costs as much as my vehicle."

"Take it and get used to it," I said gruffly. "It's not getting ridden here sitting in my garage. The frame size is perfect for you. Lauren is about your height. I'm not fitting this body onto that small bike. You said you needed a new bike."

"Not a bike that expensive," she shot back.

"Fuck! I'm not asking you to pay me for the bike, Hannah. I *want* you to have it."

It absolutely shouldn't, but the fact that she wouldn't take a gift from me annoyed the hell out of me.

I flipped the steaks over, and reminded myself that Hannah Griffin was no longer mine to give gifts to anymore.

We weren't a couple.

Right now, we weren't...anything.

And that was my own damn fault.

"I'm sorry," I said remorsefully as I flipped the steaks. "Sometimes it's hard to break old habits."

"Habits like bossing me around?" she said with an amused laugh.

I relaxed a little.

I'd promised that I'd do whatever it took to gain Hannah's trust, and I'd meant it.

"As I recall," I said drily. "You were never very good at taking orders."

"I only did it when I wanted to or if those orders made sense to me," she said lightly. "And I was a lot more compliant years ago than I am now. I'm used to being solo and making my own decisions."

Okay, so maybe I was a little overprotective and overbearing about her safety when we'd lived in New York.

"Was I really that bossy?" I asked.

"Absolutely," she told me. "But it was part of your charm. I knew you did it out of concern for me, so it never really bothered me. I just like to give you a hard time about it."

"I'm used to bossing people around. It's my job," I informed her.

"I'm not your employee," she retorted.

No she wasn't, and she was even sassier than she'd been years ago.

My lips twitched as I wrapped the steaks to take them into the house.

Hannah had changed some, but I actually liked her new attitude.

The sweetness that was inherently Hannah was still there, but I sensed that *this* Hannah would have zero issues with telling me to go screw myself if I really pissed her off.

"I'm assuming you still like medium rare," I said as I opened the slider.

"Yes," she confirmed as she got up and followed me into the house. "I'll heat up the beans. The steak smells amazing."

She opened the refrigerator and pulled out the beans and potato salad.

"How did you know that I got beans?"

She shot me a knowing look, but didn't comment.

Hell, I guess I was still pretty predictable.

I watched her as she warmed up the beans and pulled the potato salad out of the fridge.

Hannah was an amazing cook, so she looked at home in my kitchen.

She probably should since she'd planned out every square foot of it herself.

I tried hard not to notice how beautiful she looked today. Every time she reached for something, the material of that fitted top strained against her perfectly formed breasts and exposed just a strip of her soft skin at her abdomen.

Her hair was in a ponytail because she'd been biking on the trails, but whisps of hair had escaped from that confinement and were now curving around her beautiful face.

I highly doubted that Hannah knew what she was wearing was provocative to me. It was appropriate for our bike ride, and truthfully, anything she wore made my cock hard.

It's probably hard because I know exactly what's beneath that clothing.

Hannah and I had always had the most explosive sexual chemistry I'd ever experienced, and it was natural to think about that once in a while, right?

Pissed at myself, I tore my eyes away from her and put the steaks on plates.

Hannah added the potato salad and beans.

By the time we sat down to eat, I'd pulled my shit together.

A little.

I was going to *have* to separate the relationship I'd had with Hannah before and focus on who she was now.

She wasn't mine.

I'd treated her badly when she *was* mine.

And my mission was to be her friend and try to show her that I wasn't the same asshole who had treated her like shit before she'd left.

The truth was, Hannah *had* been my best friend.

My biggest supporter.

She had bent over backwards to help me reach my goals, and she'd encouraged me when I had doubts.

I'd probably never given her as much of myself as she'd given me. Now that I knew that she'd actually left me because of my behavior and not some other guy, I wanted everyone to know that the breakup had never been Hannah's fault.

It had nearly killed me when she'd told me that I'd hurt her. Her sobs of pain had wrecked me, and at that moment, I would have done anything to be able to go back in time and fix it.

I needed to keep my dick in check, and my carnal instincts to myself.

This was about Hannah now, and what *she* needed.

"Your grilling skills are outstanding," she said as she started to eat.

I picked up my utensils as I realized I hadn't even started to eat.

"Thanks," I said as I started to consume my steak.

One thing I realized was that I couldn't be someone I wasn't to gain Hannah's trust. I was going to have to be the man I was now, and hope that she could trust me.

I probably still got distracted with work occasionally.

I was probably still bossy sometimes.

But one thing I'd always do was listen to her.

"So tell me about what you want to do for a career now that you're not in your partnership in Seattle anymore," I asked, genuinely interested in her plans.

She smiled. "Do you really want to hear all of that? I have a pretty ambitious dream that might never be attainable for me, so it's probably not worth talking about."

I actually wanted to know everything about her life, especially her dreams.

"I'd like to hear about all of it, but you can start wherever you want."

Chapter 10

Hannah

I eyed Tanner for a moment, trying to figure out if he really wanted to hear about my career, or if he was just being polite. I was relieved when I realized that he really wanted to know.

He was waiting until I was ready to talk, but he wasn't the least bit distracted.

It actually felt almost uncomfortable to have all of his attention focused on me because I really couldn't remember what that was like.

I took a deep breath. "I'd really like to build something similar to what I had in Seattle. I know the population in Montana is smaller, but the competition wouldn't be as fierce. The traveling would be difficult, but I'm hoping that I can eventually get to a place where I can hire contractors in different cities like I did in Washington. I guess I could work somewhere in Billings to pay the bills, but I loved what I was doing. Weddings were my specialty, and it meant a lot to me to be able to give the bride and the wedding party exactly what they wanted. A bride needs to feel beautiful on her special day, and it's rewarding to be part of something that's so important to a woman."

"I'm sure you were incredible at it," Tanner mused. "You have a special talent for connecting with people, Hannah. You always did. Is there some reason why you can't just start launching that business now?"

"Quite a few of them," I said earnestly. "I need to raise capital, which means I need to get my personal freelancing off the ground and make some money. I also need to gain a reputation here first. I'll have to do advertising, which is a huge expense. It would be helpful if I could get business by referrals from other weddings I've done here. I have decent savings because I sold my part of the partnership, but without some groundwork first, I could run through that money in a hurry."

"Can you take on partners like you did in Seattle?"

"Possibly," I considered. "But I'd have to find and get to know those potential partners first. Quality was everything in our business. We got a lot of special event referrals from previous clients. Honestly, it would probably be better if I do this on my own. We don't have the big cities here that we did in Washington, and I'm not sure if this business could support a few partners. I'd be better off expanding with contractors in the future."

"Did you do individual clients and not just weddings?" he asked.

"We did in the beginning," I explained. "But we got so busy with special events that we focused more on those. We were also occupied with coordinating the events we weren't handling personally. I really wanted to expand and streamline things online so we could do more contracting for individuals who needed home service, but my partners were happy with the money we were making from big events. I think we were all afraid that the business would become impersonal, and that letting a ton of people we didn't know personally sign up to contract for us could kill our reputation."

"Not necessarily," Tanner contemplated. "I understand that quality has to be your main focus, but you could keep it controlled with vetting standards and a required company training. That could be done by video. You live close to Billings, which is the most populated city in Montana. You could trial it there and a few other cities where those services might fly well, and build from there. You could have a mobile app built, and use a website online."

Honestly, that was the dream for me. Eventually, I wanted to branch out nationally to cities that would be more profitable. "Going national is the big dream, but I need to build a brand. That can take a long time. Weddings and special events will still be important if I go that route eventually, but I'd like mobile services to be accessible to everyone. I think the services would appeal to working moms, busy professionals, people with mobility issues, and elderly people who have a hard time getting out to a salon."

"Is this already being done by other companies nationally?" he questioned.

"Yes. But I honestly think we're behind in this country on mobile services accessibility, and the business is in demand. I'm not saying I won't have competition, which is why branding as the best and most recognized company in mobile services is important."

"How would you feel about having a silent partner? Basically just an investor to fund the startup for the trial in Montana?"

I looked at him in surprise.

It took me a moment to realize that he was talking about himself.

I shook my head. "Tanner, the company could fail. It's a risk. Building slowly is a lot safer."

"I'm willing to take that risk. I believe in your expertise and your business savvy in this business to make this work and grow in the future. I can help in some areas. It is my job to buy businesses and restructure them. I'm also an expert on branding."

"I realize that," I said hesitantly. "But you build huge corporations. What this company could make would be peanuts to you."

"I'm not looking to make a profit, Hannah. I want you to be happy, and this is important to you. I'll fund anything you need for your startup and carry the company expenses until you're profitable. You don't have to pay me back."

I looked at him, appalled at the suggestion. "No," I said adamantly. "That is not what an investor does. There has to be a profit in it for you if the company succeeds, and you need to be paid back for the money you'd be investing."

His expression was stormy, but his voice was calm as he said, "It's what a friend does for a friend. I'd never miss the money. Think about it. You could start this business soon. It would take a while to do the prep work, but wouldn't you rather be working on your dream while the market is still emerging and developing?"

"Obviously, I would," I admitted. "But not at the expense of someone else."

He shrugged. "Fine. We'll work something out. I'll take a small partnership percentage until I'm paid back, and then step out of the business altogether."

That idea was completely insane. If he was taking the risk, he deserved to keep a partnership percentage, even if he was a silent partner.

"What kind of percentage are we talking about here?"

He threw out a number that was so miniscule that it was laughable. "Do you know how long it would take to just get your money back?" I asked.

It would probably take him decades to recoup his investment.

"It doesn't matter," he said nonchalantly.

"It matters to me," I answered.

"I was a total dick to you at one time, Hannah. I'd like to make that up to you by being a good partner of some kind. This isn't exactly a sacrifice for me," he said obstinately.

God, I'd forgotten how stubborn Tanner could be at times.

While it would be nice to start my business immediately, it wasn't practical, and I didn't want to take money from Tanner.

We weren't friends.

We didn't even know each other anymore.

I had no idea what his motivations were right now, and they weren't making any sense to me.

Even if my company took off, there was no guarantee it would fly high. Salons failed every day.

"I'll think about it," I said noncommittally.

Really, there wasn't much to think about.

Tanner and I were essentially strangers now, and I couldn't be partners with someone I didn't know and trust.

I was attracted to him, and part of me wanted to believe that he'd changed and that he wasn't the man he'd been when we'd broken up. But my brain was still telling me to run as far away from Tanner Remington as I could get.

Tanner shot me a frustrated look, but he changed the subject. "What does your schedule look like this week?"

I shot him a puzzled look, wondering why he wanted to know what my week looked like. "It's not as busy as I'd like it to be. I don't have anything major happening until Saturday. I have a big wedding in Helena. I do have a long appointment tomorrow with Anna Remington and Lauren. I take it that I have you to thank for that appointment tomorrow."

"I'd like to take credit, but I can't," he answered. "I told my entire family the truth about what happened with us. I'm sure Kaleb told Anna, and she researched the reputation of your old business. I haven't actually talked to her about it. I'm glad you're going to meet her though. You'll like her. Lauren just relocated, and I know she doesn't like going to the local shop. She hates the relentless gossip that happens there."

I knew exactly how she felt.

I'd worked in that shop, and although the people were kind sometimes, they loved to speculate about other people's lives while they were getting their hair done.

"I like Lauren," I said with a smile.

"She became a big city girl, and I think the gossip makes her crazy. She probably forgot what it's like to live here," Tanner said with a chuckle. "You two should get along well."

"We always did," I said wistfully. "We just never got to spend a lot of time together. I hope she didn't hate me when she thought that I left you for another guy."

"It's good to have her back," Tanner commented. "And she's happy to be back home except for some of the small annoyances of living in a small town. And no, she doesn't hate you. I'm sure the news has gotten around about what really happened by now. She and Anna have become pretty close, and they seem to get tighter every day."

That made sense. Both of the women had come from a big city and were now trying to adjust to living in a small town.

"What made you decide to tell your whole family the truth?" I asked curiously as I pushed my plate away and reached for my water.

"I was wrong," he said gruffly. "I own up to my mistakes. Mom already knew the truth. She and Joy are tight. I'm starting to think the only one who completely believed that you took off with another man was me."

"And a large part of this town who didn't know me very well," I reminded him.

"I didn't come out and tell anyone in town about my theory," he said unhappily. "But I wasn't willing to talk to them about you, either. So there was plenty of room for them to make their own conclusions."

He was right.

Given no explanation, some of the people in this town would make their own assumptions in a heartbeat.

"It's over, Tanner," I said softly. "Maybe there were some things I should have done differently, too. I guess I didn't think you'd listen, and that I'd tried everything to make you remember that we were supposed to be a couple. Maybe I should have gotten in your face and made you listen. I was younger and I ran from my heartbreak."

Tanner shook his head. "I understand why you did what you did. I think you gave me plenty of chances. You were there for me for years, Hannah, and I took that for granted. I think I convinced myself that I was working hard for us, but I got caught up in the company's success and forgot what was really important. I don't blame you for leaving. I wasn't there for you. I left you emotionally and physically while I was pursuing world domination."

He sounded genuinely remorseful, and as much as I'd hurt back then, I didn't want Tanner to beat himself up. "It was a long time ago, Tanner. You've apologized, and we've both moved on with our lives. I don't think anyone goes through life without making some mistakes, and it was a crazy time for you."

"It's hard to forget that I wasn't there for you, and you sacrificed a lot for me," he said grumpily. "I always knew I had your support, but I never supported you and what you wanted. Hell, I didn't even listen to you."

I could feel his remorse, and I hated it.

What he'd done to me was eating at him, and there was no reason for that anymore.

"It wasn't always that way," I said quietly. "You were a good man, Tanner. I think anyone could get lost in the kind of success KTD had so quickly."

Deep inside, I really wanted to believe he was the amazing man I'd fallen in love with at one time. After all, I *had* seen more of that man during our long relationship than I had the business obsessed Tanner.

"I was a dick. I made you promises I never kept. Think about the possibility of that partnership, Hannah. I can't change the past, but I'd like to make up for it by helping you reach your goals here in Montana."

Is that what that offer was all about?

Did he feel guilty about not supporting my career so many years ago?

That seemed pretty pointless since I went on to become successful beyond my wildest dreams in Seattle.

Tanner had never held me back.

I'd done that to myself.

I shook my head. "You don't need to do that. We haven't even seen each other in over seven years, and I did end up in a successful business. We're basically strangers now."

He caught my gaze, and the look in his eyes was so intense that a shiver ran down my spine.

"You'll never be a stranger to me, Hannah," he said huskily before he stood and started taking the dishes to the kitchen.

He didn't explain that comment or add any details.

In fact, he didn't say another word about it as we cleaned up the kitchen together.

Chapter 11

Tanner

"How did it go with Hannah?" Devon asked the next morning.

Kaleb and Devon were in my office in Billings. We'd just finished going over some possible acquisitions.

This Monday morning meeting had become habit for all of us. It helped us center on our goals for the week.

For some reason, we changed up whose office the meeting took place in every week, even though all our offices were similar.

Hannah had left my house soon after we'd cleaned up last night, using the excuse that she usually met her mom early for coffee in the morning before Sweet Mornings opened.

"She tolerated me yesterday. We rode the trails, and we had dinner at my place," I said, my mind still going over the way she'd rejected my offer to help her reach her career goals here in Montana.

I knew that her saying that she'd think about it was her way of politely telling me to fuck off.

"You obviously don't think she's forgiven you," Kaleb said drily.

"She's not going to forgive him that quickly," Devon mused. "She needs to learn to trust him first. Trust takes time."

"She doesn't trust me," I said unhappily.

Rationally, I knew I couldn't regain Hannah's trust overnight, but I fucking hated the way she looked at me sometimes like she couldn't figure out my motives.

At one time, Hannah had looked at me like I'd hung the moon and stars just for her.

Now, she looked at me like she wasn't sure that she trusted a single word I said.

Maybe it was unreasonable to want anything different, but I did.

"I know you're trying to clear up the misunderstanding in town," Kaleb said. "I get that. It's the fair thing to do since Hannah needs to live here, too, but it feels like you're taking this personally."

"How can I not take it personally coming from her," I said irritably. "We were together for years, and we were engaged. I loved her."

"Years ago," Devon reminded me. "Are you sure you ever got over that breakup?"

"It has been years, and you've never dated another woman," Kaleb observed, eying me like he was trying to figure me out.

I stared him down. "Obviously, I moved on. We've made this company into one of the most successful holding companies in the world. Maybe I've just never met someone I wanted to be with."

"That was an expert evasion of that question," Devon observed. "Hannah is pretty special. I think she'd be a hard woman to get over."

I sent my little brother an annoyed glance. "Even if I wasn't over the breakup, she's already put me in her rearview mirror. I hurt her, and I can't take that back."

"Be straight with us, Tanner," Kaleb said solemnly. "You've never really talked much about what happened with Hannah, not even to us. I knew you were hurting, but I didn't want to force you to discuss it if talking about her made it harder for you."

I took a deep breath. "I didn't want to talk about her. I didn't want to think about her. Especially if I had to picture her with another guy. I wanted to bury the entire relationship."

"How did that work out for you?" Devon asked in a serious tone.

"It worked out fine," I lied. "Until I saw her again and realized that I'd lost her because I was an idiot. Hannah was my everything. I knew that soon after we met. I think my anger about her leaving me for another guy made me irrational, which is why I didn't go after her. I wasn't listening to her, so it was the only explanation that made sense at the time."

"Honestly, it didn't make sense to me," Devon mused. "Don't get me wrong, I believed you, but it never made sense. Hannah was crazy about you. And I never took her for the kind of woman who would just up and leave you for another man. But my judgement when it comes to females has always sucked."

"Truthfully, it didn't make sense to me, either," Kaleb admitted. "Hannah was like family, and her devotion to you was obvious. Like Devon, I believed your theory. But I was caught in the same obsession over KTD that you were at the time, so in my mind, it was the only explanation that seemed plausible. Looking back, I'm glad I wasn't in a relationship at the time. I don't think I could have balanced a relationship and the demands of our company at the same time."

"She was really supportive of KTD. She had a lot of patience," Devon said thoughtfully. "But I think she must have felt like she wasn't important to you anymore. Everything we did revolved around this company at the time."

"I made her feel like she wasn't important," I said hoarsely. "I didn't listen to her. I was so distracted that I didn't keep any of the promises I made to her."

And I hated myself for that now.

"And you regret that now," Kaleb stated. "But you can't go back and change that, Tanner. We all acted like idiots back then. The only difference is that Devon and I weren't in a committed relationship at the time, but I have some regrets over not paying attention to the important things in life, too. I get it. What do you want from Hannah now?"

"She doesn't owe me anything," I said in a graveled voice. "And I can't expect anything from her. I want her to trust me again. I want to help her reach her own goals since I didn't do shit for her when she needed me."

"Then support her goals now," Devon suggested. "What's stopping you?"

"Her," I replied, frustrated. "She doesn't want my help, and she doesn't need my support. She doesn't need *me*. She's been successful, and she can do it again on her own. Hell, all I want is to make it easier for her to achieve that goal."

I explained to my brothers about what Hannah's plans were for her business, and about my offer to help finance it, which was flatly refused.

"It might be a little soon to make her an offer like that," Kaleb advised. "You two need to get to know each other again. Luckily, none of us are the idiots we were when you two broke up."

"I plan on getting to know her," I rumbled. "But I'm not so sure she has the same intentions."

"You're the most persistent guy I know," Devon informed me. "Wear her down."

"This isn't a business transaction, Devon," I said in a disgusted voice.

"No," Kaleb argued. "He's right. If this is important to you, make it happen. Just go a little slower."

Devon snickered as he looked at Kaleb. "Like you should be talking about going slow? You don't think your relationship with Anna happened at warp speed after you figured out that the two of you were supposed to be together?"

Kaleb shrugged. "I knew what I wanted once I pulled my head out of my ass. Tanner just wants to right some wrongs. His romantic relationship with Hannah is over, but I get why he wants to make things right."

Devon eyed me with a knowing look. "Is it really over?" he asked, the question hanging in the air ominously.

When Kaleb's questioning gaze landed on me, too, I started to feel a little cornered.

I was a man who always liked to be in control.

But my brothers knew exactly how to put me on the spot.

They'd been doing it since we were born.

"What do you want me to say?" I asked impatiently. "Hannah was done with me a long time ago."

"But are you done with her?" Devon probed.

"I can't rewind what happened," I growled. "Hell, I wish I could, but I can't."

"Mistakes can be forgiven," Kaleb disagreed. "It might take time and patience, but none us are the same men that we were when we were building this business like it was the only thing that mattered. You just need to prove to her that you're still the same guy she fell for years ago. She's not married or involved with someone else, so you have a shot. I guess you're the only person who can decide if all that work is worth it to you. If you still have feelings for Hannah and she doesn't end up feeling the same way, it might be hell on you."

"She's worth it," I answered without hesitation, my voice raw with emotion. "She was always worth it."

"Then be a pain in her ass until she forgives you," Devon suggested. "You're pretty good at that."

"It might not work out," Kaleb warned. "It's been seven years. You might find out that your feelings have changed or that her feelings have changed. But if I was in this situation with Anna, I'd have to know there was zero chance of us getting back together before I gave up."

"I don't plan on giving up," I told my brothers. "But I can't jump ahead of myself and think about anything else but regaining her trust right now."

"That should be your first priority," Kaleb agreed.

"She can be stubborn when she wants to be," Devon said. "I still think you're going to have to wear her down. If she basically told you to screw off about the partnership, then you'll have to be charming and persistent."

"I'm not a charming guy," I grumbled.

"But you definitely know how to be persistent," he said with a grin. "And she must have thought you were charming at one time. She was crazy about you."

"I was lucky," I answered grumpily. "My college education was the only thing I had going for me when we first met. I wasn't wealthy, and I definitely wasn't charming. Persistence was the only thing I had."

Devon was the Remington who could charm women easily.

I'd been serious, goal oriented, and introverted, even as a much younger man.

It probably wasn't surprising that I'd gravitated toward someone who was my complete opposite.

Hannah had fascinated me from the very beginning.

She always worked extremely hard, but she'd known when it was time to quit and pay attention to what was important to her.

Most of the time, *I'd* been what was important to her.

I'd soaked in her sweetness and attention like a damn sponge.

And I'd fallen for her so fast and so hard that it had made my head spin.

"She never cared that you weren't rich," Kaleb answered. "She cared about you."

"She also thought you were the hottest guy on the planet, which I personally never understood," Devon joked. "But you could use that to your advantage if you decide you want a romantic relationship with her."

I couldn't be pissed off at Devon for that comment because I'd never understood it, either, but I'd always felt like the luckiest asshole on the planet because Hannah had felt that way.

I'd always stayed in shape physically, but I wasn't as pretty as Devon, or conventionally handsome like Kaleb.

I was a normal guy with average looks and a visible scar over my eyebrow from a hard fall off a horse when I was younger.

I was the middle Remington brother who people didn't really notice most of the time.

And I was okay with that since I usually didn't want to draw attention to myself.

Hannah was a stunning woman with her dark hair and mesmerizing dark eyes, and a curvy body that would make guys look twice… or several times.

She probably could have picked a better man than me in New York City to fall for, but like I'd just told my brothers, I was lucky.

She had loved *me,* and she'd proven that over and over during the years we were together.

I just hadn't been smart enough to keep appreciating her when my life spiraled out of control.

"I'll just have to take things one step at a time," I informed my brothers before they got up to go to their offices.

I planned on taking things slow, even though I wasn't always a patient man when it involved something I really wanted.

But a little persistence wouldn't hurt, as long as that persistence didn't scare her away.

Chapter 12

Hannah

"So tell me exactly what you want," I instructed Lauren as we sat in front of the mirror in the enormous master bathroom at Anna Remington's house.

Anna was sitting in a chair right next to Lauren's, waiting for the color I'd put in her hair for highlights to be finished.

I had to admit that it had been a little unnerving to be standing next to an international pop star, but Anna was so nice that I'd soon forgotten that she was a superstar.

She and Lauren had been so kind to me, and I'd really appreciated that enthusiasm and kindness since I'd rarely had that kind of reception in Crystal Fork since I'd returned here.

I'd really missed being treated like a welcome guest, and being with people who acted like they really wanted me to be here felt really good.

Lauren took a deep breath and let it out as she looked in the mirror. "I'm not sure. I just want something…different. Anna talked me into getting contacts, so I look better than I did when I was wearing my clunky glasses, but I want something more…sophisticated and chic.

I've looked frumpy since I was a teenager. I've lost a few pounds since I got back to Crystal Fork because I'm more active here, but I hate my hair, and I suck at doing makeup. I guess I just want to feel more attractive and confident. I know I can't really fix my boring image, but it would be nice if a guy would look at me and actually see me."

"You are not frumpy," I insisted. "Maybe you're just tired of the same look. Sometimes it helps to change things up a little. How do you feel about going shorter?"

Lauren had beautiful, dark blonde hair, but it was thick and long. For as long as I'd known her, she'd usually worn it in a very long braid to keep her long hair manageable.

She also had incredible blue eyes that had been understated by her glasses, and they were stunning now that she was wearing contacts.

She'd spent a lot of years studying in college to get her doctorate degree, and she was intellectually gifted.

I had a feeling it wasn't her looks that scared men away.

It was the fact that she was much smarter than the average guy.

In my mind, all she needed was a man who could keep up with her intelligence level, or one who wasn't intimidated by it.

I'd do everything I could to make her feel better about herself and boost her confidence, but I certainly would never tell her to dumb herself down just to attract a man. Her intelligence was a gift, and she was perfect exactly as she was.

"I'm up for whatever you think will help this mess," Lauren said gratefully.

I ran my fingers through the hair she'd unbraided. "I think we should highlight it, and do some layers. I'll take some length off so you don't feel weighed down by your hair. After we're done, I'll show you how to do your makeup and write down what we used so you can order it or pick it up somewhere."

"I think that would be amazing," Anna commented from her chair.

Lauren smiled at me in the mirror. "I'm beyond ready for this makeover."

I mixed the color I was going to use for highlights, and then started highlighting her hair.

I could switch back and forth from Lauren to Anna if I timed it right.

"I feel guilty," Anna said unhappily as I worked.

"Why?" I asked as I shot her a quick, sympathetic look.

"Before I found out what really happened between you and Tanner, I blamed you for the breakup."

Lauren nodded slightly. "I hate to admit that I jumped to conclusions, too. Tanner never really talked to me much about the breakup, but Devon mentioned that Tanner thought you'd left him for another man. Part of me found that hard to believe, but I felt bad for Tanner. He's like a brother to me."

I smiled at both of them. "Do you think I'd ever blame either of you? You didn't know me that well, Lauren, and you were close to Tanner."

"I knew you," Lauren argued. "Maybe I didn't know you well, but something in my gut told me that you'd never do that, and I didn't listen to that instinct."

"He hurt you pretty badly, didn't he?" Lauren asked in an empathetic tone. "Anna told me about what Tanner told Kaleb about the real reason for the breakup."

I nodded slowly. I was getting to really like both of these women, and I didn't want to lie to them because they'd been so nice to me. "He did. But it happened a long time ago. He apologized, and I think he's genuinely remorseful for what happened. I'm okay with it."

"I love Tanner," Lauren said. "He's been like an older brother to me since I lost my own brother. But I think he was a major asshole. I know how much he changed during that time in his life. We spoke occasionally, but he wasn't the same guy he'd been before KTD exploded. I knew it wasn't because he didn't care about me or how I was doing, but his interest in listening to me was nonexistent. I was grateful to get the Tanner I knew back into my life after his father died. It was like he suddenly came to his senses and snapped back to being the Tanner I knew and loved."

I mentally filed that information.

Apparently, I wasn't the only one who had noticed how much Tanner had changed during that period in time.

"It took a little longer for Kaleb to let go of his workaholic ways," Anna mentioned. "He was still struggling with it when we met, but I don't think he was as obsessed as they'd all been when KTD suddenly started to become a mega company."

Lauren sighed. "I think Kaleb worked like that to keep busy. I don't think he wanted to think about his father's death. Finding closure would have meant that he had to accept that his dad was gone. I'm glad he finally found that closure after he met you. He was extremely close to his father."

"And Devon?" I asked curiously. "Do you think he found closure?"

Lauren shrugged. "Devon is...Devon. He's charming and funny sometimes, but it's hard to read his emotions or motivations. He doesn't open up very often. He covers his emotions in sarcasm, cynicism, and bad humor most of the time, but underneath all that, he's a decent guy. I just don't think he wants anyone to know that."

"I heard that Tanner is trying to make up for what he did," Anna said. "Is that true?"

"Yes," I confided. "He's trying to dispel the rumors that I dumped him for another man. He wants to be friendly so some of the people in town stop treating me like dirt."

"I really hate the gossip in this town," Lauren griped.

"I guess I'm used to having rumors spread about me," Anna explained. "But what's happening around town since you got back is ridiculous. I have to admit that I've heard kinder things going around since you had drinks with Tanner at The Mug And Jug Saturday. I think you should be friendly with him. He owes it to you to make sure those rumors are completely gone."

"He's been very willing to do that," I assured her.

"But?" Lauren questioned.

"But doing that is a little complicated for me," I explained. "I guess I still don't trust him, and I'm not sure being around him is good for me."

"You're still attracted to him," Anna guessed. "That's why it's complicated, right?"

"How did you know?" I asked, surprised.

Anna smiled ruefully. "I kind of went through that same problem after I met Kaleb. I didn't trust him in the beginning, and I barely knew him. But I wanted to get him naked almost from the first moment I met him. That chemistry was there almost right away. We wanted to just be friends, but that didn't work out well for either of us."

"Tanner and I were together for a long time," I explained. "But that chemistry never faded away for me. I guess that attraction was so strong that it's hard to shake."

"Then a friendship might not be possible," Anna warned. "If Kaleb and I ever separated, I sure as hell couldn't be his friend."

Finished with Lauren's highlights, I turned to work on Anna's hair. "But it's been over seven years for Tanner and me. I think I'm over everything except my lingering attraction to him."

Okay, I wasn't exactly sure that was true, but I wanted to think it was the truth.

As I started shampooing her hair, she answered, "I think you should let him clear things up regardless. Be seen with him, let the gossip disappear. I adore Tanner. I don't think he'd ever intentionally hurt you again, but I know what it's like to try to be a man's friend when you want to jump him every single moment of the day. Just be careful, Hannah."

"I completely agree," Lauren added.

My heart warmed as I realized that Anna and Lauren were trying to protect my heart.

They both knew and loved Tanner, but they wanted to make sure that I was okay, too.

I'd ached for this kind of relationship with female friends again, and they probably had no idea how much their comradery meant to me.

"Can you manage to be with him without getting hurt?" Lauren asked softly.

"I think so," I mused. "It feels pretty awkward right now because we're both used to another type of relationship, but there was a strong friendship component to our relationship, too."

"Tanner is pretty stubborn," Lauren commented. "I doubt he's going to give up until everyone in this town treats you the way you should be treated."

"We haven't actually made any plans for this week," I shared. "I'm not even sure we'll see each other."

"He'll show up somewhere," Lauren said. "He has an overinflated sense of guilt and honor sometimes. I also think he probably wants to be there for you when you need him now. He really is different, Hannah. He isn't the same guy he was when you broke up. He hasn't been for a long time."

"Do you really think he's changed that much?" I asked cautiously.

"You know Tanner," Lauren replied. "Even when he was being a jerk, he was generally honest, and he was faithful. He's not a manipulator. If he says he wants to help, he's doing it for the right reasons. He obviously *wants* to help make things right."

Her statements made sense to me.

Maybe Tanner had neglected our relationship, but he'd never tried to gaslight me or manipulate me.

I wasn't sure if doing something like that was even in his nature.

It was probably totally wrong for me to think that Tanner had any ulterior motives.

He never had before.

What you saw was what you got with Tanner.

"I guess we'll just see what happens this week," I said as I dried Anna's hair with a towel.

"You don't just have to count on Tanner to help," Anna said. "We can go out around town together when I get back from New York. If people see us together, it will be further proof that there's no hard feelings between you and Tanner or his family."

"I'll go, too," Lauren offered in an enthusiastic voice.

"But you're both so busy, and—"

"Not that busy," Anna insisted. "I'd honestly like to be friends with you, Hannah, if you'll let me. My best friend in the world was my stylist back in Los Angeles. We hardly get to see each other anymore. This world in Crystal Fork is so damn new to me, and I could use genuine friends."

"Me, too," Lauren added. "Anna and I could use an addition to our 'getting used to a small town after living in the city' club."

I'd been so damn lonely since I'd gotten back from Seattle, and it seemed incredible to me that Anna and Lauren were both adamant about being my friend.

I genuinely liked both of these women, and it would be so nice to have friends I could talk to again.

"Let's meet up at The Mug And Jug for coffee when I get back," Anna suggested. "I can never get enough coffee."

"I'll end up having one of the cinnamon rolls," Lauren said like she was disgusted with herself. "I can't resist them."

"I'll split one with you," Anna offered. "Since I got married and went on a honeymoon that was like an eating orgy, I'm barely squeezing into my stage costumes."

"I suppose that would be better than me wolfing down the whole thing myself," Lauren replied.

"Carbs and sugar are my downfall, too," I shared.

We commiserated for a few minutes about how unfair it was to love food but not be able to eat many of the things we loved without putting on weight.

By the end of the long appointment, we'd found that we had a lot of other things in common, too.

I was incredibly grateful that I was going to see these two women again soon.

It was the most enjoyable appointment I'd had in a very long time.

Chapter 13

Tanner

"Do you really have a friend you're visiting in Helena on Saturday, or are you making up that excuse to take me there?" Hannah asked as we ate dinner at Charlie's on Thursday night.

I didn't blame her for asking that question since I'd been persistent about spending time in her company over the last few days.

As usual, she looked beautiful without really trying.

She'd arrived at Charlie's after doing some errands.

Her hair was slightly tousled like she'd been rushing to get here on time, and she was dressed in ass hugging jeans and a bright colored sweater.

Just like every other day that I'd seen her this week.

Hannah was big on color, the brighter the better. She'd always insisted that wearing bright colors made her dark hair and eyes less boring.

I'd always argued that her hair and eyes were gorgeous regardless, but I'd usually gotten an eye roll whenever I'd told her that. Personally, I did think that colors suited her personality. She always looked like a bright ray of sunshine, even on the crappiest of days.

Luckily, I'd been able to see her several times this week so far.

On Monday, we'd gone grocery shopping together after work, where I'd discovered that some things about Hannah had never changed.

If I tossed crap food into my cart, which I usually did, she'd quietly take it out and replace it with something healthier. If I tried to switch them back, she'd wait until she thought I wasn't looking, and switch them again.

It was a ritual we'd probably gone through thousands of times in the past.

I'd just forgotten how damn cute she could be when she was concerned about my health.

I'd finally grinned at her and let her mostly have her way. She hadn't touched a few of the junk items that she knew I loved, and I *was* getting older. I probably didn't need to be eating like a college guy anymore.

Hannah wasn't exactly a health food nut. She indulged in junk food, but she didn't live on it like I did.

On Tuesday, I'd picked her up to get ice cream at the local shop in the evening because ice cream was one of her favorite things at any time of year.

Yesterday, I'd gone into work a little late because I took Hannah to The Mug And Jug early to get coffee.

She'd adamantly refused to get a cinnamon roll, but she'd ended up snagging a few bites of mine, telling me the calories didn't count if it wasn't her cinnamon roll.

I'd found that comment to be absolutely adorable, and I would have fed her the entire thing if she'd let me.

Tonight, I'd insisted on dinner at Charlie's.

"I planned on going to Helena," I hedged.

Honestly, I hadn't planned on seeing my friend in Helena for lunch until after I'd heard that Hannah was doing a wedding there on Saturday. But it was planned now.

Helena was a long drive. She was leaving tomorrow evening so she could get up early for the wedding preparations on Saturday. That would put her on the road after dark alone. I could get her there on my private jet in a fraction of the drive time, and she wouldn't be driving on the remote roads and highways by herself at night.

Yeah, the roads were still good right now, but that could change at any time.

The weather could change in Montana in the blink of an eye, and it often did.

I'd told her to cancel her bed and breakfast reservation because I had a two bedroom hotel suite.

She'd pushed back on canceling her own reservation, but I'd eventually convinced her that it would be more practical for us to stay at the same place since I planned on getting a rental car.

Okay, so I'd booked that suite on Monday night, after I'd learned more about her plans, but I hadn't been lying.

Not *exactly*.

I had, in fact, already booked the hotel before I'd asked her to cancel her reservation.

Hell, I knew I was stretching the truth, but I was fucking desperate.

There was no way she would have agreed to let me take her to Helena to avoid driving alone for a long distance at night.

Hannah pushed her empty soup bowl away and reached for her toasted turkey sandwich that had just gotten to our table moments ago. "How is our going out of town together going to improve my standing in this town?"

I grinned. "How long do you think it will take for word to get around that we left together in my jet? We'd have to be on very friendly terms for that to happen."

She sighed. "I suppose you're right. But I don't want to give people the wrong idea. What if they think we're together again because we went away for the weekend? Things are already different for me here, and it's only been a few days. I've booked more appointments in this town in the last day or two than I've booked since I've been home in Crystal Fork. You probably don't need to keep putting yourself out to be seen with me as much anymore."

Yeah, well, I had a problem with that possibility.

I wanted to be with Hannah.

Every. Single. Fucking. Day.

Maybe I'd forgotten what it was like to be with her on a daily basis, but now that I'd been reminded what that was like, I was getting completely addicted to that feeling all over again.

Even though I'd been a dick to her at the end of our relationship, I had missed her.

Thinking back on it now, all I'd wanted was to hear Hannah's voice when I'd called her the last time we'd talked before she'd left. Maybe I had been severely distracted by work, but I'd missed hearing her voice.

I got my wish.

I had heard her voice from Tokyo.

Unfortunately, I hadn't really been listening to what she was saying. If I had listened, she never would have been out of my life in the first place.

I took a slug of my water to wash down a huge bite of my sandwich before I spoke. "I honestly don't give a flying fuck what people think. The nature of our relationship is none of their business. The whole point was to let people know we didn't have hard feelings between us. What if I told you that I want to be with you in Helena just because it's nice to be in your company again? I thought I'd take the bikes and we could do a bike path up Mount Ascension on Sunday. There's no snow in the forecast."

The brief look of excitement on her face made it worth stretching the truth about my trip to Helena.

"I'd love that," she said with a smile that made my damn cock sit at attention. "But we weren't planning on spending another night."

"I'll extend my reservation."

All right, now I was blatantly lying. I'd *already* reserved until Sunday.

Fuck! I hated bullshitting Hannah, but I wanted to spend time with her. She didn't seem eager to spend more time together than necessary, even though I had offered to be a real friend to her.

I couldn't blame her for that, but the more time we spent together, the more comfortable she seemed with me.

I didn't want to screw that up by missing an entire weekend that I could easily be spending with her.

"Are you sure you can do that?" she asked.

"Yep," I said confidently because I was already booked for Saturday night.

"I've never ridden in Mount Ascension, but I've heard it's a nice ride."

"I've hiked there before," I told her. "But that was a long time ago."

"Are you sure you don't mind?" she asked hesitantly.

Hell, no, I didn't mind.

I realized at some point Hannah would decide we'd spent enough time together to prove to people that we didn't hate each other.

Before that happened, I was going to have to convince her that I really wanted to spend time together simply because I wanted to be with her.

"I did suggest the trip," I reminded her.

"I guess I just don't want you to feel like you have to do it. I know you're trying to make up for what happened in the past—"

"This has nothing to do with the past, Hannah," I said abruptly. "Is it so hard for you to believe that I've enjoyed the time we've spent together this week?"

In some ways, Hannah was the same person she'd always been, but there were differences, too.

I wanted to know everything about the Hannah who was sitting across the table from me *right now*.

She shrugged. "Maybe that is hard to believe sometimes," she said softly. "We've been out of each other's lives for a long time."

"Which means we have a lot of catching up to do," I said firmly. "I want to know who you are now, Hannah."

"I've told you about most of my life in Seattle. Other than my business, it wasn't all that exciting."

She hadn't told me about her life in Seattle.

Not really.

She'd told me about her business and her previous business partners, but very little about her personal life.

Maybe she wasn't comfortable talking about the men in her life
with an old flame, but there must have been relationships for her.

Hannah was too damn beautiful and warmhearted. If I was a
stranger who had run into her in Seattle, I'd definitely want to know
her better.

Hell, now that I thought about it, maybe it was better if I didn't
know about *that* part of her life.

"You told me about your business. What did you do for fun?" I
asked curiously.

"I had a great circle of friends there," she said after she'd swallowed
the last of her sandwich. "Most of them were in my field. In the
beginning, I did all the tourist things. Later, I visited the museums
and I really liked Pike Place Market when I had the time to get there.
When it was nice weather, I wanted to check out biking paths. There
was never a shortage of things to do in Seattle. It has a pretty vibrant
nightlife scene, but I got tired of the clubs pretty quickly. I did love
the comedy clubs, concerts, and going to the theater."

"You didn't get enough of the theater in New York?" I asked.

Hannah and I had gone as often as possible to see the shows in
New York.

She smiled. "Never. You know me."

I did. She was always clamoring to see a new performance, and I'd
tried my best to get her there because it made her happy.

I'd enjoyed every new show we'd seen, but I'd never loved Broadway
like Hannah.

"Do you ever miss all that excitement of the city?" I questioned.

"Sometimes," she admitted. "But I miss the peacefulness and the
scenery of Montana when I'm in the city, too. I guess there are trade-
offs no matter where you live. I was born and raised here. Despite
the fact that the people in this town weren't happy with me, it feels
like home."

Christ! I still hated that the people in this town hadn't all wel-
comed her back with open arms.

She was one of their own.

"But things are improving?" I asked.

She nodded. "Some people are acting like the misunderstanding never happened. I can't say everyone was awful. Silas, Charlie, and some of the people I knew from growing up here were nice to me from the beginning."

Probably because they were smart enough to realize that Hannah didn't have a mean bone in her body.

Even without my help, others would have eventually realized the same thing.

It might have taken a while, but Hannah was a hard woman not to like.

Fuck knew I was still drawn to her.

It had always been that way for me with Hannah.

Maybe I'd been able to put her out of my mind when I'd thought she'd left me for another guy, but now that I knew the truth, I was completely screwed.

I was just as mesmerized by her as I had been years ago.

Could I be her friend now?

I had no damn clue, but I also knew that I couldn't stay away from her now.

I also knew that she didn't trust me, and that was my biggest hurdle to get over at the moment.

If she could learn to trust me again, I'd worry about everything else…later.

Bottom line: I wanted Hannah to be happy here, and I knew her career opportunities were more limited here than in a bigger city.

She'd helped me and supported me when I was trying to get my career off the ground.

I wanted to be there for her like I should have been years ago.

And that wasn't going to happen until she learned to trust me again.

This time, *her* happiness came first.

"Are you okay, Tanner?" she asked, her voice concerned. "You look like you're thinking pretty hard about something."

I lifted a brow and caught her gaze. "I was lost in thought. I was thinking about you."

Her eyes widened and she looked flustered.

Had I really been such an asshole that I'd forgotten to give Hannah the attention she deserved?

She looked like she was bewildered that I'd been thinking about her instead of something else...like maybe KTD Remington.

She hadn't asked me exactly what I'd been thinking about, which was unusual because Hannah was inquisitive by nature.

I hated the fact that she didn't feel like she knew me well enough to ask what I was thinking anymore.

Hannah might feel more comfortable with me, but not comfortable enough.

I picked up the check, and Hannah instantly reached for her purse. "Let me give you some money."

She'd tried the same thing at the ice cream shop, and at The Mug And Jug.

"Not. Happening." My voice held a warning that would intimidate my most senior of employees.

She rolled her eyes. "I know you're incredibly wealthy, but I'm used to paying for myself. We're not together anymore."

"Get used to it," I informed her. "If we're going somewhere together, you're never going to pull money out of your purse."

I didn't have the right to take care of Hannah anymore in any other way. I'd be damned if she was going to toss me money to pay for her food.

I stood to go pay the check, and Hannah scrambled out of the booth.

"Thank you for dinner," she said after I'd paid the bill and we'd stepped outside.

"You're welcome." I knew she wasn't happy, but Hannah had known me long enough to know that I wasn't going to change my mind about taking her money.

She could be stubborn at times, too, and I'd learned her boundaries.

Been there.

Done that.

And we'd learned to compromise.

We were past the point of arguing over things that were pointless.

"What time are we leaving tomorrow?" she asked.

I walked her to her car, which wasn't far from my own vehicle.

"I'll head over to your apartment after I get off work. I'll pick you up this time," I insisted. "There's no point in you leaving your vehicle at the airfield."

There was no public airport in Crystal Fork. Most people just flew out of Billings.

My brothers and I had constructed our own private airfield on a strip of land that we owned jointly. It was convenient to all of our homes.

"Okay," she agreed easily. "I've never flown in a private jet. I'm kind of excited about that."

Kaleb had been the first to purchase a private jet and helicopter. The three of us had traveled together for a while out of Billings before Devon and I had purchased our own jets and helicopters because we often had to be in different places at different times. We'd built the airstrip in Crystal Fork after Hannah and I had broken up.

She'd never had the chance to fly private with me.

I grinned. "Don't get too excited. It's a pretty short flight."

She shrugged and smiled back at me. "I don't care. It's a first for me."

I gritted my teeth as my dick twitched from watching her enthusiastic response.

All Hannah had to do was smile at me, and my damn cock was hard.

There was no other woman in the world who could elicit that response.

As Hannah drove away, I knew I was completely fucked with this whole friendship thing.

The problem was, when I was close to her, I had absolutely no desire to save myself from the heartache I knew was probably headed my way in the future.

Chapter 14

Hannah

"This is incredible," I told Tanner honestly as I took a seat and fastened my seatbelt the following afternoon.

The cream leather seats and furniture were so luxurious it was ridiculous, but the bedroom, bathroom, and galley kitchen that I'd just toured were way over the top.

It made sense for Tanner to have the jet, and to be comfortable while he was traveling, but it was stunning to realize just how much outrageous wealth he actually had now.

Yes, he'd been wealthy by the end of our relationship, but he hadn't spent much of that money, and they'd put a lot back into their business at the time to keep gobbling up more assets.

He'd still been busy trying to conquer the world.

"I don't travel as much as I used to," Tanner said as he took the seat next to mine. "But when I do travel, it's nice to get to where I'm going feeling rested."

"No more jet lag?" I asked.

Tanner had battled with jet lag from traveling internationally, so I knew exactly what he was talking about. He'd never slept well on a commercial plane, so he always drank a lot of coffee to compensate for his lack of sleep.

"Not anymore," he said drily. "It's hard not to sleep in a dark bedroom with a comfortable bed, and I eventually got used to switching time zones."

"Are you still acquiring new companies?" I asked, genuinely interested in how much KTD had grown.

"Yes," he affirmed. "But not like we did at the beginning. We have to have some personal interest in a company. We're the parent company for a lot of very valuable businesses now. That keeps us busy, and at some point, you have to stop acquiring businesses and focus on and perfect the ones that are already huge producers. We're picky about what we acquire these days. KTD is a mature holding company now. We don't need to pick up every company available and make them into huge, moneymaking corporations. Life and work has changed for me, Hannah. I still work hard, but I'm not willing to sleep in my office anymore. Losing our father changed things for all of us. I think we realized that the only thing in our life was KTD. We all had a lot of regrets about not spending more time with my father while he was still with us. Granted, there was no way of knowing what would happen to him, but I think we all had to face the fact that none of us are going to live forever. Neither are our loved ones. It was time for us to step back and realize that we only have so much time, and we want to be able to say that we don't have any regrets. Mom will never admit it, but she needed us after our father died, and we're always going to be there for her."

I reached out instinctively and took his hand. "I get that. I feel the same way about my own mother. She'd never admit that she needed me here, either, but I think that heart attack scared her. I know it scared the shit out of me. I guess it's just hard to imagine you living a quieter life. You always needed more hours in the day for KTD."

He squeezed my hand. "Actually, I didn't. I just didn't realize it back then. We didn't need to build KTD at a breakneck pace like we did. I think success got to all of us, and we lost our minds. I don't think any of us were prepared for that kind of success, and we got caught up in that. KTD could have become successful at a slower pace, but we were all too bullheaded to realize what we were sacrificing at the time."

I was finally willing to admit that it seemed that Tanner *had* changed.

Just like me, he'd grown up while I was out of his life.

He'd actually left work a little early to pick me up today, and judging by his frequent appearances to take me places, he wasn't obsessing over KTD.

He or one of his brothers stopped by the ranch to check on Millie every single day.

Honestly, it was a miracle that he was taking me to Helena for the weekend because he was visiting an old friend.

That wouldn't have happened after his business had started to grow at a crazy pace.

He seemed…settled and at peace with who he was now.

He was comfortable with his outrageous wealth, and he didn't seem like that money ruled his life.

Tanner drove a luxury SUV, and he had the perks of his wealth like this crazy, extravagant private jet, but he didn't have as many toys as some billionaires.

The house I'd helped him plan was large with some features that most people couldn't afford, but it wasn't an opulent mansion dipped in gold.

Nobody that met Tanner in person would know that he was extraordinarily wealthy.

He was a nice guy who didn't mind getting his hands dirty to help a neighbor who needed him.

Suddenly realizing that I still had a tight grip on Tanner's hand, I immediately started to pull back, but he held on tighter, and I simply relaxed.

Even though I was starting to crave this kind of closeness with Tanner, it was still dangerous, but I decided to just trust my instincts.

"How long will you be tied up with the wedding tomorrow?" Tanner asked casually.

"All morning and afternoon," I explained. "I can't leave until the bride is ready to walk down the aisle, and I'm doing makeup and hair for her maid of honor and two bridesmaids. It's an important family, and they're paying me a fortune to be there. It was a referral from a wedding I did in Washington. I'm hoping it might get me more business here in Montana."

"If you had contractors in Helena, you could be managing this wedding from Crystal Fork," he said lightly. "Have you thought about my partnership offer at all?"

"You just said that you're picky about acquisitions," I teased.

"It wasn't a business proposition or a proposed offer from KTD," he said huskily. "You wouldn't be partnering with KTD. You'd be partnering with me. It was a personal offer."

I leaned my head back against the comfy headrest and let out a long breath. I felt like I should be honest with him. "Give me some time, Tanner. I want to build my reputation here in Montana. This business could fail miserably. Do I want to go back to having a successful business? Yes, of course I do, but I've had the experience of being successful before. Part of that satisfaction was knowing my partners and I had done it on our own."

How could I possibly partner with Tanner anyway?

Every time I looked at him, I wanted to rip his clothes off and explore that hard body of his in the most carnal ways possible.

As hard as I'd tried, I couldn't seem to shake the desire to be a lot more intimate with him.

I liked this new Tanner a lot, but I wasn't sure I could be his friend and business partner.

"What if I just give you an interest free business loan that you can pay back whenever you can afford it?" he questioned.

"I'd think you were crazy," I said wryly. "You're a business genius. You of all people know that would be a horrible deal for you."

I finally pulled my hand from his, and I felt that loss of contact almost instantly.

He took my hand back and rested our joined hands on the big arm rest between us. "This isn't about business or making a profit," he said in a graveled voice. "I want you to be happy. Believe it or not, I still care about you, Hannah. I can't just turn that off because we aren't together as a couple anymore."

God, I still cared about him, too. Probably more than I should. But I couldn't just take his money. "If I did decide to take you up on your offer, we'd have to work out better terms for you. This would be a huge risk on your part. And I'm not ready to take that risk quite yet. I'm not even established here yet."

"The offer is always going to be open, Hannah," he said. "Take your time."

I let out a sigh of relief that he'd backed down and given me some space.

One thing I could say about Tanner is that he knew me.

I think he sensed that I wasn't ready, and he wasn't going to push me any harder yet.

I relaxed as the jet started down the runway, and I knew we were about to approach takeoff.

I loved to fly, and this was an experience I was going to enjoy.

I hadn't gotten the opportunity to travel much in the past, but it had always been my dream to see more of the world. Especially the places that really intrigued me.

I closed my eyes as the jet started accelerating down the runway.

"Still dreaming about visiting Australia?" Tanner asked as we went airborne.

I opened my eyes and looked out the window as we climbed. "Yes," I confessed. "I haven't gotten there yet."

Australia was the first on my list of places I wanted to go, and Tanner knew it. I'd been talking about it from the day we'd met.

We'd been planning that destination for our honeymoon because he'd never been, and he'd wanted to go there, too.

"Someday, I'm going to make good on my promise to take you there. I haven't been there, either."

I turned my head to look at him in surprise. "You've never had to travel there?"

He shook his head. "It wouldn't have been the same without you there. Devon and Kaleb have been there on business, but I stayed behind and held down the fort at the headquarters."

I almost melted as our eyes met, and I saw a flash of regret in those gorgeous eyes before he could shutter it.

He'd actually avoided going to Australia? Because it had been *our* dream vacation?

"You made that promise a long time ago," I said softly.

"I guess I never forgot that I promised to take you there on our honeymoon," he grumbled. "I couldn't muster up much enthusiasm about seeing The Great Barrier Reef with my brothers."

"I can't just go with you to Australia."

He grinned. "Of course you can. I have a private jet. It would actually be quite easy to arrange."

He was insane, but there was something sweet about the fact that he wanted to fulfill an old promise to me.

"I'll get there someday," I said. "There's no reason for you to feel like you have to make good on a promise you made a long time ago, but thank you for offering."

"We will go there together at some point in the future, Hannah. But I can be a patient man when I want something badly enough."

I would have laughed if he hadn't sounded so serious.

Tanner Remington was not usually a patient guy.

"If that's true," I replied. "Then you really have changed."

"Maybe I've learned that some things are worth the wait," he mused.

He didn't explain that comment further, and I didn't feel like I could ask him exactly what he meant.

However, I was pretty sure that he was biding his time, waiting for…something.

If he was waiting for me to tell him that I was willing to go on what should have been a very romantic honeymoon trip for the two us, he was going to be waiting forever.

At one time, that had been one of my dreams, but going with Tanner to Australia as a friend would be more like a nightmare for me.

It would be an excruciatingly painful experience for me.

I was finally beginning to realize that I'd never quite gotten over Tanner Remington.

It was a bad situation for me to be in because I knew we could never recapture the intimacy we'd once had between the two of us.

Yet, I still wanted to be near him. I wanted to know this intriguing man that had apparently changed profoundly since our last year or so together.

I'd put myself in this dilemma by agreeing to spend time with him. The question was, what in the hell was I going to do now?

Chapter 15

Hannah

Our first night in Helena had gone well.

We'd picked up takeout food for dinner because I had to get up early the next morning and go to work.

Staying together in the same suite on night one had been pretty easy. I'd retreated to bed early because I had to get up early.

It was today, day two, that was a little more awkward.

I'd finished with my duties at the wedding in the afternoon, and Tanner had picked me up in his rental vehicle after his lunch with a friend.

I'd been excited when we'd played like tourists in the area for the rest of the afternoon.

We'd gone to the Gates Of The Mountains Wilderness Area, and taken a breathtaking boat ride on the Missouri River because neither of us had ever done it before.

I'd always wanted to visit the spot that Meriwether Lewis had first documented during his explorations, and to my delight, that was something that Tanner had never forgotten about me.

We'd lingered there as long as possible because it was peaceful before we'd headed back to downtown Helena for dinner.

We'd arrived back at our suite after dinner.

Although Helena was the capital of Montana, and was considered a city, there wasn't a lot to do at night unless one wanted to hit the clubs or bars.

"Thank you for the incredible day," I said to Tanner as I sat down on the sofa with a glass of wine in the common area of the suite.

He'd picked up one of the wines that I liked, and had gotten himself some beer earlier in the day.

Everything had been planned today with my preferences in mind.

His thoughtfulness was touching, but I still wasn't quite sure how to react to this new Tanner who was focused on me and what I wanted.

In some ways, he reminded me of the Tanner I'd known in the earlier years of our relationship, but it wasn't exactly the same.

I'd changed.

Tanner had changed.

He was a lot more mature and sure of himself than he'd been years ago.

Yeah, I found that incredibly attractive and alluring, but a little more intimidating than the Tanner I'd known years ago.

The way that he seemed to be able to focus entirely on me was captivating.

While it was flattering to have his complete attention when we were together, I wasn't exactly sure how to handle it.

Tanner had been considerate in our earlier relationship, but he'd been a guy who was still building his career and establishing himself. He'd always been determined, but he'd had his insecurities about KTD and his abilities at times.

He wasn't that man anymore.

He was a billionaire who recognized his own worth and skills in business.

Tanner had given up everything to get to this point in his life, and now he seemed much more focused on other things in his life.

Namely…*me.*

A big part of me relished that attention, but it was so much more intense than it had ever been before.

I knew I was losing my wariness of Tanner, and even though I knew that was dangerous, I couldn't help it.

It was so easy to be drawn to the man Tanner was right now.

His eyes swept over me thoroughly before he answered. "It was my pleasure. I enjoyed it, too."

God, the way that sexy baritone could make any response sound sensual made me half crazy.

Tanner was seated on the other end of the sofa in jeans and a T-shirt that matched his gorgeous blue eyes. The shirt was just snug enough to bring attention to his muscular biceps and tight abs.

He had the body of a guy who liked to be outside and do heavy physical labor.

It wasn't the physique of a male who had sculpted that fit body in a gym.

Tanner Remington was ruggedly handsome and ripped, which had always appealed to me more than a man who pumped iron or ran on a treadmill indoors.

There was nothing wrong with someone who kept in shape by using a gym, but Tanner had always seemed to have a much more raw sensuality than the average male.

There was something about that aura of his that made me want to move up close to him and set those primitive instincts free.

Probably because I knew exactly what it was like when Tanner was untamed and raw.

I forced my gaze from him and took a large sip of wine, disgusted with myself because I was salivating over Tanner Remington.

I *did not* need to learn all of the mysterious secrets of this new Tanner.

The old one had nearly killed me.

"What are you thinking about?" he asked huskily.

I could feel his eyes on me, even though I wasn't looking at him.

I'd taken a quick shower after we'd gotten back from the wilderness area, and changed into my pajamas. I was dressed in my sleep shorts and a comfortable, cotton shirt, which weren't exactly sexy.

However, I now wished I was covered from head to toe at the moment.

I felt half naked and vulnerable, but it probably had nothing to do with what I was wearing.

"I don't really think we need to talk about the past anymore," I said softly.

"We do if that's what you were thinking about," Tanner insisted. "I don't think we can start over until you've forgiven me for the past."

"We can't ever start over," I told him. "We have way too much history that was incredibly painful. We hurt each other, Tanner. It's hard to get over that."

"I hurt *you*," he corrected. "Any pain I felt was brought on by my own actions."

It touched me that Tanner was so willing to take accountability for everything that had happened between us, but it was also troubling because he wasn't completely at fault.

I shook my head. "I don't think that's completely true."

If it was time for us to get real with each other, then I was going to have to be completely honest about *my* issues that had played a part in our breakup. I'd told him some of it when I'd had that meltdown after our first visit to The Mug And Jug, but it was probably time for me to share everything.

He deserved that. He'd already done everything possible to prove himself to me.

I continued, "I think I always had insecurities about us, and that wasn't your fault. You were so driven and determined to be successful. You were educated. You were incredibly handsome. There was part of me that always wondered if you'd leave me for a more educated and sophisticated woman someday. I think those insecurities got even bigger the more successful you became."

"Why didn't you say anything about that?" Tanner asked. "You never even hinted that you were insecure."

"I don't think I ever wanted to acknowledge those feelings myself," I told him honestly. "When I first got to Seattle, I went through a pretty bad depression. Our breakup felt like it verified all those feelings I had about myself. That I wasn't good enough. That I wasn't woman enough to hold your attention. I had problems even getting out of bed in the morning. I finally had to seek help, Tanner. I was a mess, and I didn't want to keep living that way. I learned a lot about myself over a few years of counseling. Yes, you were a jerk, and my attempts at communication failed. But my insecurities ate me alive inside, too. There was something wrong with me. It wasn't just your actions. If I'd had the self-confidence I'd pretended to have, I would have smacked you in the head to get your attention."

"You shouldn't have had to do that," Tanner grumbled. "I should have noticed."

"Not necessarily," I said earnestly. "I was pretty good at hiding those insecurities. I didn't face them myself until I sought help for my depression. That period in my life was pretty scary, but that crisis probably needed to happen to get myself to where I am now. I was weaned off my antidepressant medication once I pulled my mental health together, and I'm careful about my mental health now. I have to be. I don't ever want to go to dark places like that again. You weren't the cause of that mental collapse, Tanner. Our breakup was just the catalyst that made it happen."

By the time I'd stopped talking, I was surprised to feel a tear roll down my cheek.

Maybe I had worked through my issues, but there was obviously some pain and regret about our failed relationship that still lingered inside of me.

I did regret that I hadn't been strong enough to fight harder for our relationship.

Tanner and I had shared some very good years together. The relationship had been worth fighting harder for when Tanner went through that phase.

But I'd been too busy fighting my own demons at the time.

B. A. Scott

I gasped as I felt myself being bodily lifted gently until I landed in Tanner's lap.

He wrapped his arms around me protectively as he rasped, "Christ! I'm so fucking sorry, Hannah. Where in the hell was I when this was happening to you?"

I curled into his warm, muscular form like my body was made to be plastered against him. He felt good. So. Damn. Good. "You're missing the point, Tanner," I said quietly. "I'm trying to tell you that this *wasn't* all your fault. Maybe if I'd been confident enough to tell you that you were hurting me, you would have listened. I didn't. I just kept trying to be the woman you thought I was. That happy-go-lucky, supportive woman you'd always known."

"Is that why you broke down and told me that I'd hurt you the first night?" he questioned gently.

"Yes," I confessed. "I guess I couldn't hold it in anymore. I was mad at you, but probably more angry with myself that I'd never been able to voice those emotions when we were together."

"Do you think you were depressed earlier in our relationship?" he asked, his voice concerned.

"My insecurities and low self-esteem were always there, but the depression hit me like a freight train when my whole life fell apart. Being depressed about our breakup would be normal, but this was different. I was clinically depressed. I think it was a warning that I needed to fix the mental health issues that I'd hidden for so long. At some point, even if we'd stayed together, I would have melted down in the future. You can only bury those issues for so long before you have some kind of meltdown."

"Do you have any idea how much I hate the fact that you went through that alone?" he asked hoarsely.

I shook my head as I wrapped my arms around his neck. "Don't. This was something I needed to face myself. Mom raised me right, and she did everything she could to support me. I just never felt good about myself. I told you that I was overweight in high school, and that I had terrible eczema. You've seen the scars from that period in my life. I'd just get over one flare, and my anxiety about the way I looked would bring on another almost right away."

Those eczema flares had finally stopped by the time I got into my senior year, but the small scars on my face were still visible. When I'd gone to Seattle, I'd sought treatment from a dermatologist to minimize the scarring as much as possible. After that, I'd learned to accept and love myself the way that I was and always would be.

I'd dropped the extra pounds and started experimenting with the magic of makeup during my senior year in high school. I'd learned that there were things I could do to my crazy hair to make it look better, and that I could conceal my old scars.

I'd been excited that I could improve the way I looked on the outside, which had prompted me to want to help others do the same by becoming a cosmetologist.

Unfortunately, I'd never worked on the emotional issues I'd experienced during those awful years in my early life.

"Those scars were always barely visible. I never saw them," Tanner said in a raspy voice. "The scars weren't noticeable to a guy who has a very large and very visible scar on his own face. You're beautiful Hannah, inside and out."

God, that was one thing that had always made me love Tanner even more.

He'd never seen a single one of my flaws because he'd loved me.

I smiled because he was hell-bent on defending me. "That doesn't matter when you're a teenager and you're struggling to fit in with everyone else. I wasn't old enough to realize my strong points. I just knew that I wasn't like the popular kids, and I struggled to be likeable since I wasn't very attractive. Maybe I wasn't bullied outright, but my hearing was fine, and I could hear the whispered comments and laughter about my appearance. Nobody really wanted to be my friend, and I wanted friends so badly in high school."

"That was their loss," Tanner rumbled as he stroked a soothing hand over my hair.

"I know that now. But I was still pretty damaged from those earlier challenges, and I never dealt with that. All of my issues spilt over into my adulthood. Those ingrained insecurities, anxiety, and low self-esteem became part of my psyche. But that's in my past now, Tanner. I painfully moved through those issues in Seattle so that I could come out stronger on the other side."

"Do you feel strong, Hannah?" he asked as he put his fingers under my chin and urged me to look at him.

The moment our eyes met, the warmth of his gaze nearly made me melt.

"Most of the time," I whispered, a shiver of awareness creeping slowly up my spine. "My occasional insecurities are normal now, and not some drama from my past."

I'd never felt closer to Tanner than I did at that moment.

Maybe because I'd never allowed myself to be completely honest about my issues with him before.

I'd hid them behind the façade of a woman that I thought he could love.

Now, I was just…me.

I could tell from the look in his eyes that he cared about what had happened to me, and that he didn't think I was crazy because of what I'd gone through.

In fact, there was admiration and understanding in his heated gaze, and something else I couldn't quite decipher.

"Tanner?" I said breathlessly.

Before I could blink, he lowered his mouth to mine.

I'd probably kissed Tanner thousands of times, but there was something about this embrace that was completely different from any other.

I closed my eyes, and let myself fall into the most magical, all-consuming kiss that I'd ever experienced.

Chapter 16

Tanner

I fucking knew that I shouldn't kiss Hannah, but after her fearless disclosures, there was nothing that could have stopped me from claiming what I thought was mine.

The moment I claimed those gorgeous lips, I knew I was fucked.

I just didn't care.

The embrace wasn't particularly carnal.

It was a slow and thorough exploration that was emotionally charged.

On my part, there was definitely a desperation to thoroughly acquaint myself with this woman, and to reach her emotionally when words had failed me.

I wanted her to know that I felt and understood every word that she'd said, and that I was here for her in a way that I hadn't been before.

Christ! Hannah was probably the bravest woman I'd ever known.

Maybe she didn't see that, but I did.

She'd walked through hell alone, clawing her way to get to the other side when it would have been far easier to just give up.

She put her hand on my chest as my tongue explored her beautiful mouth, but she wasn't pushing me away.

She opened for me, and started to boldly rediscover me, just like I was relearning her.

I couldn't say the kiss didn't get heated.

With Hannah, it was impossible to be this close to her without my cock clamoring for more, but there was so much more to this kiss than just…sex.

Mine!

I wanted to claim her.

Hannah Griffin *was* mine.

She'd *always* been mine.

Strangely, I felt that certainty now even more than I had when we were together. And that was saying something because I'd been a pretty possessive asshole when it came to Hannah.

Every muscle in my body tightened as Hannah moaned against my lips.

My arm reflexively tightened around her.

Mine!

My emotions started to war with my carnal instincts.

Hannah wanted, and I immediately needed to satisfy my woman's needs.

My dick and the rest of my body suddenly realized how much I needed physical satisfaction myself, but…

Now is not the time for that, idiot. You need Hannah's trust more than you need to fuck her.

When I forced myself to end the intimate contact between us, Hannah was panting, and the raw need in her eyes almost broke me.

I only saw that vulnerability for a second before she looked away, but I *had* seen it, and for just a moment, she'd let me in.

Hell, she'd let me in by telling me about what had happened to her in Seattle, and about her mental health issues.

Okay, maybe that didn't mean she completely trusted me, but it was…something.

She made a brief attempt to climb off my body, but I held her there with brute strength. "Don't," I said, my voice husky with emotion. "You were brave enough to share what happened to you. Don't back down now. After that kiss, can we just admit that we still have feelings for each other? I'll be the first to admit that I want a hell of a lot more than just a friendship with you, Hannah. We can't get back what we had before, but I don't think either of us want that. We're different people now. But we could start over and have something different this time. Something even better than we had before. I'm done bullshitting you about wanting to be your friend. I mean, I do want that friendship, but you and I were never meant to be just friends, Hannah."

She didn't pull away.

She boldly straddled my body and looked down into my eyes. "I just confessed that I lost my mind for a while in Seattle."

I shrugged. "I was pretty depressed when my father died. I can't compare that depression with the clinical depression you went through, but I know how damn hard it was to crawl out of that hole. You're a brave, determined woman, Hannah, and that's one of the things that I always loved about you."

"I wasn't that brave before I went through that depression," she denied.

I tightened my arms around her waist. "You were. I just don't think you were able to see how brave you were before you sought help in Seattle."

She shook her head. "I wasn't able to really see any of my good qualities. I'm sorry. I should have been honest with you about the way I was feeling. But I wasn't ready to face those things myself back then. It was easier to just pretend that those emotions didn't exist."

Hell, she had no idea how much I understood burying emotions that were fucking painful to bring into the light of day.

I reached up and stroked my hand over her silky hair. "Don't be sorry for being human. We all make mistakes. We wouldn't be human if we didn't. You were as close to perfect as a person could get in my eyes. I wish I would have known that you were battling your own demons. I would have tried to help you slay them."

She shot me a soft smile that made my chest ache as she replied, "You know, you probably would have tried to slaughter those demons for me. But it wouldn't have worked. Until I was able to fix things and internalize those truths myself, nothing else would have helped. I had to believe I was worthy, deserving, and be at peace with who I was, Tanner. I finally got to that place, but it took a long time to get there. I'd gotten so good at pretending that I was okay that even I believed that I was most of the time."

I got what she was saying because I'd done that myself after we'd broken up.

She took a deep breath before she continued, "I can admit that it would be hard to just be your friend, too, but part of me is really afraid of the feelings that I still have for you. Obviously, I'm still attracted to you, but I'm not sure it's wise for us to try to start over. And you're right, we *would* have to start over. We've changed too much to have the relationship we did before. You're also correct about me not wanting that relationship back again. I wasn't honest with you, Tanner. I was so insecure that sometimes I was trying to be someone I wasn't. I don't really want to be anyone but myself anymore. I'm a little more selfish than I used to be. I still care about other people, but I take care of my own needs, too, because I know that I'm worth it. I won't sacrifice myself to make other people happy anymore."

Fuck! She had no idea how attractive that was to me.

She saw herself the way that I saw her, and she went after exactly what she wanted with the confidence that she could do whatever the hell she wanted.

Maybe some guys got off on getting their ego stroked and having a more submissive female.

But I was not one of those men.

Being challenged by her was pretty damn hot.

"I think taking care of yourself is pretty fucking sexy," I said as I grinned at her.

She snorted. "I think you're completely insane. Nobody thinks being selfish is sexy."

I shook my head. "It's not selfish to stand up for yourself and know your own worth. I happen to like that about you. You've gotten pretty sassy. It *is* sexy."

When she threw her head back and laughed, something that had been coiled tightly inside of me finally relaxed.

It was the first time I'd actually heard her laugh like that since we'd met up again. It felt so damn good to know that I was finally seeing a Hannah who wasn't as guarded with me as she'd been before.

When she'd recovered, she answered, "You're probably the only man in the world who thinks that's sexy."

I grinned back at her and winked. "Good. I think I should be the only man whose opinion really matters to you."

She lifted a brow in a flirty way that I loved. "That's a little cocky and presumptuous."

"Admit it," I drawled. "You kind of missed my bossiness."

She sighed dramatically. "Maybe I have. A little. You wouldn't be Tanner Remington without trying to take control of everything."

"I have tried to tame those instincts," I reminded her.

"Don't," she insisted. "It's part of your nature, and I can handle the real you. I'm not afraid to take you down a peg if you get too cocky."

My dick twitched because I knew she'd do exactly that.

She added, "I want us to be real and honest with each other, Tanner. Right now, I don't know where all of this is going, but we have to be honest with each other. Always."

A twinge of guilt gnawed at me.

"Okay, then I'll start by admitting that I set this whole trip up simply because I wanted to be with you for the weekend. I did have lunch with a friend here, but I wasn't planning to before I knew that you were coming to Helena. I also didn't want you driving those remote highways alone at night, and I selfishly just wanted to be with you."

I knew I was taking a risk by admitting that, but she was right. We had to be honest with each other about everything.

Her eyes widened as she looked at me, but her lips turned up in a small smile. "I think I already suspected that, but I'm glad you fessed up."

"No more lies, Hannah. I want you to trust me. My only defense is that I was desperate to spend the weekend with you, and I didn't want you to be alone on the road late at night."

"You should have told me the truth," she scolded lightly. "But to be honest, it's kind of flattering to know you went to all of that work just to spend time with me."

"I'd do almost anything to spend time with you," I admitted.

"I'm not used to that," she confessed. "Things were so much different at the end of our relationship."

"Get used to it," I told her. "I'm not the same man you knew at the end of our relationship, and I'm sure as hell not going to piss away a possible second chance."

She cocked her head as she sent me a puzzled glance. "You really wanted to be with me that much? This isn't guilt talking?"

"Hell, no," I said irritably. "I do have regrets about how things ended between us, but yeah, I just wanted to be with you because it feels good. If that makes me selfish, I don't give a fuck. It doesn't feel right when I'm *not* with you. Being with you makes me happy, Hannah, and I haven't been happy in a long time."

"I think it makes me happy, too," she said with a small sigh.

"You *think* it makes you happy?" I teased.

She blew out a long breath. "Okay, since we're being honest, I do like being with you, Tanner, and sometimes that scares me. I'm also starting to trust you, and that terrifies the hell out of me, too."

My gut ached as I ran a thumb over the soft skin of her cheek. "I know, sweetheart. It's going to take time to lose that fear, but know that I'd rather cut off my balls than to hurt you again. I never meant to hurt you the first time."

She nodded. "I think I realize that now, and I forgive you for making a mistake. I made plenty of my own in our relationship. But this is a little scary for me, and I'm not sure that we can start over again."

"I'll wait," I vowed. "I'll eventually convince you that it's possible."

"You're that sure of yourself?" she teased as she lowered her forehead to mine.

"Yep," I said as I reached behind her head to hold our position because the playfulness and my contact with her felt so damn good. "My persistence and stubbornness is one thing that's never changed."

"You're bullheaded," she accused playfully.

"Guilty," I conceded readily.

When I really wanted something, I could be a pain in the ass, and I'd never wanted anything more than I wanted Hannah.

She *was* going to be mine.

It wasn't conceit or cockiness that made me believe that.

It was the knowledge that my future happiness and my life depended on making that happen.

She climbed out of my lap as she said shakily, "Then I guess we just take this one day at a time. You should probably know that if I wasn't starting to trust you, I never would have told you all of the things I did tonight."

I didn't try to pull her back to me, even though every instinct I had was screaming at me to do just that.

I had to get some physical distance from her before I did something I would probably regret.

Something Hannah wasn't ready for right now.

It was going to have to be enough that I was making some headway in gaining her trust.

My father had always said that the best things in life were worth the wait.

My father had been a wise man, and I knew that he was right, but he'd never mentioned just how torturous that wait could be.

And I hadn't even started the long campaign to get Hannah back into my life for good.

Chapter 17

Hannah

"What an incredible view," I told Tanner after we'd reached the top of Mount Ascension.

We'd spent the entire morning and part of the afternoon riding the interconnecting trails after starting at the trailhead.

We'd dressed warmly for the ride, and the weather had cooperated beautifully.

Someone had already been there with our bikes, which I was starting to realize was one of the perks of being incredibly wealthy and powerful.

Things just magically showed up where and when Tanner Remington wanted them.

We'd taken off almost immediately after we'd arrived at the trailhead.

The ride wasn't especially challenging. Mount Ascension was more like a giant hill than a mountain, but the areas to explore through the woods were vast.

We'd stopped to eat a picnic lunch earlier that Tanner had arranged to take with us, and the time I'd spent with Tanner was more relaxing than any other day I'd spent with him.

Maybe getting real with each other had helped dissolve the tension.

Even though we'd had one spectacular kiss, and I'd had an extremely vulnerable interlude with him, Tanner wasn't pushing for anything more.

No more kisses.

No real physical intimacy.

But there were some changes in our relationship, and the chemistry between us was finally out in the open.

Honestly, my head was still spinning from the night before, so I appreciated the fact that he'd backed off a little to give me time to think and get my head together.

He wanted to start over.

Deep inside, I desperately wanted the same thing.

I wanted to believe that we really could start over.

We'd both made mistakes in the past, but we were older and wiser than we'd been years ago.

I'd finally decided to just take it slow and see what happened.

If I ran away because of my fear now, I'd always wonder what could have been if I'd just given the whole starting over thing a shot.

"It is a nice view," Tanner said as he strolled around the summit. "And the trails are a lot quieter than I thought they would be. I haven't seen anyone up here since we got to the top."

We'd seen a few hikers during our ride, and only one group of people on mountain bikes.

"Helena isn't exactly a huge tourist city, and summer has been over for a while," I pointed out. "I'm sure the people who come here are mostly locals, and there are tons of trails to explore."

Yes, it was really nice weather for Montana in the fall, but most people who visited Montana came here for Yellowstone or Glacier National Park during the warmer months.

I sat on a large rock, and Tanner sat beside me.

The rock wasn't big enough for personal space, but I realized that I really didn't care.

I liked the feeling of being this close to him right now.

It had been an amazing day, and it was a peaceful, quiet moment with beautiful scenery that I was glad that I was sharing with Tanner.

The awkwardness between the two of us was gone.

Unfortunately, that made the chemistry between the two of us ever more intense for me.

I opened my backpack and took out a bottle of water.

I took a long drink to hydrate myself before I said softly, "I missed this."

He turned his head to look at me and our eyes met. "You missed what?"

"This," I answered as I waved my arms out toward our surroundings. "Sharing space and new experiences with you."

"You never found another guy who likes to mountain bike?" he asked, his voice rough.

Since honesty was now our policy, it wasn't difficult to tell Tanner the truth.

I shook my head. "Nope. I rode solo in Washington. I didn't date much in Seattle, and those dates were first dates only."

"Why?" he questioned. "You're an incredible woman, Hannah. There had to be men lining up to date you."

I snorted. "I never saw that line. It wasn't that I didn't hope I'd meet someone I'd connect with, but it just never happened. What about you? I'm sure you're inundated by women who want to date you."

"Most of those women just want to date a billionaire," he said drily.

"I'm sure that's not true," I protested.

"It is true," he replied. "I haven't had the slightest interest in dating since we broke up. I've never met anyone who changed my mind about that. You were the only woman who ever felt right to me."

Incredibly, what I'd heard was true. He *hadn't* been with anyone else since we'd broken up.

God, I knew that feeling of nobody else feeling right because I'd felt the same way.

"We had a pretty tight connection at one time," I agreed. "And it happened really fast. That hasn't happened for me again, either."

Tanner and I had clicked almost from the moment we met.

As different as we were, for some reason we just seemed to…fit.

I'd been drawn to Tanner for some inexplicable reason, and I was pretty certain he'd felt the same way.

"All the more reason for the two of us to start over," he teased. "I'm not sure there's another woman in the world who would actually put up with me."

I laughed. "You have plenty of great qualities once a person gets past your bossiness and your desire to control everything and everyone around you."

"I can't say that I don't still attempt to do that," he mused. "But I realize now that controlling everything isn't really possible. It's an illusion. Sometimes, shit just happens, and there's nothing you can do about it."

He was right. No matter how much we tried to control things, shit did just happen sometimes. Things that we had zero control over. Like his father's death. I had a feeling that Tanner had learned that lesson the hard way, and knowing that made my heart ache for him.

"I think there's times when we have to let go of our desire to control everything," I told him gently. "If we don't, it will make us crazy, and we get mired down by guilt over the things we could never have prevented."

"Like my dad's death and your mother's heart attack?" he asked gruffly.

"Exactly," I said with a sigh.

"I'm still going to try to control things and prevent bad things from happening to you," Tanner warned me.

I smiled. "Of course you will. You wouldn't be Tanner Remington if you didn't."

Tanner would be protective to the point of overbearing if someone let him.

But I knew those tendencies came from a place of love and fear of something happening to someone he cared about.

He didn't do it simply to be an asshole.

"Do you think you'll ever be able to get past the way that I treated you before you left?" he asked in a grim tone.

"I already have," I replied honestly. "It wasn't all your fault, and your distraction and total focus on KTD and my insecurities were a recipe for disaster. I think you're having more problems with forgetting it than I am. You have to let it go if you really want to try starting over. We can't move forward until we both let go of our past. I think I'm ready to move on. Are you?"

"When you put it that way, I guess I'm going to have to let it go," Tanner answered. "But it's not easy to forgive yourself for pushing away the best thing that ever happened to you."

"Maybe it wasn't all bad," I said thoughtfully. "It was painful, but I came out of that experience a lot more emotionally healthy. That breakup forced me to deal with issues that had been holding me back and tormenting me for a very long time. I'm not sure how long I could have lived that way if it hadn't happened."

"I don't know anyone else who can always find a positive in a really shitty situation," Tanner grumbled.

"Is that really a bad thing?" I asked him lightly.

He shook his head. "No. But it's not something I can do. I guess I'm an asshole who likes to wallow in my misery."

I snorted. "I can wallow for a long time before I see a silver lining in a bad situation. It's not always readily apparent."

"I tend to like to leave the shit behind instead of evaluating it," he joked.

"Sometimes I wish I could do that instead of evaluating things half to death until I find something good about it," I said earnestly.

"Don't," Tanner insisted. "Your way is probably better. Your ability to find something positive even in the most challenging of situations is something I always loved about you. It kept me from becoming a cynical asshole."

Tanner wasn't cynical.

Granted, he was intense and serious sometimes, and driven, but Tanner had an amazing heart if someone was brave enough to find it.

He rose from his seat on the rock. "Should we head back down?" he asked as he held out his hand.

I nodded and let him pull me to my feet.

It was getting late, and we still had to fly back to Crystal Fork.

Tanner had to work tomorrow, and I had appointments scheduled for most of the day.

"Thank you for this weekend," I said as I walked back over to my bike. "It's been good for me."

I felt more relaxed and at peace with Tanner than I had for a very long time.

I also liked this different Tanner so much more than I'd thought was even possible.

"It's been good for me, too, Hannah," Tanner answered as he retrieved his bike.

"Are we really going to try to start over?" I blurted out as I mounted my bike right next to him.

He shot me a mischievous grin that made my heart stutter as he answered, "If you haven't noticed yet, I'm already trying. I think you'll have to make your own decision about that when you're ready."

He nodded for me to take the lead, just like he always did.

Tanner always preferred for me to go ahead of him so he could watch my back.

There were so many things I wanted to say to him, but now probably wasn't the time.

We'd just had an amazing day together, and I wanted to bask in that happiness for a while.

I took the lead and started back down the path.

I wasn't sure I'd ever be ready to jump headfirst into another relationship with Tanner Remington, but the temptation to try it was going to be nearly impossible to resist.

Chapter 18

Tanner

"Have you thought about my business offer?" I asked Hannah as we were flying home. "Now that we're starting over and leaving the past behind us, there's really no reason for you to turn me down."

She squirmed a little in the leather seat beside me, which wasn't a good sign, but I'd decided I wasn't taking *no* for an answer anymore.

Hannah had her own dreams, and those dreams weren't going to happen without an initial influx of capital.

She'd helped me reach my goals under much tougher circumstances. I'd be damned if I'd let her refuse to let me do the same for her.

She didn't answer immediately, so I continued, "I think the best solution is to let me become your angel investor. No paying me back. Just a straight percentage of the business. You'll need all of your profits, especially in the beginning."

"That would be completely insane," she insisted. "You wouldn't get paid back unless I eventually sold out."

I shrugged. "That's the way it works. Hannah, I do angel investing all the time, and so do my brothers. If we see a startup that has potential, we roll the dice. If that business succeeds, we have a small ownership in a very lucrative company."

"What if the business fails?" she asked, her voice slightly panicked.

"Angel investing isn't about the money for me," I explained. "Some businesses succeed, some don't. But there are a lot of worthwhile ideas that need to get off the ground and have a chance at success. I've made a lot more money than I've lost with angel investing. And your business won't fail. With your knowledge of the industry, and my help with some of the details, it *will* be successful. If I didn't think that was true, I would try to dissuade you."

Okay, that statement probably wasn't completely accurate.

I'd dump an endless amount of money into whatever she wanted without a second thought if I thought it would make her happy, but I did think the success of her company was entirely likely.

Hannah was driven and savvy. She'd already made this type of business a success, and she'd wanted to push for more, but her business partners had held her back. I trusted her knowledge of the industry. I wanted her to reach for whatever she wanted with her own business.

The roads were still good in Montana, but winter was going to hit shortly.

She couldn't keep traveling alone across the state in the shitty weather once the snow started to fly.

Just the thought of her driving the treacherous winter highways to get to a job made me crazy.

I'd already decided Hannah was going to be mine, so everything I had was going to be hers as well, eventually.

Was I completely sure that was going to happen?

Maybe not immediately, but it *was* going to happen.

I'd do everything in my power to regain her trust and take care of her the way I should have done years ago.

"What percentage are we talking about here?" she queried.

"Three percent for the capital you need to do the startup," I tossed out.

She turned to me as her jaw dropped. "That's not even rational," she sputtered. "This business doesn't even have an evaluation yet. Even if it did, that wouldn't be a wise investment."

I met her stubborn gaze with one of my own. "It's the only offer I'm making. This isn't about the goddamn money. We agreed to start over. You can accept the offer. The venture in Montana isn't going to be that costly."

She lifted a brow. "Maybe not to you. It's a fortune to me. And if this ever goes national, I'll probably need additional funding."

"And I'll be there to provide it," I said smoothly. "We'll figure that out when it happens. I own a property not far from Sweet Mornings. It's the old offices of an accountant who relocated. I originally bought it for Lauren to use for her remote business, but she set up an office at home, and she prefers to work from her home office. Those offices are just sitting there empty. Using that office for your business will lower your overhead. It will also keep you close to your mom. You'll be able to check in with her whenever you want. You'll always have peace of mind knowing that she's okay."

She folded her arms over her gorgeous breasts as she inquired, "And I suppose you're offering that office rent free?"

"Of course," I said nonchalantly. "It's an investment toward your future success."

"You realize that you're offering me everything I want right now with absolutely no downside to accepting that offer. The risk is all on you."

Obviously, I knew that.

I wanted this to be an offer she couldn't refuse.

It wasn't a risk for me. While Hannah knew I was a billionaire, I didn't think she had a good grasp on just how wealthy I was now.

Me funding her business was no different from her buying a cup of coffee at The Mug And Jug in the morning.

It was literally nothing to me.

It meant everything to her, and I'd dump my entire fortune to make her happy if necessary.

I could make more money, but there wasn't another Hannah for me.

I grinned at her. "I didn't get rich by not taking chances with a lot more money than it would cost to fund this new business venture of yours."

"Twenty-five percent," she said firmly.

"Not happening," I answered as I folded my arms over my chest, too.

This was her business, and I wanted her to feel like it was hers.

"Twenty," she said hopefully.

"Nope," I replied as I sent her a look that would terrify anyone else I was negotiating with.

She let out an exasperated breath. "Don't give me that look, Tanner Remington. I'm not one of your potential buyouts or your employee. I know you. There's always room for negotiation."

Fuck! I loved her boldness and her lack of fear in challenging me, but she was not going to win this particular argument.

I shook my head. "Not this time. That's my final offer. Take it or leave it."

Her body relaxed and her arms dropped to the armrests on the seat of the jet. "I think you know I want to accept. You're offering my dream with very little risk. But it's not fair to you."

"It's completely fair," I replied. "Considering how much you supported me at one time, this is practically nothing from me in return. Is it really so hard for you to believe that I want to support your dreams without gaining an enormous profit?"

"Maybe it is sometimes," she answered bluntly.

Okay, that hurt, but I knew I'd never given her a reason to believe that I cared about her ambitions before we'd broken up.

I'd been a selfish prick about what I'd wanted without giving a shit about what she wanted at one time.

While I hated the way I'd been years ago when it came to Hannah, there was nothing I could do about that behavior now.

All I could do was show her that I did care.

Someday she'd realize that her happiness meant everything to me now.

The tears of confusion that I saw forming in her eyes nearly gutted me.

"Hey," I said in a gentler tone as I wrapped an arm around her shoulders. "I thought we agreed to start over as the two people we are now. This guy cares about you, Hannah. He wants to support you in any way possible. The amount of money you need means nothing to me. I know we struggled together for a long time, and you only got to see the beginning of KTD's success. I'm a billionaire now with unlimited resources."

Rationally, I knew she understood that, but having spent so many years with me when I was struggling, I wasn't sure she'd totally internalized that fact yet.

She sighed. "I'm not sure that's totally sunk in for me," she admitted. "Everything changed so fast for us at the end of our relationship."

Yeah, things had happened so fast that I'd never gotten the chance to make sure her needs were met before we'd separated.

I regretted that, and I planned on making that happen from now on.

"Accept it," I advised. "I plan on spoiling you outrageously in the future."

Hell, I wanted to make sure she never needed or wanted another man except...me.

I'd screwed up once.

I was a smart guy.

Maybe it had taken me a while to get my head back on straight again, but I knew what my priorities were now.

That wasn't going to happen again.

I'd been living half a life without Hannah.

A big part of me had died when she'd left me.

I'd been going through the motions for years, but I hadn't really been fully living my life.

Probably because I wasn't capable of doing that without *her*.

When Hannah had sauntered back into my life, I'd remembered what it was like to be alive again, and I wasn't fucking up a second chance.

"Money isn't that important to me," she said softly. "Don't get me wrong, I want to make a good living. I got used to having the money to take care of myself, and I liked it. I also like being successful. But having more money than I know what to do with isn't my priority. I just want to be happy doing something I love."

I knew that, and it was one of the many things I'd loved about her. Hannah wanted to love and be loved, and I'd been that lucky bastard who had been a recipient of that love.

And, fuck me, I wanted that back again.

I'd probably never realized just how lucky I was until I wasn't the center of her life anymore.

"Money can't buy happiness," I agreed gruffly. "But it doesn't hurt."

She let out a genuine laugh that made my gut ache.

"I supposed it doesn't if that money doesn't rule your life," she answered, amused.

"It doesn't," I assured her. "Not anymore. But you can do good things with that money sometimes, too."

"You and your brothers donate a lot of money," she said approvingly. "I've read about some of your charities, and I know you give a lot to make Crystal Fork a better place to live."

"There's no point in being obscenely rich if you can't better other people's lives with that money somehow," I answered.

"I really admire the fact that you feel that way," she said as she shot me an adoring smile.

Hell, that smile did it for me.

I'd give away a lot more money if it meant she'd keep looking at me like she adored me for the rest of our lives.

"Somehow, we managed to get off the subject of you accepting my offer," I reminded her. "I'm not going to leave this alone until I have the answer I want."

I was determined to get that acceptance before we left my jet.

"I'd have to be an idiot to decline the offer," she said, her tone serious now. "Besides the fact that it isn't really fair to you, maybe

I'm also a little nervous. One step at a time seems a little safer. I've never done this without partners, Tanner."

"You're perfectly capable of doing it without partners," I assured her. "I get that hesitation. I've always had my brothers as partners. But in this case, you'll have me, Hannah. Maybe it might be hard to believe, but I'll be there for you this time."

"Fifteen percent," she ventured.

I had to force myself not to smile.

Fuck! I loved her persistence and stubbornness, even though it could be annoying when I wanted something.

This was part of the new Hannah, and it was intriguing because she'd never been this obstinate or business minded before.

Part of me wanted to just agree if it made her happy, but I had no desire to take away what should be hers.

"Four," I rumbled.

She shot me an irritated look. "That's not negotiating or meeting in the middle," she complained.

"Sweetheart, I'm Tanner Remington. That *is* the way I negotiate, and I always get my way these days."

She snorted. "Not with me, you won't. That hard-ass attitude won't fly with me. Twelve."

Hell, if things went my way, we were going to own everything together someday.

Hannah was about to give me exactly what I wanted.

I didn't want to press my luck.

"You're at twelve. I'm at four. I'll meet you in the middle. Eight. Final offer."

She sent me a satisfied smile, like she'd gotten exactly what she'd wanted. "You've got a deal."

She leaned over and kissed my cheek before she murmured, "Thank you."

It took everything I had not to pull her gorgeous mouth to mine, but I gritted my teeth and stopped that instinct.

Patience!

I wasn't going to get what I wanted from Hannah without some fucking patience.

I'd waited close to eight years.

My dick could wait longer.

I was glad she thought I'd compromised sufficiently in this battle.

She had no idea that I was actually the winner this time.

Hannah might not know it yet, but I'd just closed the most important deal of my life.

Chapter 19

Hannah

"If I would have known going to the spa was this amazing, I would have done it a long time ago," Lauren said as we sat in the quiet room of a day spa in Billings waiting for our pedicures.

It had been almost three weeks since Tanner and I had sealed our deal on my business, which I'd decided to name Glam Anywhere.

The business had proceeded at warp speed once we'd signed a contract.

Of course, that wasn't difficult to do when someone had Tanner Remington as a partner.

He'd put an entire team of people on the office, the business structure, and the website development.

Surprisingly, he'd been personally involved in every step, and he hadn't approved anything without getting my approval first.

My office was set up, all of the business details were done, and we were getting very close to launch.

I'd been working long days recruiting some basic contractors in the most important cities in Montana.

All of the structure was in place.

The most important things in my future were branding, bringing in new contractors, and advertising to make the business fly.

"This was all Tanner's idea," I reminded Lauren. "Personally, I thought I was way too busy to spend a day at the spa. But Tanner found out that I did a spa day on a routine basis in Seattle to manage my job stress. The next thing I knew, he'd arranged for us to go to a spa day because he thought I was working too hard."

I'd balked at the idea, but Tanner hadn't taken *no* for an answer.

Anna was out of town, or she'd definitely be with us today.

I had gotten closer to Lauren and Anna over the last three weeks, and I valued those blossoming relationships more than they'd ever know.

They'd both been so supportive of my new business.

Their expertise in economics, branding, and marketing were invaluable when I wanted to pick their brains for information.

Lauren let out a contented sigh. "I think it's one of the best ideas Tanner has ever had. I already feel so much better since you started giving me your beauty advice, and this pushes my wellness right over the top."

I turned my head and smiled at Lauren.

She looked amazing.

She had always been an attractive woman, even though she'd never saw that in herself.

Honestly, it wasn't the makeup, new hair, or her weight loss that was actually making her glow.

It was the newfound confidence that she was radiating that made a difference.

That was the funny thing about wellness and feeling like you were the best version of yourself physically.

It helped boost your mental perception of yourself, too.

That was probably why I enjoyed what I did so much.

Genetics and the beauty a woman had gotten by the luck of the genetic draw wasn't really important, but feeling like you were putting your best face forward could be life-changing for a woman. No matter what a woman had gotten in the genetic lottery.

"I'm a firm believer in spa days," I told Lauren honestly. "Women don't take the time for self-care in a world where they desperately need it, physically and mentally. It's always been a mood booster for me."

"I think I get that after today," she said as she smoothed down her white spa robe and sipped at her water. "I think I'll be a regular here now. That facial and the massage were amazing."

She was right, and I was now thankful that Tanner had insisted on this spa day.

I'd forgotten what it was like to take care of myself.

I'd been too busy stressing over my mom and my future in Crystal Fork to even think about revisiting a spa.

"We'll make a promise to remind each other that we need to do this," I told her. "We'll drag Anna with us next time."

"She was bummed that she couldn't come," Lauren mentioned.

"I just feel bad that Tanner insisted on paying," I said unhappily.

Lauren shot me a puzzled look. "Why? Tanner is richer than a god, and he really likes treating people to things they love."

I shook my head. "I'm just so used to taking care of myself."

Lauren let out an amused snort. "You haven't realized that Tanner thinks he's the caretaker of everyone he cares about? I'm used to taking care of myself, too, but you'll eventually have to accept that Tanner is...Tanner. I gave up on that battle a long time ago. Since he became a billionaire, his favorite thing is to give everyone what he thinks they need, regardless of the cost. You're lucky that he hasn't bought you a house or a new vehicle yet. Yes, it's exasperating at times, but I finally realized that it actually makes him happy. He feels like he's doing something to help the people he cares about, and he expects nothing in return. I only argue with him now if it's something extreme, like my new house. He's still a little pissed off that I wouldn't let him pay for it outright for me. But he's done so much to help me in the past that I flatly refused. I make more than enough money to pay for it."

"He's always been generous," I admitted. "Even when he wasn't a billionaire."

"Ha!" Lauren exclaimed. "You haven't really seen his madness yet. He was just coming into his money when you two separated, and he was too obsessed with KTD to spend it. Let him do things for you sometimes, Hannah. It honestly does make him feel like he's useful, and his only motivation is to make people happy."

"He doesn't have to give me things to be useful," I argued. "He's been by my side every step of the way in my new business."

"You're surprised," she guessed. "It's taking you a while to see how much he's changed since that KTD obsession he went through."

"It's hard to get used to," I said softly. "I think he's more interested in helping me than furthering his own business interests right now."

"You told me that you and Tanner wanted to start over being the people you are now," Lauren said gently. "That's the man he is now, Hannah, and has been for quite a few years now."

"More like the old Tanner?" I questioned.

"More like the old Tanner on steroids," she said with a chuckle.

"I kind of noticed that," I confessed. "Tanner was always thoughtful during the majority of our relationship, but now I feel like he anticipates my needs before I do."

Lauren nodded. "I swear he spends a lot of time thinking about what's best for his loved ones. He's scary observant now."

He was, and it was almost unsettling.

It wasn't that I didn't like that kind of attention from Tanner, but I wasn't used to it.

"Get used to it," Lauren said like she'd been reading my mind. "Tanner takes care of the people he cares about, and I don't think that's going to change. And he's pretty pigheaded about it, too."

"He's given me enough," I informed her. "I couldn't have started my new business without him, and he negotiated ridiculously stupid terms for a business tycoon. Since that deal, he's dedicated his time and energy to Glam Anywhere, and he's given me an obscene amount of things he thinks I'll need."

This trip to the spa was only one more thoughtful thing he'd done in a long line of thoughtful gifts.

Some of those things I'd needed, like an updated computer with plenty of storage and speed.

Some of the things he'd given me were definitely over the top, like a brand new mountain bike that was nicer than the one he had at his house.

I'd argued adamantly, but the big lug didn't budge an inch when he really wanted me to accept something, so that bike was now stored at my apartment because he'd refused to take it back.

"You'll get used to it," Lauren said nonchalantly. "I've been a grown woman who can take care of herself for a long time, and he still shows up at my place with stupidly expensive things he thinks I need."

"But you're like a little sister to him, Lauren," I reasoned. "That makes a lot more sense."

She raised a brow. "Does it?" she questioned.

"Yeah," I mumbled. "I'm just a previous love interest of his from years ago that he's now...helping."

"If you think that's all there is to your relationship, you're crazy," Lauren said drily. "I've seen the two of you together. I've also seen the way he looks at you. Tanner is trying to gain your trust back, and I don't think that's just because he wants to be your lifelong friend or something. He's biding his time until he knows exactly what you want from him."

I sent Lauren a startled look.

Tanner hadn't given me any reason to think he wanted anything more than we had right now.

Yeah, we'd talked about starting over in a relationship, but that amazing kiss we'd shared in Helena hadn't been repeated.

We'd grown closer emotionally, and we'd gotten to know each other better, but he'd never given me a clue that he wanted anything more.

Unfortunately, it was hard for me to be around Tanner without wanting to get him naked, but I'd learned to squash those desires to the best of my ability.

That approach wasn't working as well as I wished it would.

The more I got to know the man Tanner was now, the more I adored him.

"I think you're crazy," I muttered to Lauren.

"And I think you're in denial," she said with an amused chuckle. "Tell him you're completely ready for a romantic relationship with him, and he'll pull out all the stops to get you back. I think he's just waiting until he thinks he's made up for some of the crap he's done to you in the past. I guess the question is…do you want him back, too? I have zero doubts about what Tanner wants. I've known him for a long time. He doesn't talk about it to me, but he seems so happy when he's with you, like he's finally exactly where he wants to be."

"We forgave each other for all of the things that happened in the past," I told her. "We've started over."

Lauren shook her head. "I don't think he'll let go of that until he knows that you trust him. That takes time."

"We're just getting to know each other again," I said.

"I think it's good that you're taking your time," Lauren replied. "He did hurt you, Hannah. I know you're starting over, but those wounds needed time to heal. You needed to get to know Tanner again because he's changed. But if you decide that you're willing to trust him completely, you're totally screwed. That man will do anything for you. I don't think there's ever been anyone for him *but* you, and he knows he took your relationship for granted. He's not going to screw that up again if you give him another chance."

"We can never go back," I said earnestly. "I was a different woman seven years ago."

Lauren took a deep breath. "I know I'm not a person who should be giving advice on relationships, but I know Tanner. He is like a brother to me. You're right. Things would be different. You're different people. But is that really a bad thing? You spent a lot of time sacrificing your own needs for Tanner's ambitions back then." She held up a hand as I started to object. "Hear me out. I know Tanner didn't insist you do that, but you wanted to see him happy, and you willingly put a lot of his needs and wants first without much compromise. I honestly don't think it would be all bad if you had something new and better than it was before. In fact, I don't think Tanner will do it any other way now."

I sighed instead of arguing.

In a lot of ways, she was correct.

I'd lost some of myself in our old relationship, which wasn't Tanner's fault.

It was mine.

"I let myself get caught up in his success," I explained. "I wanted him to be happy."

"I understand that," Lauren answered. "You're a giving person, Hannah, but it doesn't have to be that way anymore. Let Tanner give back. I know he's very willing and able to do that. Take what he's offering and know that he wants to do it because he cares. It's really just that simple. Take all the time you need to be sure of what you want. Believe me, Tanner is going to be there when and if you're ready."

I shook myself back to reality.

The truth was, Tanner hadn't shown me anything but friendship since that night in Helena.

"I'm not sure that Tanner really wants a romantic relationship," I said hesitantly.

"Because he hasn't made a move on you?" she queried.

I nodded slowly.

"Anyone who knows him can see what he wants. Everyone except you. If you make one move to show him what you want, he'll be all over that. I don't think he wants to push you, but that man is getting desperate."

I snorted. "Are you telling me to seduce him?"

"I don't think you need to do that," Lauren said drily. "Tell him you want him and that you trust him, and it's over. No seduction necessary."

"We've gotten close over the last few weeks," I murmured. "I don't want to screw that up."

Tanner and I saw each other every day, on both a professional and a personal level.

We spent almost every evening together, and he made sure we left some time to play on the weekends. He'd insisted on it.

I cooked because I liked to cook.

He helped clean up.

We'd talked about anything and everything on those evenings and weekends together.

I'd gotten to the point where I longed to see his handsome face every day.

I wasn't sure what I'd do if things suddenly changed for us.

I couldn't say that we were dating.

But I couldn't say that we were just friends, either.

Tanner and I were somewhere in between.

Was it really possible that Tanner was waiting for me to decide what I wanted?

Maybe?

In Helena, I had been a little uncertain about whether we could have a romantic relationship again.

I also remembered him mentioning that he was letting me decide if I was ready for that.

Lauren put a comforting hand on my shoulder. "I don't think it's possible for you to screw things up with Tanner unless you decide to start seeing someone else."

I was about to tell her that would never happen when the nail technician arrived at the door of the quiet room to pick us up, abruptly ending our conversation.

Over the last few weeks, I knew I'd started to fall in love with Tanner Remington all over again.

Maybe there had never been anyone *except* Tanner Remington for me, either.

Chapter 20

Tanner

"I'm surprised that you actually accepted my invite to have dinner," Devon said drily. "I was sure you and Hannah had become attached at the hip."

I was prepared to dig into my chicken fried steak that had just been delivered to our table at Charlie's when I grumbled, "Hannah and Lauren went to the spa in Billings today. They're going to stop to have some dinner there."

"So I'm your backup plan?" he asked jokingly.

"Basically, yes," I shot back. "Mom ate already, and Kaleb is out of town with Anna. And Hannah and I are not attached at the hip. We don't spend every night together."

To my regret, we'd missed a few nights together in the last three weeks.

Devon grinned as he picked up his burger. "Okay, *almost* every night. Not that I blame you. She's a lot prettier than I am. How are things going between the two of you?"

"Good," I said with shrug. "Her business is almost up and running."

He frowned. "I'm not asking about business, Tanner. I'm talking about you and Hannah. I've seen the two of you together. We all have. It's blatantly obvious that you'd like a lot more than a business arrangement or a friendship. Sometimes you look almost desperate for a whole lot more. Your balls must be bright blue by now."

Hell, I was hoping I wasn't *that* obvious.

Getting myself off every night wasn't working for me.

It didn't even take the edge off for me anymore.

My dick was hard the moment I saw Hannah, and that condition didn't stop until she was long out of sight.

"I'll handle the blue balls as long as necessary," I told him. "I want a lot more than a bed partner with Hannah, and I'll get that, eventually."

Devon looked up from his food. "How much more?"

I'd talked to Kaleb and Devon about Hannah, but I'd avoided telling them exactly where I wanted our relationship to go.

"Everything," I said huskily as I met Devon's inquisitive gaze. "I'm getting her back. Hannah was always meant to be mine."

I knew that with every breath I took.

I just wasn't exactly certain how to accomplish that goal.

Trust took time, but I was starting to lose my battle for sanity when I was around Hannah.

Surprisingly, Devon didn't look the least bit fazed by my admission.

"Glad you finally realized that," he said as his attention went back to his burger. "When you get her back, I'll be the first one to celebrate. You've been a cranky asshole for the last seven years. I'm not going to bullshit and say that you're a ray of sunshine now, but you're a lot happier since Hannah came back into your life. Plus, she'll finally be my sister-in-law. Win-win."

"I wish it was that easy," I rumbled.

"It is easy," he contradicted. "The feelings are still there. Just pick up where you left off, but don't be a dick this time."

"I'm not going to be a dick," I informed him. "But we can't just pick up where we left off. It's been seven years, and neither of us are the same as we were before."

In a more serious voice, he answered, "Don't make this more complicated than it needs to be, Tanner. You were always the most thoughtful Remington brother. You analyze things to death when it comes to Hannah."

I shot him an annoyed look. "When you want something bad enough, you want to make sure you don't screw it up. Hannah doesn't completely trust me anymore."

"Yes, she does," Devon countered. "If she didn't trust you, she never would have made a business deal with you. This business means a lot to her."

I'd thought about that, and those thoughts had made me a little more hopeful. "Just because she trusted me in business doesn't mean that she wants to be with me personally again."

"Like I said," he answered. "You make things way too complicated. You don't have to be the same people you were years ago. People change over the years. The feelings just still have to be there. You and Hannah both feel the same way you did a long time ago. Seduce her and get it over with. That kind of sexual tension will make a guy insane."

I shot him a curious look. "How would you know what it's like to want a woman you can't have?"

"I probably know more about getting burned than you might think," he replied evasively.

"Are you ever going to tell me who she was?" I asked.

Devon might act like he never wanted entanglements of any kind, but all of that was bravado.

I'd always known that.

He dated, but he always managed to keep things simple and uninvolved.

Devon only dated women who wouldn't tie him down or ask for more than he wanted to give, and I knew there was a reason for that.

There had been a woman he'd cared about at one time, but it must have been so short-lived that his family had never known what had happened.

"Nope," Devon quipped. "And nothing really happened. You're going to have to accept that I just don't want the same thing that you and Kaleb do. I'm happy with my life, Tanner. I like my freedom. Just let it go."

Kaleb and I had tried to figure out what was going on with Devon for years, and he hadn't budged. We'd had a few theories, but I didn't think what we assumed was actually true.

Whatever it was, there was something that had happened to Devon that we didn't know about.

I didn't buy that nothing had happened to change him.

In college, he'd wanted to meet someone in the future that he could share his life with.

For some reason, that had changed, and he'd become more than a little jaded about relationships and commitment.

It was a little perplexing that we'd never been able to wring the truth out of him.

For the most part, we'd always told each other everything.

Devon might act like he didn't care about anything, but there was a heart buried under that cynicism of his.

He'd taken our father's death just as hard as Kaleb and I had. He joked about prowling around Mom's ranch because he wanted food, but I knew the truth.

Just like Kaleb and me, he was protective of the parent he still had.

"Fine," I finally conceded. "But I'm here if you ever want to talk about it."

He swallowed the last of his burger before he replied, "There's nothing to talk about. I think we need to get your love life straightened out before anyone worries about the one I'll never have. What's your plan with Hannah? I care about her, and I don't want to see you mess up this second chance."

"I won't," I assured him.

"What would you do if she started to date someone else?" he asked. "It's not like she's not free to do that right now. You're treating her like one of your buddies, and you haven't spoken up about exactly what you want."

I ground my teeth and tamped down the urge to throttle my younger brother.

He was trying to get to me.

And it was working.

"That. Won't. Happen."

Devon shrugged. "It could. Hannah is a beautiful, talented woman. Everyone in Crytal Fork adores her now. Hell, she just did a free makeover and haircut for Lisa Thompson a few days ago because Lisa was sick for a while. I heard through the gossip channels that Lisa wants to fix Hannah up with her single brother now."

"Not. Happening," I growled.

Devon raised a brow. "You think not? There's a gorgeous single woman in town, and the single guys are noticing her, Tanner. You know how things are here. The whole town wants to play match-maker when they see a single woman that they accept as one of their own."

"I don't see Hannah accepting a date with Marvin Thompson," I said tersely. "Or anyone else in this town for that matter."

I had nothing against Marvin or any of the single guys in Crystal Fork, but Hannah was fucking mine. Any single guy in this town would have to be crazy to touch a woman who was already mine.

"What?" Devon said with irritating innocence. "Do you think everyone knows that you want Hannah? Sure, there's speculation because everyone in Crystal Fork loves to speculate, but nobody really knows, and you two act like you're just friends."

The thought of some man asking her out and actually laying a hand on Hannah made my blood pressure spike.

I slammed my fist down on the table. "I'd destroy the first man who lays a hand on her," I said in a guttural voice.

Devon sent me a satisfied grin. "Now you sound more like the older brother I know."

"Are you trying to piss me off?" I asked gruffly.

He shook his head. "No. I'm trying to get you to shake off your fear of losing Hannah and make you realize that you can't lose some-one who's not yours...yet. Make your move, bro, or somebody else might beat you to it. Crystal Fork might have given up on hooking us up, but they're going to try to find a match for Hannah. And you know the matchmakers can be relentless. Hannah doesn't have to agree to the date. The busybodies will make sure she's in the right place at the right time to 'run into' whoever they're trying to set her up with. They've done it a million time to both of us in the past."

Fuck! He was right. This town had written the Remington brothers off as hopeless a long time ago, but I knew the way those matchmakers operated. I'd been manipulated into having dinner with more daughters, nieces, and friends than I could count in the past.

And Hannah was too damn nice to leave an awkward situation.

"I hear you," I acknowledged. "I'll warn her in case she's forgotten how persistent the matchmakers in this town can be."

Everyone had started to accept Hannah as one of their own, and they'd hound her until they found a 'nice guy' for her.

Devon nodded. "I'd definitely warn her, and make your intentions known, even if it has to be subtle for now. I know how important Hannah is to you, Tanner. Let everyone else know, especially her. You're not going to scare her off."

I cocked a brow. "How do you know that?"

"Hannah doesn't scare that easily, and she feels the same way you do," he stated simply. "I think you're both just afraid to be the first one to admit it."

"I'm not afraid to tell her how I feel," I argued. "I'm just not sure she's ready to hear it. I basically left the ball in her court, and I'm not sure where she stands right at the moment."

"You'll never know until you try," Devon reminded me. "I'm not saying you have to marry her tomorrow, but put yourself out of your misery and tell her the truth. Tell her you're losing it. This whole friendship and business partner thing is making you half crazy."

"Is it really that obvious?" I asked reluctantly.

Devon pushed his empty plate away and picked up his water. "Probably not to everyone, but you're my brother. I know you, and I make it my business to make sure that you're happy. I know you're happy having Hannah back in your life, but I know your frustration when I see it, and I hate that for you. Especially when I know it could be easily resolved. Just rip the Band-Aid off and do it, Tanner.

It's not going to get any easier. The uncertainty of this situation is killing you."

I had to admit that my patience was getting razor thin.

It was hell being with Hannah and not touching her.

At this point, Hannah was either going to trust me...or she wouldn't.

She'd said that she was starting to trust me in Helena.

These last few weeks had either pushed her to the point where she could trust me to start over...or not.

Being in limbo and not knowing my fate *was* killing me.

I nodded as Devon sent me an empathetic glance.

My younger brother might act like an insensitive asshole sometimes, but when it was really important, he dropped that persona and acted like a brother who gave a shit.

I might not always like his methods, but I couldn't argue about how much he cared.

"I'll return the favor someday," I promised him.

"I'm never going to need advice on my love life because I don't have or want one," he said nonchalantly.

I didn't believe that.

Some woman was going to knock Devon on his ass someday.

Devon wasn't as cold as he wanted people to think he was.

He just buried his heart under a whole lot of bullshit.

It would take a tough female to reach the real Devon, but when she did, all hell would break lose, and I looked forward to watching that particular show when it happened.

Chapter 21

Hannah

"I can't possibly go to New York for the weekend," I told Tanner the next day. "Glam Anywhere is getting ready to launch. I'm too busy."

It was Thursday, and we'd just had dinner at Tanner's house.

He'd just casually dropped the fact that we were going to New York for the weekend like it was already a done deal.

I was settled on the couch when Tanner handed me a glass of wine and seated himself next to me with a bottle of beer from a local microbrewery.

"You can and you will. The business is ready to launch. You don't need to be fretting over things over the weekend," he said firmly. "I got the best tickets in the house to see Wicked on Broadway. We never got a chance to see it, and you mentioned that you never saw it in Seattle. I know it was at the top of your wish list. I knew you'd refuse to take enough time off to go to Australia, but this is something we can do. When we signed our contract, you promised not to work on weekends unless it's an emergency. And you have Reese now to manage the office."

"We're so close to launch. It is an emergency," I informed him.

All of the things he'd said were true.

At his insistence, I'd hired a manager because it made sense. My duties were extensive as the new owner, and even though I'd argued that I could manage the office myself to lower overhead, Tanner would have none of it. Since his reasoning had made sense, I'd hired Reese to take care of the day-to-day duties and issues so I could focus on branding and marketing the business.

And yes, I had promised not to work weekends because I didn't want to get burned out and unfocused because I was exhausted.

However, the closer we got to launch, the more things I had to get completed.

"Did you really get tickets to Wicked?" I asked, touched because he'd done that just for me.

Tanner didn't mind the theater, but he didn't love Broadway shows nearly as much as I did.

He nodded. "I also booked us restaurant reservations."

When he named one of the most expensive and exclusive restaurants in New York, I almost swallowed my tongue.

It was a place we never could have dreamed about going to when we were together as a couple in New York because it was obscenely expensive.

It took me a moment to remember that Tanner had unlimited resources, and he could do or buy anything he wanted without a second thought.

"Come with me, Hannah," he said in a low, seductive baritone. "We'll have a great time."

That was indisputable.

I had a great time whenever I was with Tanner, and he was offering me something I really wanted because he was a thoughtful guy.

"It's a crazy idea," I said weakly. "We'll have to fly."

He grinned. "And I just happen to have a private jet. It's not complicated. We get on the jet. It takes us to New York. We see an incredible show and have a nice dinner."

He mentioned the accommodations, and I had to remind myself one more time that Tanner was a billionaire.

He was planning on staying in the Presidential Suite at one of the most expensive hotels in the city.

Honestly, I still wasn't used to this new Tanner.

I'd seen him reach success, and we were in the process of building an expensive home, but I'd never really had a chance to experience this powerful business tycoon who wore that success like the billionaire he was today.

God, I really wanted to go with him.

Not just for the experience, but to be with Tanner for an entire weekend without any other distractions.

Really, there was no reason I couldn't go, but it would really feel more like…a romantic date.

It wouldn't be easy for me to be with Tanner that way and not want a lot more than his friendship.

Like he could read my mind, he said offhandedly, "Consider this our first date."

I turned my head and found him watching me intently, like he was nervous about my answer.

"But we aren't really dating," I said breathlessly.

"And that's a problem for me, Hannah," he rumbled. "I don't want to be just your friend. I want more, and I'm hoping you do too, and that you'll give me another shot at treating you the way you should have been treated a long time ago. Being with you without touching you or treating you like you're my woman is making me lose my mind."

My heart stopped for just a moment as I looked into his eyes.

His expression was so fierce and mesmerizing that my core clenched viciously with a need that almost consumed me.

God, I wanted that.

I wanted him so badly, and I wasn't going to even try to deny that anymore.

I probably had never stopped wanting Tanner Remington, even when we weren't together.

Now, he was laying his emotions on the line with no reservations, not knowing how I'd respond.

"We don't have to rush things," he assured me. "I just can't handle not being able to touch you anymore. It's killing me."

I took a deep breath and inhaled Tanner's tantalizing, masculine scent.

Everything about him overwhelmed me sometimes, and the urge to touch him, get closer to him, was nearly unbearable.

Tears filled my eyes, and a single tear dropped onto my cheek.

"Christ!" Tanner swore. "I didn't mean to make you cry. Forget I said anything."

I shook my head and reached out to grab a fistful of his pristine, custom shirt.

I pulled him closer to me, and he certainly didn't resist.

I closed my eyes and savored the feel of his warm breath on my lips before I said, "It's been killing me, too. I want to be with you, Tanner. I trust you, but I was afraid of ruining what we've gained in the last several weeks."

A powerful arm wrapped around my waist to pull me against his massive body before he lowered his mouth to mine.

Tanner kissed me like a man possessed, and I relished every second of it.

My hands speared into his hair, absorbing the intimacy like I needed it to keep on living.

Tanner and I had always had an explosive chemistry, but this time it was different. That chemistry was still there, but it was much more…intense.

The embrace was desperate.

Possessive.

Demanding.

It felt like he wanted to possess me, and God, I really wanted to let him take everything he wanted and more.

Probably because I felt the same way, and I couldn't get close enough to this man to satisfy that longing.

When he finally let me come up for air, I was panting, and my heart was racing like it was going to pound out of my chest.

"I can't seem to go slow when it comes to you," he said huskily. "But I'll try. Tell me you'll go with me to New York. I want you all to myself for a few days, Hannah. I'm not asking you to sleep with me, and I'm not asking for more than you want to give. I just want to be with you."

My heart squeezed so painfully that it physically hurt.

I let out a long sigh as he rearranged our bodies until I was leaning back against the front of his body with my head resting on his shoulder.

I'd get Tanner naked without a second thought, but maybe he was right.

Maybe it was too soon for that.

My body didn't think so, but my head said we'd barely gotten to know each other again.

"I want to go," I answered honestly. "I want to spend that time with you, too."

I felt his body physically relax. "Then it will be our first date."

I opened my mouth to tell him that we'd had our first date a long time ago, but I closed it again.

Really, it was a first date for us.

I was different.

He was different.

This relationship felt different.

I was probably more giddy than I'd felt when we'd first met.

So, it was a first date for us.

"It's a little fancier than our real first date."

We'd met having coffee, but our previous first date was going to a movie and dinner at a casual diner.

"I don't really have anything to wear, and we're leaving tomorrow," I added. "That's not a casual restaurant, and I haven't been out on the town for a long time."

"We'll go early so we can stop on Fifth Avenue," he replied. "I'll get you whatever you want. Let me take care of you for a change, Hannah."

I wanted to protest, but I suddenly remembered what Lauren had said at the spa.

If buying things for the people he cared about made Tanner happy, then I'd let him get me a dress.

This time.

"Thank you," I said softly. "I'll try not to break your credit card."

He chuckled as he toyed with my hair. "Sweetheart, that would be impossible to do, but I'd enjoy watching you try."

"What if I decided to go on a massive shopping spree with your credit card? I'm sure you have an endless amount of credit," I teased.

"Then I'd be the happiest asshole on the planet," he said seriously. "I want to give you all of the things you should have had a long time ago. I promised you the world, Hannah, and I never got a chance to deliver."

My heart melted because there was so much regret in his tone.

I squirmed until we were facing each other.

Because we were so close, I couldn't help but fall into his beautiful blue eyes.

I could see and feel his remorse, and that wasn't what I wanted.

Before the meteoric rise of KTD, Tanner had always been good to me. He'd been the boyfriend that most women wanted but could never find.

My heart in my throat, I put a palm against his cheek. "No more regrets," I whispered, wanting to soothe him. "We talked about this. We both made some mistakes." I put my fingers against his lips when he began to protest. "I'm a different woman. I'm all grown up, and I can handle my emotions. I don't want material things, Tanner. I just want to be with you. A new relationship, and a fresh start without regrets anymore."

It was just that simple, and just that complicated.

I was falling in love with Tanner all over again.

The way that I felt about him had probably never changed, but this relationship felt...different.

Maybe I was old enough and wise enough to notice all of the things I never had before.

Tanner had changed over the years, too.

Whatever it was, this relationship was intense, but I was strong enough to stand up to him and be the partner I couldn't be a long time ago.

"The past is the past," I added. "I'm looking forward to an incredible future, but if you hurt me, I'll be in your face about it."

He grinned, and my heart did a somersault.

God, more than anything, I wanted things to work out for us this time.

"Are you saying that you can handle me now, sweetheart?" he asked in a low, sensual voice that sent a jolt of electricity down my spine. "I'm pretty used to getting my way."

That sensation landed directly between my thighs.

Oh, hell yes, I could handle Tanner Remington.

"You're not always going to get your way," I told him.

"I'm going to try," he warned me.

I smiled.

Tanner was a powerful man now who was obviously used to getting what he wanted when he wanted it.

Once he'd completely worked his way through his remorse about the past, he was going to be a bossy, demanding partner.

Surprisingly, since that was actually Tanner's nature, I didn't want it any other way.

Chapter 22

Tanner

"I think I'm ready," Hannah informed me as she walked out of her bedroom late on Saturday afternoon with a radiant smile on her beautiful face.

I'd been ready for over an hour, but I'd been content to sit in our hotel suite and wait for Hannah with a tumbler of good whiskey.

It took me a moment to respond because Hannah literally took my breath away.

She was always beautiful, no matter what she was wearing, but in the designer, ruby red dress she'd gotten on Fifth Avenue yesterday, she was stunning.

I'd left my card with the store she'd chosen, and insisted on her not knowing the price of any of the things she wanted.

I'd left with the assistant falling all over Hannah to find her anything and everything she wanted.

My woman had good taste.

She'd chosen a designer gown with sheer sleeves and a plunging neckline.

And, of course, it had to be red.

My cock was already having a field day.

I decided that I was going to have a love/hate relationship with that gown almost immediately.

That silk top barely covered her gorgeous breasts and the entire gown molded to her body like a second skin.

There was also a slit up the side that showed a flirty amount of her long, shapely leg whenever she moved.

Hannah was average height for a female, but she had the legs of a runway model.

I had to stop and reassure myself that she was *my* woman.

My date.

She was going to draw the attention of more than one interested male glance, but as long as they didn't touch her, I'd have to roll with it.

She was, after all, dressed up to go out with *me.*

My possessive streak was soothed a little when those thoughts finally computed in my brain.

I stood, already dressed in a dark suit and tie.

As I moved closer to her, I caught the scent of her subtle but sensual perfume, and I nearly lost it.

This isn't the time to give in to your cock, Remington.

This night was for Hannah, and I wanted to make it a night she'd never forget.

This was the date she'd never gotten years ago, and I was going to make damn sure it was unforgettable.

I ran my hands down her arms. "You look stunning, sweetheart."

Those words didn't do justice to her radiance, but there really weren't words to tell her how I felt right now.

She smiled broader. Her eyes sparkled as she put a palm to my cheek affectionately. "You look incredibly handsome yourself, Mr. Remington."

I let her go and swiped a box from the coffee table. "I want to give you something before we go," I said as I handed her the box I'd picked up yesterday while she was shopping. "You might want to wear them."

She looked at the box and then up at me again.

The gorgeous smile left her face.

"Harry Winston?" she said breathlessly. "Please tell me that whatever you bought is just in a Harry Winston box."

Fuck! I hated that look on her face.

I tossed the box back on the coffee table, took her hand, and led her to the sofa.

"I think we better talk before you open the box," I said gruffly as we sat.

"Tanner," she said hesitantly.

"Just let me talk, Hannah. I think we need to get a few things cleared up now that we're starting over again."

She nodded slowly.

"I'm not a young guy who doesn't know what my priorities are, and I'm not the man you knew who couldn't pull his head out of his ass long enough to realize what really mattered. The urge to be a good provider for you was always there for me. Not because you can't take care of yourself. You did a damn fine job of doing that for yourself in Seattle. But it doesn't matter. I think every man wants to take care of the people he cares about, and that instinct to take care of you and make you happy has gotten even worse for me with age and maturity. My obsession with KTD started out with me wanting to take care of you, but I got caught up in the game of trying to be the best. That's not where my head is anymore, and it hasn't been for a long time. In my mind, I don't see the point of having the money I have now if I can't use it to make people happy. I have everything I could possibly want or need. Maybe my obsession with wanting to make you happy, provide well for you, and needing to watch out for your safety is old fashioned, but it is what it is. That's who I am now. More than likely, I'll be a pain in your ass in the future, but I can't change who I am. I'm going to buy you the stuff I want you to have in the future, things I couldn't afford when we were together last time, and I hope to hell you can learn to just accept that."

She shook her head. "It's not really that…"

"What is it then?" I demanded to know.

"I'm used to taking care of myself, Tanner. I'm not used to some-one caring about my safety or my happiness anymore."

"Get used to it," I grumbled. "As long as we're together breathing the same air, I'm always going to be thinking about ways to see that gorgeous smile of yours, and I am *always* going to be protective. We spent years on a tight budget, Hannah. Now I'm obscenely rich and I can give you anything your heart desires. Let me?"

"Has it ever occurred to you that I want you to be happy, too," she said stubbornly. "I'm not a billionaire, so what can I do to make *you* happy?"

Hell, there was only so much honesty a man could do.

I didn't think she was ready for that answer.

"Accept everything I want to give you?" I suggested. "And just be with me. If you do, I promise you that I'll be ecstatically happy."

She slapped me on the shoulder. "You know that's not what I'm talking about."

I shrugged. "It's the truth."

"You're impossible," she said with a small smile. "Now tell me what I can do to make you happy if I'm going to readily accept what you want to do for me."

"I'd think that would be pretty obvious, sweetheart. I haven't dated anyone since the day we broke up. I just want *you*. Always have. Always will."

She let out a happy sigh, and that smile I loved was back on her face again. "You're an incredible man, Tanner Remington. Have I told you that lately?"

I grinned at her. "No. But you just made my fucking day."

"Then I'll make sure I remind you of that every day," she shot back. "And I'll figure out how to make you happy without being a billionaire."

Hell, I was easy. All she had to do was crook a finger and let me know she wanted me.

I'd get her naked and be the happiest guy on earth.

She didn't crook her finger, but she leaned into me, wrapped her arms around my neck, and put those plump, warm lips against mine.

She hadn't gotten naked, but this was the next best thing.

My patience snapped almost immediately.

I wrapped my arms around her waist, pulling her as close to me as she could get, and took complete control of the embrace.

I wanted Hannah more than I wanted to take my next breath, and I ravaged her mouth in the way only a lover should.

She urged me on, giving back exactly what I gave her, and it made my cock as hard as a pipe.

Somehow, I needed to brand Hannah as mine, and this kiss was my only option at the moment.

I savored the possessive connection with a primitive satisfaction that I'd never experienced before.

I felt like a caveman, but I really didn't give a fuck.

Hannah was mine, and if I got my way, which I planned on getting, she'd be mine for the rest of our lives.

Reminding myself not to be a selfish prick, I finally eased up.

We had an incredible night planned, and Hannah was going to get exactly what she deserved.

She was panting and my heart was pumping like I'd just run a marathon when I finally released her mouth.

Hannah and I had always had incredible sexual chemistry, but the way I wanted my cock inside her warm, welcoming body to claim her was beyond incredible sexual chemistry right now.

But that obsessive need was going to have to wait.

I'd have to be content with taking her out as my woman at the moment.

The way she was clinging to me soothed those carnal instincts. A little.

I didn't want to rush this whole dating thing, and I didn't want to go this quickly. I wanted Hannah to be sure of exactly what she wanted from me before she ended up in my bed.

"Does that answer your question about what will make me happy?" I questioned huskily as I swept my lips along her temple, savoring her sexy scent.

"No," she whispered. "I think that kiss swept every thought out of my mind for a moment except for the carnal ones. Sometimes I wish you weren't so damn hot."

She sounded so disgruntled that I chuckled as I finally released her.

"Personally, I'm glad you think so, because it's hell keeping my hands off you," I shared.

She sent me a sensual smile. "Did I ever ask you to keep your hands off me?"

"Hannah," I growled, warning her that my control wasn't a sure thing.

"Okay, okay," she said with a musical laugh as she smoothed her dress out with her palms. "I'll try to behave."

Hell, I'd rather she didn't, and I really needed to change the subject. "Are you ready to open that box now?"

She nodded. "I think so."

I picked it up and handed it to her.

She took a deep breath and popped the lid.

Hannah gasped, even though I was pretty sure she knew exactly what she'd find.

Since the collection had first come out, she'd covertly eyed the lily cluster necklace and earrings from Harry Winston like it was the most beautiful jewelry she'd ever seen.

I'd known that she'd never expected to own it herself, but she'd admired it from afar.

I'd seen her face every time she saw it in a magazine or an advertisement in New York.

She'd had the same look on her face that almost any guy had when he saw an expensive Ferrari or a Bugatti he knew he'd never own.

She'd viewed it with reverent appreciation but with realistic perception.

I'd made a vow to myself to get her a piece or two of that collection one day.

Today, I was finally making good on that promise I'd made to myself so long ago.

"Oh, dear God," she said in an awed voice. "I probably should have known you'd go big."

"No reason not to," I answered. "And I know those are the pieces that always caught your eye."

I hadn't bought a simple pendant and earrings.

The necklace was a series of interconnected, diamond lilies that went completely around the platinum setting.

The earrings were matching diamond lilies and platinum.

The necklace was finely crafted and delicate, and it wasn't a gaudy piece, which was probably what Hannah had loved about it.

"Tanner," she said as she gingerly traced one of the flowers. "This was the most expensive piece."

"It was also the one you loved," I reminded her.

I took the necklace out of the box and started securing it around her neck.

"You noticed," she said like she was surprised that I'd paid attention.

"I wasn't always a dick," I said jokingly.

"You weren't, but you were working so hard," she answered.

"I loved you, Hannah. I hope you never doubted that. Of course I noticed."

Once the necklace was secure, I handed her the earrings because there was no way I was going to try to stick an earring into her pierced ear.

She removed the earrings she was wearing and deftly put on the earrings without ever looking in the mirror.

It was probably a mystery to most men how women could put on a pair of pierced earrings so quickly without a single hesitation or misstep.

"Let me go look in the mirror," she said brightly. "I need to fix my lipstick and we can go."

She swiped a finger over my upper lip as she added, "You have lipstick on your mouth."

She'd probably performed this task a thousand times in the past, and I instinctively gave her the same answer I'd given her a thousand times before. "It's your fault."

She sighed with an unrepentant look on her face. "I have to agree with you this time. I did attack you."

"I wasn't exactly complaining," I said with a smirk.

"Thank you for the gift, Tanner," she said softly as she pulled her hand back. "It means more to me than you'll ever know. Not because of the monetary value, but because it was so thoughtful. I'll always cherish it because of that."

She lightly kissed my cheek so she didn't transfer any more of her makeup onto my face before she stood and sauntered into the bedroom.

Damned if her words hadn't made me feel like the king of the world.

I decided I liked feeling that way, and that she was going to have a lot more to cherish in the future.

Chapter 23

Hannah

"So what do you think of the food?" Tanner asked as the waiter walked away for moment.

We were on our millionth course, or at least it felt like it.

"It's exquisite," I replied honestly. "But the service is a little over the top. It's almost uncomfortable. I'm not quite sure it's my thing."

He cocked a brow. "What do you mean?"

God, I probably shouldn't have said that, but Tanner and I were making it a point to be honest with each other.

Most women would kill to be in my place right now.

It was one of the most elegant and expensive restaurants in New York, but I hadn't loosened up since we'd sat down.

And Tanner and I hadn't been able to speak in private until this moment.

I wasn't used to people catering to my every need and hovering over me to anticipate those needs. And the protocol for a fancy dinner like this was out of my wheelhouse.

Luckily, Tanner had handled the wine pairings. I really liked wine, but I wasn't versed in expensive vintages and years.

I felt awkward.

I probably should have looked up the etiquette for fine dining. The silverware was a total mystery to me.

I'd already used the wrong utensil for one of my courses, and our waiter had looked slightly horrified before he'd recovered quickly like the professional he was.

I'd also offered to use the same fork for the next course, and the same waiter had quickly picked up that fork, placed it on my plate, and hastily taken it to the kitchen like it was a faux pas to use the same fork twice.

Finally, I'd just decided to watch what Tanner did so I didn't make any further mistakes.

I'd heard about this restaurant of course, but I'd never known it was this complicated to eat a meal here.

This was also the longest meal I'd ever eaten. The small bites were delicious, but I wondered if it wouldn't be wiser to bring them all so we could consume them faster.

"Don't get me wrong," I reassured him. "The food is probably the best I've ever eaten, but I'm not sure when these courses will end, and I don't know the etiquette of fine dining like this. The silverware thing is confusing. And it's a little weird to have someone hovering over me all the time. And each course is just a bite or two. Do you do this often?"

Tanner smiled like he was highly amused. "Not often," he shared. "But I got used to it since I dine so much with wealthy business owners. I'm a guy who would rather dig into my meal because I'm usually starving. Relax. Enjoy the food. You're the customer, and the customer is always right. Eat with whatever silverware you want. The waiter can bring you more silverware."

Easy for him to say.

The waiter wasn't looking at *him* like he was an alien from another planet who ate like a barbarian.

Truthfully, people treated Tanner like he was a god.

Other than the few weird looks I'd gotten, the waiter had treated me like a princess, too, because I was obviously close to one of the richest men in the world.

I took a deep breath and tried to relax.

Tanner was right.

He was paying a lot of money for this meal.

I needed to just ignore the reactions to my ineptitude.

"Does it ever make you uncomfortable that people treat you like a god?" I queried.

He shrugged. "It was definitely something I had to get used to in the beginning. I guess I don't think about it much anymore. The people who care about me treat me the same way they always did."

Of course. I supposed it was something one got used to after years of being treated this way.

Just the fact that Tanner had been able to simply stop and pick up my necklace and earrings without a hitch told me he could arrange almost anything with a snap of his fingers.

He was a very powerful man now, and I doubted that many people told him there was something they *couldn't* do for him.

Really, it amazed me that Tanner was still...Tanner.

He'd obviously never let that power or the money get into his head.

Yes, he'd changed, but he'd changed for the better.

When he'd leveled with me in the suite about who he was and how he viewed life and his wealth, his explanation had just made me admire him more than I already did.

Did I object to his slightly old-fashioned attitude about providing for me and wanting to take care of me?

No, I really didn't.

In fact, it felt incredible to have a man who cared about me that much.

I hadn't quite gotten over wearing a jewelry set that I'd always admired but never dreamed of owning myself. But I was starting to get used to the fact that Tanner didn't see gifts like that as expensive. He bought and gave things to people to try to please them.

He wasn't a guy who ever had to worry about the cost.

I'd never had time to adjust to that fact in our earlier relationship. KTD had just been starting its meteoric rise when we'd separated. Yes, we'd been building an amazing home, but that home had been his first major purchase. He'd been too busy to think about the money in New York. He'd been too busy chasing the success of KTD when we'd lived here to spend any of that money he was accumulating.

Maybe I didn't need his money, and maybe I could take care of myself. However, his honesty and clear acceptance of who he was now had touched my heart.

I could accept his protectiveness and his desire to make me happy and keep me safe because I realized that taking care of people had become an integral part of his nature.

It was a quality that I adored about him now.

"If you don't like this place, we can blow it off and go get something else," he said seriously.

I shot him an astonished glance.

"We can't leave in the middle of a dinner like this," I said, appalled at the thought.

"Of course we can," he said nonchalantly. "As long as the dinner is paid for, we can do any damn thing we want."

"I think our waiter would have heart failure," I advised him.

"He won't as long as he gets a good tip," Tanner said with a grin. "Do you really think that rich people care what their waiter thinks? They don't. Not when they're paying for the services. It's just a restaurant, Hannah. If we want to leave, we leave. If you want to try that dessert they're preparing right now, we stay. Your choice."

Dessert? Okay, that made me relax. We were about to get the best part of this delicious meal.

I shook my head. "There's no way I'm missing dessert," I told him adamantly.

It might only be a bite or two, but it would probably be the best bite I'd ever had.

There was a mischievous look on Tanner's face as he replied, "If it's good, lick the spoon. If you really like it, ask for another one. This is your dinner, Hannah. Eat it however you want with whatever utensil you want. You don't have to get hung up on etiquette. It's not necessary."

"You do all the right things," I reminded him.

"Only because I had to learn," he answered. "I do business dinners, and it's probably become habit for me. I don't do these restaurants for pleasure most of the time because it's not really my thing, either. I like being fed great food in large portions. I'll probably grab a hot dog on the way to the theater tonight. I usually have to get something more substantial after a dinner like this."

A startled giggle left my lips before I slapped a hand over my mouth to stop it.

I was full, but I could see why Tanner might not be.

The man had a huge appetite.

"Did you really do that?" I asked.

"Every single time," he said.

"Then why are we here?" I questioned curiously.

"It's an experience you deserve," he replied seriously. "Only the best for my woman."

My heart squeezed inside my chest, and I wanted to fly over the table and kiss him.

This obviously wasn't exactly his scene, either, yet he'd wanted me to experience the best that New York could offer.

"Thank you," I said in a heartfelt tone. "The food has been a gastronomical delight. It's my first time dining like this. I guess I was just a little nervous about making mistakes."

My entire body relaxed as I realized my fear was all about embarrassing *him*.

This was Tanner's world now, and I'd wanted to fit in.

I wasn't a sophisticated woman.

Most men with his wealth probably didn't date beauticians whose idea of elegant was eating at a nice Italian restaurant with a huge plate of pasta.

"If I'd known it was going to make you nervous, I would have taken you to a different restaurant," he grumbled. "One that serves gigantic portions of good food without the pretentiousness."

"No," I said immediately. "This was an experience, Tanner. Something I've never done before. It means a lot to me that you wanted me to experience this, and the food is something I'll never forget."

"Even if you barely got to taste it," he teased.

"Absolutely," I answered, completely relaxed.

I viewed this dinner much differently now.

Tanner had wanted this to be a food experience for *me*.

He didn't give a damn if I ate like a woman who wasn't used to being treated like royalty.

All he cared about was making this evening special.

I suddenly realized that Tanner would give me the world on a platinum platter if I wanted it simply to make me happy.

My nervousness I'd experienced was completely *my* issue.

This world wasn't the way he lived his life, but he'd learned to adapt because of his enormous wealth and his business.

I didn't have to fit into this world because the real Tanner was the same small town guy I saw every single day.

Maybe he did wear that custom suit like he was born to it, but he was still the thoughtful man I'd come to adore.

Our dessert was presented with aplomb.

I picked up whatever spoon I wanted and savored those two bites. It was so decadent that I did lick the spoon.

Several times.

"Hannah," Tanner said in a warning growl.

"What?" I said innocently. "You told me to lick the spoon if it was good. It was heavenly."

"I changed my mind," he said. "You're driving me crazy."

I smiled as I realized that he was imagining something a little more carnal than chocolate ganache.

He was looking at me like he wanted to devour *me* in place of dessert.

A thrill of anticipation shot through my body. It had been so damn long since I'd seen that particular look.

My body ached with longing, and knowing that Tanner wanted me with the same desperation made me completely insane.

My hand shook just a little as I put the spoon on my empty plate. "Then I guess I won't have another one," I said teasingly to try to dispel the sexual tension between the two of us.

"Do it," he grunted. "I'll probably enjoy watching, but I might lose it."

Tanner and I had always been flirty, especially in the beginning of our relationship.

But we'd lost some of that in the last two years of our relationship when he'd started to get preoccupied with KTD's success, and it had *never* felt like this.

I was definitely falling in love with the new Tanner all over again, and it almost felt like a brand new relationship that was so much deeper than it had ever been before.

Maybe I'd been too mentally unhealthy to completely let him in before, but I was wide open and vulnerable now.

It was both scary and exhilarating at the same time.

However, I wasn't going to put up a wall to block those emotions.

I wanted to feel Tanner.

I wanted to experience that kind of intensity in our relationship.

"I'll spare you," I said in a sensual voice I didn't recognize. "This time."

He sent me a heated look of warning that told me that I'd pay if I kept pushing him.

Scorching heat flooded between my thighs as I held his gaze, telling him silently that I'd welcome that kind of punishment.

I wasn't a woman who was going to back down from this kind of heady sexual banter anymore.

It was way too intoxicating for a woman who hadn't been attracted to another man since I'd separated from Tanner.

That intimate moment was broken when the waiter came to ask if our dessert was acceptable.

When Tanner told the man it was the best he'd ever had and then winked at me, I had to stifle a laugh.

It was probably shockingly inappropriate in our current setting, but I loved the fact that Tanner didn't seem to give a damn.

I didn't openly laugh until later, when Tanner did, in fact, grab two hot dogs on the way to the theater.

When I refused to eat one, he devoured both of them like a man who hadn't just eaten a gazillion course meal at one of the most exclusive restaurants in the city.

The rest of the night was magical, filled with laughter and romance.

It was the most incredible date I'd ever had.

Chapter 24

Tanner

"I thought you went to bed," I said to Hannah as I walked out of my bedroom and into the living area of our suite. She was in a pink, modest, cotton nightgown that shouldn't look sexy, but on her, it did.

I was restless after showering, unable to sleep, so I'd decided to go into the kitchen and have a drink.

I'd found Hannah sitting on the couch, gazing out the window, which had three hundred and sixty degree views of the city.

She was hugging one of the throw pillows with a faraway look on her face.

She turned to me with a smile. "I tried to sleep. I guess I was still wired up from this evening. The show was amazing. Plus, I didn't want to miss my last chance to watch this view at night."

"If you like it that much, we can stay for another night," I suggested as I walked into the kitchen with only a pair of sweatpants on.

I poured a glass of wine for Hannah and grabbed myself a beer before I walked back to the living area.

I put the drinks on the coffee table and settled myself behind her, my arms around her waist so she could lean back against me.

She tossed the pillow onto the couch and put her arms and hands over mine.

Now that I was here, I wasn't going to miss the chance to have her sweet body against mine, even if it was fucking torture.

She let out a sigh of contentment that made the restlessness inside me settle down almost immediately.

"This really is an incredible view," she murmured.

"It is," I agreed. "Do you ever miss New York?"

The lights of New York were stunning, but all I could look at was Hannah.

I couldn't remember a time when she'd looked quite this happy.

"Not usually," she explained. "I mean, views like this make me appreciate it, and I do miss Broadway and some of the incredible food here, but I don't think I'd want to live here again. I guess there's a big part of me that likes being in a small town. What about you?"

"If I want the city, I can get there by jet or helicopter," I told her. "I probably have the best of both worlds, but I always missed Crystal Fork when I was here. I was raised there. Granted, I didn't miss the gossip or the things that drive me crazy about that town, but I missed the sense of community and most of the people. I also missed getting on a horse and getting away when I needed it."

"And actually being able to see the stars at night," she added.

"That, too," I said with a nod as I reached for my beer.

"We had big dreams when we lived here," she said as she picked up her wine, took a sip, and set it back on the table.

"In the beginning, that was about all I had," I said drily. "I don't think I ever understood why a woman like you wanted a guy like me. I was broke with nothing but an entry-level job and a shitload of dreams."

"And a lot of ambition," she added. "I knew you'd make your dreams a reality. Besides, I thought you were the hottest and most charming man I'd ever met."

"I wasn't charming. I'm still not. And I definitely wasn't the best looking guy around," I disagreed. "I was crazy about you, but I could never quite seem to find the words to tell you how I felt in the beginning."

"Which is exactly why you were so charming," she informed me. "You were a serious guy with no bullshit. That's pretty refreshing here in the city. I was completely charmed."

Okay, I wasn't going to try to talk her out of thinking that I was charming. "And the scar on my forehead? And the fact that I'm just an average looking guy?"

"You are no such thing," she scolded angrily. "You have the body of a god, and the most beautiful blue eyes I've ever seen. That scar on your forehead was the only thing that kept you from absolute physical perfection, which was good. No woman wants to date an Adonis. They're usually boring. To me, you were and still are… perfect. I had my own scars."

Hell, I wasn't about to try to get her to look at me realistically. If I was lucky enough to have that title with her, I wanted to keep it.

"Like I've told you before, I never saw those scars, Hannah. I thought you were the most beautiful woman I'd ever seen. Still do, and that is never going to change."

We were silent for a moment before she finally asked, "Why did your mother never tell you that I didn't run off with another guy? I've been wondering about that. It's not like my mother didn't know the truth, and those two are best friends."

Hannah and I had talked a lot about our past over the last few weeks, but maybe there were still a few things to say before we could leave it behind.

"She didn't know what I was thinking, Hannah," I said huskily. "I didn't talk about our breakup. I couldn't. I had to compartmentalize it to survive. The only thing that kept me from coming after you was my fucking pride. I avoided your mother for a long time. I didn't want to hear about your life with someone else. When we did speak, I didn't ask about you, and she could hardly give me any news about your life without me asking first. It's not like you and I were old friends."

"Your mom never said anything about me?"

"Not to me," I grumbled. "I made it pretty clear that talking about you was off-limits for me, and you knew my dad. He wasn't going to ask unless I wanted to discuss it. He slapped me on the back in sympathy when it first happened and told me if I ever wanted to talk about it, he'd listen. We never discussed you again. I traveled a lot, and went on with my obsession about KTD for a few more years. In my mind, there was nothing I could do about your choice. I didn't have my shit together back then. It took me way too long to grow the hell up."

If I'd had my priorities in order, I would have known that Hannah was sending me a message by leaving.

Instead, I'd taken it as a rejection, making an immediate assumption that was never remotely true.

"I didn't have my shit together, either," she said remorsefully. "But we're here together now. It almost feels surreal to me."

It actually felt like a fucking miracle to me, and I'd never take this second chance for granted.

Hannah was mine, and she was going to stay mine.

"If that ever happens again, I'll find you," I said in guttural voice.

She squirmed so she could turn around and face me.

Her actions were almost torture for me because that shapely ass was wriggling against my already hard cock.

Her beautiful eyes met mine with a vulnerable expression that made my gut ache.

"I'm not the kind of woman who runs away anymore, Tanner," she promised. "I'm looking forward to the future too much for that. I could beat myself up for forever for not leaving a note, or not trying harder to get you to listen to me, but I can't. I'm too happy right now to look behind us. Everything that happened brought us to where we are right now, and to the woman I am today. Would I handle things differently now? Of course I would, but I was pretty young and pretty messed up all those years ago. We're both in a much better place to be together in a better relationship."

Hell, she was probably right.

I hadn't appreciated her back then, and I definitely hadn't deserved her.

"I accept that," I conceded. "But did it really have to take that many years apart?"

She wrapped her arms around my neck. "I'm not complaining. I'm pretty happy exactly where I am right now."

I lifted a brow and tightened my arms around her waist. "That wasn't exactly a complaint. I'm happy where you are right now, too."

The only thing that would make it better is if we were both naked and in my bed right now.

Then it would be absolutely perfect.

As much as I wanted to just be close to Hannah, I also wanted her coming hard and screaming my name.

I hadn't been with another woman since college.

I hadn't wanted to be with anyone except Hannah since the moment we'd met.

And now that I was with the object of every one of my sexual fantasies, it was damn hard not to try to get her into my bed.

But it was going to have to be Hannah who made that decision, and I wasn't going to rush her.

"I couldn't sleep because all I could think about was you," she said in a seductive voice that made my cock twitch. "I got myself off in the shower thinking about you, but that didn't cut it for me."

Holy! Fucking! Hell!

I *didn't* want to rush her, but I wasn't sure I could handle *this* conversation.

There was only so much a guy could take.

However, I must like torture, because I asked, "How long have you been getting yourself off thinking about me?"

It wasn't like Hannah and I had never been intimate, and I wanted to know.

"Almost from the moment we saw each other again," she said without an ounce of hesitation.

I grunted with satisfaction. "Same. I can't look at you without wanting to bury my cock inside you until you're thinking about nothing else but me."

Hannah buried her hands in my hair and gazed at me with a vulnerable look in her dark eyes. "Do it," she said suggestively. "Do it before I lose my mind. I want you, Tanner. I've always wanted you, but that longing is worse than it's ever been before. I don't care about our past or our future right now. I just want you to fuck me until I can't think straight anymore."

She put her hand between our bodies and stroked boldly over my hard cock before she added, "I think you want exactly the same thing."

The desire in her liquid brown eyes broke me.

Hannah wanted me, and fuck knew I couldn't go through another night without her.

I gripped her silken hair, holding her head to keep her looking directly into my eyes. "Be sure this is what you want, Hannah. Once I take your gorgeous body, you *are* going to be mine. No turning back. Ever."

Her gaze burning into mine, she reached for the hem of her nightgown. "Then I hope you're ready for a long night," she said in a low, tremulous voice.

That was her answer.

No hesitation.

No fear.

Christ! She was bolder than she'd ever been, and that confidence ramped up my possessive instincts even more.

I *needed* Hannah, and I didn't give a fuck about admitting that to myself.

My heart nearly stopped when she raised that demure nightgown up and over her head and tossed it onto the floor without looking away from me.

I broke eye contact then.

I couldn't help it.

The woman had the body of a curvy, sexy goddess, and she'd been completely naked underneath that gown.

She raised a brow, an action that was almost a challenge.

A what-do-you-plan-on-doing-now-that-I'm-standing-here-naked challenge.

I had her on her back on the couch, my body over hers, before she could take another breath.

I gripped her hair, tilted her head, and growled, "I'll make you pay for being a tease."

"Oh, God, I hope so," she said breathlessly.

"Count on it," I vowed right before my mouth slammed down on hers in a greedy kiss that almost made my head explode.

Honestly, it wasn't really a kiss. It was more like a desperate claiming of the only woman I'd ever really wanted.

I needed my cock inside her, but I wanted to possess her in every other way possible before that happened.

She moaned into my mouth, and fisted my hair.

She was panting by the time I released her lips to explore the soft, sensitive skin of her neck.

My mouth explored its way down her body until I finally got to the most delectable pair of breasts I'd ever put my hands or lips on.

I sucked one nipple into my mouth and lightly pinched the other.

The sexy gasp I heard come from Hannah's lips told me that she still liked some of the same things that she had when she was younger.

Her hips lifted, and she started to grind against me.

"Please don't tease me," she insisted. "Not this time. I can't take it."

I could have reacquainted myself with her breasts for much longer, but the desperation in her voice was echoing my own.

Hannah wanted.

I needed to satisfy that desire.

I reached between our bodies and finally touched her soaked pussy, stroking a finger over her distended clit.

"Oh, God, yes!" she moaned. "Touch me. Please."

Fuck that! I knew what made Hannah insane, and I was going to use that knowledge until she was coming so hard that all she could do was scream my name mindlessly.

There was going to be no satisfaction for me until I heard that happen.

Chapter 25

Hannah

I was about to lose my mind.

My body was already on fire, desperate to climax.

All he had to do was touch me to make me crazy.

I gripped Tanner's hair tighter as he started to move away.

"Noooo!" I protested, my head thrashing from side to side.

Ignoring my fierce grip on his hair, Tanner moved down my body.

He put one of my legs over the back of the couch, and the other over his shoulder.

It took a moment for my frenzied mind to realize exactly what was going to happen.

I didn't have a chance to think about it or prepare myself, and I literally squealed as Tanner's hungry mouth started to devour my throbbing pussy.

Every nerve in my body responded to the feel of his hot, wet tongue sliding over that sensitive nub.

Nothing. Absolutely nothing felt like this, and I'd fantasized about it a million times.

Tanner knew exactly how to bring me to the brink of climax, and then keep me there until he finally pushed me over the edge with that wicked mouth of his.

"Tanner," I panted. "I can't."

My body was so ready that I wasn't sure I could stay in this state of arousal for very long without completely losing my mind.

"You can," he demanded with his mouth against my pussy.

Every stroke of his tongue pushed me higher, and when he slid one finger inside me, and then two, moving them in a rhythm that matched the stroke of his tongue, I screamed, "Oh, God, Tanner. Please!"

I needed just a little more pressure, a little more stimulation, and I'd fly over the edge.

I craved it, but Tanner wasn't going to let me come until he knew I was on the brink of losing it.

My skin was sweaty and slick against the leather of the couch, and my body was pulsating, pleading for release.

Right now, Tanner Remington had complete control, something that I sensed that he needed at the moment.

It was arousing as hell, but it was also killing me.

He'd always teased, but this was...different.

There was an emotional intensity between us that had never been quite this strong before.

"Tanner," I screamed. "I can't take any more."

He must have sensed that I was serious, because he sped up his motions, lifted my ass until he was pressing harder against my pussy, and ate me out like his life depended on it.

"Yes," I cried out. "Yes, Tanner, yes!"

My orgasm was so intense that it was almost frightening.

Wave after wave pounded at me as I clung to Tanner's hair like it was my lifeline.

Tanner curled his fingers and found my G-spot, which almost sent me through the ceiling.

My entire body was shaking as I recovered, my mind blown, and a warmth spreading over my body that I'd never experienced before.

Maybe because Tanner still had his head between my thighs, licking every drop of that powerful orgasm like he couldn't get enough of me.

"Enough," I said insistently. "Fuck me! I need you, Tanner."

My climax was satisfying, but it hadn't soothed that aching need to have him inside me.

He moved like lightning. He shoved his sweatpants off, picked me up off the couch and wrapped my legs around his hips. "Condom," he said hoarsely.

"I'm on birth control," I informed him hastily, my arms around his neck for balance. "No need. I've never been with someone else."

"I haven't, either," he grunted as my back hit the wall. "It's going to be hot, hard, and quick this time, Hannah. My patience is gone."

"Sounds perfect to me," I panted.

With one powerful surge of his hips, Tanner was inside me, buried so deeply that I let out an audible gasp.

My soul relished the sensation so much that the moment of slight discomfort barely registered.

He was a big man, and it had been a long time for me.

"Fuck!" Tanner said with a groan. "You're so tight and hot, Hannah. You okay?"

"Yes," I whispered against his ear. "Don't hold back. I need this. I need you."

"You've got me," he said, his words sounding more like a promise than a statement.

Gripping my ass tightly, he started to pump into me like a man possessed.

I reflexively tightened my legs a little, wanting to capture the raw passion that burned between the two of us.

I buried my face against his neck, savoring the way our bodies slid and slapped together furiously, like they were made to be fused together like this.

God, his cock felt so good inside me that I could feel another orgasm starting to curl tightly.

"I need you to come for me, Hannah," Tanner commanded as he thrust harder and deeper.

"I don't think—"

"Don't think," he rasped. "Touch yourself. I want to feel you milking my cock, and I want to see you get off this time."

I wanted whatever would arouse him right now, so I reached between our bodies and felt the place where his cock was thrusting into me at a furious pace.

Feeling that connection, the push and pull of that hard cock was so erotic that my head hit the wall with a moan.

I could see the look on Tanner's face, and it was the most sensual thing I'd ever seen.

His eyes were wild.

His chest heaving.

He was laser focused on exactly what our bodies were doing.

There was something heady and delicious about watching a man like Tanner lose himself because he wanted me so badly.

I slid a finger over my sensitive clit, giving myself exactly what I needed to send myself over the edge.

I wanted to see Tanner completely lose control, and I wanted to go with him.

I sensed that was exactly what he wanted and needed, too.

My body overwhelmed with sensation, I let go.

I closed my eyes as my walls spasmed against Tanner's cock.

"Fuck, yeah, Hannah," he groaned as he buried himself inside me over and over again. "That's exactly the way I wanted to come. Just. Like. This."

His powerful body surged into me deeply as he found his own release.

"Tanner," I screamed as my fingernails dug into the skin on his shoulder.

I was so senseless that my fingers clawed at his back as his mouth claimed mine like he owned it.

I kissed him back, our tongues tangling, our bodies molded together in the aftermath of our orgasms.

It felt so damn good that I never wanted it to end.

I'd never felt quite this intimately close to Tanner, and I knew it was a feeling that was going to be completely addictive.

I gasped for breath as he released my mouth, my body totally spent. Without a word, he moved toward his bedroom.

My head dropped onto his shoulder, not certain how the man could still move.

I definitely couldn't.

I felt like a limp noodle.

He finally disconnected our bodies and laid me gently on the bed.

I felt the loss of our connection almost immediately, so I was relieved when Tanner got into the bed beside me, wrapped his arms around me, and pulled me close to his warmth again.

"It's a damn shame when a man can't control his dick long enough to make it last," he said gruffly. "But I knew the first time was going to be quick for me."

I stroked my hand over his ripped abdominal muscles.

I almost reminded him that it wasn't even close to our first time, but I didn't.

Really, it almost *felt* like our first time, even though we'd been together for a lot of years.

Things *were* different between us.

"I don't know," I teased. "It was pretty mind blowing for me. Have I told you that you're the hottest man on the planet? Times a thousand?"

"No," he said, amused. "But I wouldn't mind hearing that every day."

"Then I'll tell you that every day, too," I promised.

My heart ached that Tanner would probably never see himself like I did.

Not long ago, he'd told me that he'd always felt like he was the boring Remington brother because he wasn't as engaging or as handsome as his siblings.

He hadn't said that without an iota of jealousy or envy.

To him, it was just a fact.

In my eyes, Tanner was the hottest Remington brother and always had been.

It drove me crazy sometimes because Tanner couldn't see just how extraordinary he was or how some of his qualities were absolutely irresistible.

"Thank you," I said softly.

He stroked a hand over my bare arm. "For what exactly?"

"So many things. For being such an incredible man. For giving me this night that I'll never forget. For helping me with a business that means something to me, even though it's small compared to what you're used to doing. For being so thoughtful." In a more teasing voice, I added, "And for the most amazing sex of my life."

"Was it that incredible?" he asked. "And you know I should have—"

I put my fingers over his lips. "Yes, it was. And I'm done talking about the past. This is us now, Tanner, and you're the best boyfriend a woman could ever dream of having. *This* relationship is new and different, and after that interlude, I'm completely addicted to you."

I was relieved when he rolled me onto my back and came on top of me with a grin. "I'm glad you feel that way, because I've been addicted to you for weeks now. It's definitely different. You've gotten sassier and bolder as you've gotten older."

I smiled up at him. "Are you complaining, because if you are then you're out of luck. I was young, had zero self-confidence, and was a little messed up back then. Now I know exactly what I want, and I'm looking at his handsome face right now."

"Hell, no, I'm not complaining," he answered huskily. "It's sexy as fuck. Feel free to undress any time you feel like it."

"Now that I've had a taste of that hot body of yours, you might regret that invitation," I joked.

He shook his head. "I'll never regret it. I adore you, Hannah. I hope you already know that, but I'm leaving nothing to chance anymore."

I had an almost irresistible urge to tell him that I loved him, but I bit those words back because it was probably too soon to talk about love.

But I did love him with every breath in my body.

I'd probably always loved Tanner, even when we weren't together, but the way I felt now was almost overwhelming.

In the past, there had probably always been a part of myself that I'd held back, the messed up part that I hadn't wanted Tanner to know about.

Now, there was nothing I couldn't share with him because I wasn't afraid of my emotions and the way that I felt anymore.

I didn't feel like there was something wrong with me.

I had no walls with Tanner, and even though that was a little terrifying, I wanted him to fall in love with the woman I was now.

I put my palm against his cheek. "I adore you, too. You have no idea how grateful I am that you came back into my life."

He didn't say anything.

He simply lowered his mouth to mine and kissed me.

It was a thorough, tender embrace that touched my heart so much that it almost made me cry.

I'd been happy with my career in Seattle, but something had always been missing for me.

I'd longed for something, but I guess I'd never wanted to admit that I was longing for someone, and that person had always been Tanner.

For the first time in my life, I felt like there was absolutely nothing missing from my life and I was experiencing what it was really like to be truly happy.

Chapter 26

Tanner

"I see that you took my advice and made sure the entire town knows that you and Hannah are back together," Devon said as we chatted at an impromptu barbecue my mother was hosting this afternoon. "Did you ever warn her about the matchmakers?"

It was getting a lot colder than it had been earlier in the fall, so we were barbecuing on my mother's massive, covered patio that had infrared heaters, and my brothers and I had lit two firepits that sat on opposite ends of the patio.

Mom liked to entertain outdoors, and she made sure that cold weather didn't keep her from having the barbecues she loved so much.

It was just friends and family.

Still, there was a decent crowd here.

My mother never did quiet, lightly attended events.

She'd just hosted Thanksgiving dinner not long ago with a ton of people attending, including all of my family, Hannah and her mother, Lauren, Reese, Silas, Charlie, and anyone else in town that had no family to go to on the holiday.

So, this impromptu barbecue had been a surprise, but my mother loved a good party, and she never went long without having another one.

It had been a few weeks since Hannah and I had returned from New York, and they'd been some of the happiest days of my life.

Her business had launched successfully, and she was over the moon about the interest she'd had in mobile services in Montana.

"No need to tell her about the matchmakers," I informed him. "I'm making sure that everyone knows that she's mine."

"No doubt about that," Devon said drily. "You two can't keep your hands off each other."

He was right.

When I wasn't touching her, I was watching her.

She was on the other side of the patio at the moment chatting with my mom, her mother, Lauren, Anna, and Reese.

Silas and Charlie weren't far away. They seemed to be in a light-hearted conversation. The two of them had been friends for years, and they liked to give each other a hard time.

"I noticed that there seems to be something happening on the acreage next to Mom's ranch," I said to Devon. "Any idea what's happening there?"

I'd driven by that property today, and I'd noticed quite a few trucks coming and leaving from that location.

"You haven't heard?" he said, sounding surprised.

I finally stopped watching Hannah and looked at Devon. "Heard what?"

"The wayward cousins are moving back to Crystal Fork," he informed me. "The old house was demolished. They're building homes there."

"Asher and Cole?" I asked.

Devon raised a brow. "Do we have any other wayward cousins?"

Okay, that surprised me, and very few things surprised me anymore.

Yeah, they owned the land, but I had assumed they were never coming back to Crystal Fork.

The two of them owned one of the most successful tech companies on the planet.

It was based in Austin.

"Why in the hell are they coming back here?" I asked.

He shrugged. "They plan on breeding horses. Rumor has it that they're turning their everyday operations over to a CEO and stepping down. If that's the case, it probably doesn't matter where they live."

In some ways, that made sense. Asher was around Kaleb's age and Cole was only two years younger. They'd been busting their asses for a long time to become billionaires. My brothers and I had considered doing that ourselves, but now that our company was established, we didn't really need to turn things over. We could pick and choose our acquisitions.

Asher and Cole's tech company was a whole different business.

They'd probably spent every waking moment running that company.

My cousins were the offspring of my uncle, my father's younger brother.

My father and his brother had never been close. My uncle had been a heavy drinker, and he'd never been a pleasant person to be around.

My dad had always hoped he'd get rehabilitated at some point, but that had never happened, and he'd had some pretty questionable morals.

Eventually, my father and my uncle had stopped speaking.

My uncle had owned the land next to the ranch because it had been inherited from my grandfather. My dad had gotten the majority of the land for his ranch when my grandpa had passed away, but my grandfather had never entirely disinherited his second son, even though he'd been an asshole.

That property wasn't as vast as my dad's ranch, but it was significant acreage.

"How does Mom feel about that?" I asked.

"She's thrilled," Devon replied. "You know her. She always wants family back in Crystal Fork. Maybe our family was never close to our uncle or his kids, but she's hoping she can repair that relationship."

"The town probably won't be thrilled," I said drily. "Half of the people here still think they murdered their father."

There was a huge scandal when Asher and Cole were younger.

My uncle had been murdered when my cousins were younger. Asher had taken Cole to Austin because their mother had died years ago, and I didn't think the two of them had ever looked back.

The murder was still unsolved, but the police had never had any evidence to prove that Asher and Cole had done it.

But the gossip had been rampant in Crystal Fork.

Some believed that my cousins had murdered their father.

Some didn't.

"I don't think they did it," Devon informed me. "I talk to Cole once in a while. I think part of the reason they're coming back is to figure out who murdered their father."

"I don't think they did it, either. You talk to Cole?" I questioned. "Hell, I've tried to reach out to Asher a few times, but he's never taken my call."

We barely knew our cousins. They had both been standoffish as kids, and incredibly unsocial, just like their father.

Then again, with the father they had, I was surprised they were still sane.

"Asher is a dick," Devon told me. "But Cole is a little more social. I wouldn't say we're close, but we keep in touch once in a while."

"There has to be a reason why they're coming back," I mused. "They could breed horses anywhere. Hell, they live in Texas."

I was pretty sure that Devon was right. They had some unfinished business here in Montana."

"I hope Mom isn't disappointed if they don't really want to communicate," I told Devon. "I know they're both Remingtons, but they're not like the rest of us."

Devon grinned. "I think she'll figure out a way to get close to them. She always felt bad that they wouldn't let her or Dad help them when they were young."

"They tried hard," I reminded my younger brother. "Just like Dad tried to help his brother. None of them wanted anything to do with us."

"I'm not sure our uncle would allow it," Devon pondered. "And once those two were suspected of murder by some of the people in this town, I think all they wanted to do was see Crysal Fork and their old life in the rearview mirror."

"You're probably right," I agreed.

Asher and Cole hadn't had an easy life growing up.

Looking back at the situation as an adult, I suspected that my uncle was pretty abusive, but my cousins had never admitted to that abuse. Although I knew that my father had asked them if they were being abused. Many times.

"I can't believe you haven't heard about the return of the black sheep Remingtons," Devon commented. "The news has been a hot topic here for a while now."

"I was distracted," I said, my gaze returning to Hannah.

She was one hell of a distraction.

Neither one of us was looking back at our old relationship or the mistakes we'd made anymore.

What we had now was too damn good to be spoiled by what had happened in the past.

She'd been busy with the opening of her business, but true to her word, she'd done everything in her power to make me happy.

Hell, I still didn't think that she realized that just seeing her face made me fucking ecstatic.

She ended her busy day at my house for dinner, and to my relief, she almost always cooked.

If she'd had to eat my cooking, she might eat at my place less often.

Hannah knew when to stop working and pay attention to the people in her life.

That was one thing that hadn't changed about Hannah.

She had coffee in the morning with her mother at The Mug And Jug before Sweet Mornings opened, and they had lunch together at Charlie's at least once a week.

My mother had started driving into town to have lunch with Joy and Hannah, and Hannah checked in on my mother almost as much as she did with her own mom.

Hannah and my mother had been close at one time, and I was glad to see that they were renewing that tight relationship.

Honestly, Hannah had stepped right back into the community and my family like she'd never been gone.

She treated Anna and Lauren like the sisters she'd never had.

I knew that Lauren was relieved to have another close friend in Crystal Fork since she'd just returned here after a long absence herself.

Lauren wasn't as outgoing as Hannah and Anna, so I was glad those three were close.

Luckily, Hannah's mother had easily accepted the fact that Hannah and I were back together.

In fact, she seemed to approve, and she was treating me no differently than she had when Hannah and I were engaged.

I looked back from the group Hannah was in to find Devon scrutinizing Reese like she was a specimen under a microscope.

I knew that look.

I'd seen it every time Devon was trying to figure out a problem.

"Something wrong with Reese?" I asked Devon.

He shook his head slowly as he averted his gaze from the pretty, auburn haired woman. "There's something that isn't adding up about that woman," he said suspiciously. "And for some reason, she hates me."

I smirked. That probably pissed him off because Devon could charm almost anyone when he chose to do it.

"Hannah loves her," I told him. "And I happen to like her, too. She's a hard woman not to like."

"Have you ever wondered why she'd take a job in a place where she has no family or ties? She moved from the city to the middle of nowhere in Montana. There's something wrong with that," Devon said with suspicion clouding his tone.

I shrugged. "She said she has no close family. It doesn't seem that strange to me that she wanted a change."

"In Crystal Fork, Montana? I think she has secrets," he said seriously. "I don't like it. I'm going to figure out exactly what they are."

Devon's gaze flitted back to Reese, and I chuckled. "You're being paranoid because you can't charm her into submission. Are you attracted to her?"

He sent me a frustrated look. "Are you serious? She's probably at least a decade younger than I am."

While it was true that Devon generally hooked up with women his age or even a little older, that didn't mean that he couldn't be attracted to Reese.

Normally, he preferred women that didn't want entanglements and were married to their careers.

Reese was a sweet, quiet woman that seemed to be a lot more balanced.

"She's attractive," I said, trying to pry information out of my younger brother.

"She's a pain in my ass," Devon said in an almost hostile voice. "And she's evasive about her former life in the city."

I laughed because the woman had obviously gotten under Devon's skin, and I'd never seen that happen. "I think you're just annoyed that you can't charm her, and she won't tell you everything you want to know. She's entitled to her privacy, Devon. She doesn't know you."

"I'll get to know her," he vowed. "Hannah is like a sister to me. If she's getting close to Hannah, Anna, and Lauren, I want to know what she's hiding."

I grinned as I watched Devon continue to glare at Reese.

I'd never seen my brother get riled up by any woman, and it was highly amusing to watch.

Women didn't ignore Devon.

They generally fell at his feet.

It was interesting to see a woman who didn't fall for any of Devon's bullshit for a change.

Chapter 27

Hannah

"Hi, Hannah," Tanner's secretary said with a smile as I walked into his office in Billings with a bag of Italian food in my arms.

I'd only met his secretary a few times when I'd stopped by Tanner's office, but she was a friendly, jovial, older woman that had always greeted me with enthusiasm.

"Hi, Joyce," I answered and nodded at the door to Tanner's office. "Is he in?"

She nodded. "He said he didn't want to be disturbed. I was just about to leave for lunch. His brothers went to get something to eat, but he wouldn't leave his office today. They have a meeting late this afternoon on one of Tanner's acquisitions. You probably know how he is when he's trying to close something that's important to him."

I did, which was exactly why I was here.

Tanner wanted to acquire this particular company, and he'd been a little uptight about this meeting.

The acquisition was personal to him because it was a research company that did important medical research, and it had fallen under bad management.

Like the amazing man he was, Tanner wanted to get the company operating at its full potential again because it had so much potential to cure deadly diseases.

I'd been in Billings to meet with some of my contractors, so I'd picked up lunch for Tanner.

I knew he wouldn't be leaving his office today until that meeting happened around four o'clock.

The crazy man forgot about food when he was troubled about an acquisition.

"Well, I'm going to disturb him," I told Joyce determinedly. "He has to eat."

Tanner had been ready for this meeting for at least a week.

He didn't need to keep going through the figures over and over.

She shot me a relieved look as she stood and grabbed her purse. "I'm pretty sure you're one distraction he won't mind. Have a nice lunch."

I smiled at the woman as she departed for lunch.

While it was true that Tanner didn't let KTD rule his life anymore, there were still times when he got a little uptight about work.

I got that.

He'd given up his entire life for a long time to build this company, and it was important to him.

My company had only been open for a few months now, and there were times when I obsessed about my growing company, too.

Tanner had been there to support me every step of the way.

And I was going to be there to support him when things were stressful at KTD.

I didn't worry about his company taking over his life anymore.

He showed me every damn day that I was always his priority.

Things had been nearly perfect between the two of us since we'd returned from New York. So perfect it was almost scary.

I opened the office door quietly because my hands were too full to knock.

His office was contemporary, large, and impressive, just like the entire KTD building.

But I wasn't really thinking about his beautiful office when I peeked into the large room.

My focus went directly to the man sitting behind the desk.

Tanner was on the computer, probably going over figures for about the millionth time.

As always, he took my breath away in his custom navy blue suit, but I frowned as I saw that his hair was mussed, like he'd been raking his hands through it in frustration.

"Not now, Joyce," Tanner said gruffly without looking up from the computer. "Whatever it is, I'll deal with it later."

I smiled.

It never ceased to amaze me that Tanner could go from a congenial, small town guy in jeans to a gruff, demanding business tycoon so easily.

There were so many layers to Tanner, and I loved all of them.

Especially the demanding lover who couldn't keep his hands off me.

Our sex life hadn't cooled off, even though we'd been together nearly every single night for the last two months since our first date in New York.

It had just gotten hotter and even more intense now that we were relearning everything that made each other crazy.

"I'm not Joyce," I said firmly as I went to his desk and sat the food down on it. "You have to eat, Tanner. It's not going to help to go to that meeting without some substance."

He looked up from his computer in surprise.

And then…he grinned at me, and that pleased expression on his face made something flip over inside my belly.

Sometimes it still made me giddy that no matter how busy Tanner was, he was always happy to see me.

His distractedness immediately stopped, and he was focused on me as he stood. "Hello, gorgeous," he said in a husky tone as he looked me up and down appreciatively. "I didn't plan on seeing you this afternoon, but I'm damn glad that you're here. How were the roads from Crystal Fork?"

We'd gotten snow a few days ago, but there hadn't been a single snowflake since that storm.

I was wearing a red sweater dress and a pair of heels because I'd been in a work meeting.

I took off my coat and put it down with my purse on a nearby chair as I shot him a chastising look. "The roads are perfectly clear. Don't be sweet to me right now," I insisted, knowing I couldn't resist that heart-stopping grin of his. "You're supposed to be getting lunch with Kaleb and Devon right now. You text me every damn day to make sure I don't skip lunch. You didn't eat a single thing at breakfast. You have to be hungry."

I was aware of that fact since I practically lived at his house now.

He'd grabbed coffee this morning, but he'd refused to eat anything, even though I'd offered to fix him something.

It was the first time Tanner had left without eating breakfast with me because he'd wanted to get to his office early.

That sexy grin didn't leave his face as he came around the desk, snaked an arm around my waist, and pulled me close to him. "Are you worried about me?" he asked right before his lips touched mine.

My body reacted instantly to the kiss, and I wound my arms around his neck, even though my mind was still focused on his lack of food.

All Tanner had to do was touch me, and I immediately wanted him as close to me as he could possibly get.

This man was addictive, and I responded to his embrace, whether I wanted to or not.

My intimacy with Tanner had grown to epic proportions, and he knew exactly how to make every thought fly out of my head except *him*.

"It's not going to work this time," I murmured as he released my lips. "You need to eat, and yes, I'm worried about you. I know that you're stressed out about this meeting."

He pulled back a little, and my heart tripped as I saw the heat blazing in his beautiful blue eyes.

"Do you have any idea how sexy you look today in that red dress?" he asked hoarsely. "It reminds of that torturously sexy dress you wore in New York."

The two dresses looked nothing alike, but I'd discovered that Tanner could find almost anything sexy about me. Even when I was in dirty jeans and a shirt after being outside.

I could look like hell, and Tanner would still want me.

There was something about that fact that was incredibly sweet.

I never had to be perfect for Tanner, and he never had to be perfect for me to want him.

If he was close to me, I wanted to be closer.

"Your food is getting cold," I protested as he nipped my earlobe.

"I have a microwave," he said in a low growl. "Right now, I'd rather have you for lunch. That would relieve my stress a lot better than food."

My stomach clenched at the possessive note in his words.

Tanner was in no mood to argue or compromise, and it turned me on when he got all bossy and uncompromising when it came to sex.

"We're in your office," I squeaked.

"I don't give a fuck," he answered roughly. "It's *my* office. Did you really think I was going to let you leave now that you're here in that body hugging, red dress? Not. Happening."

My nipples tightened until they were almost painful as Tanner released me, strode to his office door, and locked it.

Heat flooded between my thighs, and judging by the look in his eyes, I wasn't leaving until Tanner was sure we were both satisfied.

Whether we were in his office or not.

Well, if that was the way it was going to be, I was going to make sure he was nice and relaxed for his meeting.

I'd make him eat.

Later.

Most of his staff *was* out for lunch, and I knew exactly how to make Tanner relax.

Doing this in his office felt deliciously wicked, but I was down for it.

Tanner removed his jacket, tossed it on the chair, and then reached for me.

I stepped back and ran my palm slowly from his chest to the zipper of his suit pants.

"Problem?" I asked as I stroked his hard cock through the material of his pants.

"A large one," he confirmed as he moved toward me again.

I stepped back again as I lowered the zipper. "I can take care of that for you, Mr. Remington," I informed him as I undid his pants and totally liberated his enormous cock. "We are in your office. Think of me as an employee who's very eager to please right now."

"Fuck!" he cursed harshly as I dropped to my knees. "My employees don't take my dick into their mouths."

"No," I replied as I wrapped my hands around his gigantic cock. "But I do."

"Thank fuck!" he said hoarsely as he gripped my hair.

I took as much of Tanner as I could into my mouth, using my tongue, lips, and suction to make him lose his mind.

He rarely let me do this, and I was going to savor every moment of it.

I could bring him close to orgasm in a matter of moments.

I knew he loved it, but he almost always preferred to come inside me, with me screaming his name. And oral sex brought him too close to the brink too fast in his mind.

"Fuck yeah, sweetheart," he said with a lust filled groan. "That gorgeous mouth of yours makes me crazy."

I rolled my tongue over the sensitive head of his cock, and sucked him more deeply into my mouth.

I gripped the root of his cock, and moved it in tune with my mouth.

There was no way I could take all of Tanner, but I wanted him to get as much pleasure out of this as possible.

"Hannah," he warned as he gripped my hair tighter.

I ignored him and gently fingered his balls.

For several moments, there wasn't a sound in the office except his harsh breathing and the sounds of me devouring his cock.

It was erotic as hell.

I got lost in the sensual pleasure of having Tanner in my mouth and at my mercy.

If I got my way, he was going to orgasm spectacularly in a way he rarely had before, and I'd be able to taste his pleasure.

Seconds after that thought had crossed my mind, Tanner forced my head away from his cock.

"Christ!" he said gutturally, his chest heaving. "Not happening this time."

Damn.

Judging by the wild look in Tanner's eyes, I wasn't getting my way after all.

He turned me around and put my hands on the desk.

I shivered as I felt the air on my legs as he lifted my dress until it was around my waist.

"You're a very bad girl, Hannah," he rasped as he ran his hands over my ass and hips. "But you've got the sexiest ass I've ever seen. You didn't really think it was going to end that way, did you?"

All of a sudden, Tanner was no longer at my mercy, and the switch was head spinning.

"What do you want then?" I gasped as he slid a finger inside my soaked panties and lightly stroked my clit.

"You already know what I want," he answered. "And you're going to give it to me."

God, right now I'd give him anything he wanted if he'd just fuck me.

My entire body was wound tight, ready to fracture.

I needed release so badly that it was painful.

With one strong tug, the delicate panties separated from my body, but to my disappointment, he didn't bury himself inside me.

Instead, he fingered my bare pussy until I was whimpering with need.

"Do you know what bad girls get?" he asked in a graveled voice.

"Show me," I panted.

My body jerked a little as he slapped my ass. Not enough to truly hurt, but enough to make me squeal with surprise.

Tanner and I had never played this game before, but it was so stimulating that my entire body was alive with sensation.

"I don't think I quite got that," I said, my voice hoarse with passion. "Show me again what bad girls get."

"They get this," Tanner told me bossily as he slapped my ass slightly harder.

"Tanner," I moaned as the shock of that action rocketed through my body.

"And then they get this," he informed me as he thrust hard and buried himself inside me to the balls.

"Oh, God, yes," I answered, my mind and body completely frenzied.

I was determined to be as naughty as possible every single day from now on.

Tanner pulled back, and surged forward again like he wanted to make sure I knew exactly who was fucking me.

Possessively.

Hard.

Fast.

And furiously.

I'd already been so aroused that I felt my orgasm pounding at the door within moments.

I tried to push back to meet Tanner's thrusts, but he was pummeling so hard and fast that I couldn't keep up.

He had my hips gripped tightly, and I just gave in to the bliss.

"Tanner," I moaned, knowing I couldn't scream.

We were in his office.

There had to be people here somewhere, and some of his employees could be coming back from lunch.

"Give me what I want, Hannah," he demanded.

I knew what he wanted.

Me screaming his name when I imploded.

I always did. I couldn't help myself.

"I can't. Not here."

"You can," he grunted. "Nobody is in on this floor right now."

When he moved one of his hands and roughly stimulated my clit, it was over.

I started screaming his name as my core clenched around his cock, and I didn't stop until Tanner had found his own release with me.

Chapter 28

Tanner

I wrapped my arms around Hannah's waist and leaned my forehead on her shoulder.

My heart was galloping about a thousand miles a minute, but my body was so satisfied that I couldn't make myself move.

Fuck! I loved this woman with a fierce possessiveness that made me completely insane.

Hannah was *mine*.

And that made me feel like the luckiest asshole who ever walked the face of the earth.

"Marry me, Hannah," I said as my heart rate slowed down again. "Put me out of my misery and marry me. We don't need two separate places. I want to be with you every moment I possibly can."

"Tanner," she whispered as she wiggled out of my grip and straightened her body.

I let go of her reluctantly and looked at her face as she smoothed her dress back down.

She looked shocked.

And then she looked puzzled.

Finally, I saw a tear start to roll down her face, and it almost gutted me.

"I wasn't expecting that," she said as she swiped the tear from her face.

"Why?" I asked, confused. "I thought it was pretty clear what I wanted."

Okay, so I'd never mentioned marriage.

Until today, I'd never mentioned living together, either, but it's what I'd wanted almost from day one.

"We've been so happy," she said tearfully. "But—"

"You don't want to marry me," I said gruffly as I fastened my pants back into place.

The knot that had been sitting in my gut tightened so hard and fast that it almost made me double over.

It had never occurred to me that Hannah didn't want exactly the same thing I did.

"Tanner, I—"

Her statement was interrupted by the loud dinging of the elevator outside my office door.

Hannah's eyes widened, and she scampered to grab the pieces of her underwear on the floor and stuffed them in her purse.

"Tanner," Devon bellowed from outside my door. "When in the hell did you start locking your office?"

"Oh, God," Hannah said, her face a little panicked. "We'll talk later, Tanner."

That wasn't a good sign.

I knew Hannah.

If she really wanted to marry me, she would have flung herself into my arms and said *yes* immediately.

"Never mind," I said stoically. "I won't throw that suggestion toward you again."

I felt like a dog with a wounded paw, and I wasn't about to let anyone touch that wound again.

I knew I was reacting like an idiot, but I couldn't seem to stop myself from going into a defensive mode.

Hannah was the one person in my life who could completely destroy me, and I'd obviously misread every one of her actions during the last few months.

How was a guy supposed to handle that?

Hannah flinched as Devon pounded on the door. "Open the door, Tanner. I want to make sure you're still alive."

"I'll just…go," Hannah said as she grabbed her bag. "You have an important meeting today. Please eat."

"Hannah?" I said hoarsely as she scrambled toward the door.

When she turned back, tears were rolling down her face so fast there was no way she could swipe them away this time.

I wanted to ask if her answer was definitely a *no* to my suggestion of getting married, but when I saw those tears, I didn't need that answer.

For some reason, Hannah didn't want to marry me.

Hell, we hadn't even said that we loved each other.

Had I gotten everything that had happened between the two of us so damn wrong?

"What?" she prompted.

I shook my head. "Nothing. I guess I'll see you when I see you."

I needed some time to think, and to come to terms with the fact that she didn't want to get married.

She nodded as she tried to rub the tears from her face before she finally unlocked the door.

Once it was open, she fled like her ass was on fire.

Devon's eyes widened as he watched Hannah step into the open elevator door, and punch the control pad.

As soon as the elevator door closed, he strode into my office. "What in the hell just happened?" he demanded to know. "Hannah looked like she was crying, and she's never *not* smiled at me and thrown herself into my arms when she sees me."

"She brought lunch," I said tightly as I waved toward the food on my desk.

Devon surveyed the items. "It doesn't look like you two touched the food."

He started opening the containers, walked to the microwave, and popped what looked like lasagna into it. "You should eat," he said seriously. "Although honestly, you look like you could really use a stiff drink. What happened?"

"I think Hannah and I just broke up," I said morosely.

Devon shook his head. "No, you didn't," he said like he didn't have a doubt in his mind that what he was saying was the truth. "I'm thinking you had a disagreement, but you two are never breaking up."

I plopped my ass into my chair behind my desk, still confused. "I told her I wanted to get married. She didn't seem so crazy about the idea."

"Just like that?" Devon asked. "You just told her you wanted to get married? Don't you think that's a little…abrupt. And where in the hell is the romantic proposal and the ring she deserves?"

Since I wasn't about to tell Devon that I'd fucked Hannah senseless in my office, and that it was a statement that I made in the heat of the moment, I simply said, "I fucked up."

"Why was Hannah crying?" he asked as he took the container out of the microwave.

"I'm assuming it was because she didn't want to marry me, and didn't really want to tell me that," I replied as I watched Devon take the food out of the microwave, curse because he burned his finger, and then plop the hot food in front of me.

"Eat," he demanded as he handed me a fork from the bag. "I think your brain is lacking some essential nutrients right now."

He took a seat in a chair in front of the desk before he continued, "Start from the beginning. I know that Hannah wasn't breaking up with you. Let's figure this out. Although I must say, your proposal delivery doesn't sound very promising. I don't think I'd want to marry you, either."

If I wasn't completely miserable, I'd probably find it amusing that my little brother was actually trying to take care of *me*.

"I didn't exactly ask her," I confessed before I took a bite of the lasagna.

Since Hannah had gone to the trouble of bringing the food, I thought I should probably eat it.

I was also pretty certain that Devon would force feed me right now if necessary.

Devon folded his arms over his chest and glared at me. "Has anyone informed you that it's customary to ask?"

"It was a spontaneous thing," I grumbled. "I suddenly realized that it didn't make sense for us to have two separate places anymore. I told her to marry me and put me out of my misery."

"Very smooth," Devon said drily. "At any time during this romantic revelation, did you happen to tell her that you loved her?"

I shook my head as I swallowed another bite of my food. "It didn't come up."

"But you have told her, right?" he asked.

"Not exactly," I said defensively. "But she knows."

Devon let out a disgusted sound. "There's a certain order to love and romance," he told me. "First you tell her you love her, and then you do the romantic proposal."

I lifted a brow. "What in the hell do you know about real love and romance. You date plenty of women, but you've never gotten serious."

"I know because I watched our father romance our mother until the day he died. He'd have your ass for this, you know."

Hell, Devon was probably right.

Dad had been a quiet man, but he'd believed in soulmates, love, and romance. The romance had never stopped for my parents.

"Mom loved Dad enough to marry him," I reminded Devon.

"Come on, Tanner," Devon said in a pissed off voice. "Do you really believe that Hannah doesn't love you? She went out of her way to bring you food because she knows you don't eat when you're stressed out. Who does that? It's the little things sometimes that tell you that someone loves you. Did she actually tell you that she didn't want to marry you?"

I thought for a minute. "Not exactly. She said she wasn't expecting me to talk about that. It sounded like a *no* to me. She didn't even know what to say."

"Maybe because you did everything ass backwards," he said unhappily. "Give her some time to digest the whole marriage thing. She did plan one marriage that never happened because you couldn't commit to a date. Maybe she a had a kneejerk reaction. Give her some time to digest the fact that you want that now, and for fuck's sake, set a date when you ask her next time. And tell her that you love her before you pop the question. I know you put the past behind you, but it may bite you in the ass occasionally."

I stopped eating and put my fork on the plate. "I didn't really think about that. I've always wanted to marry Hannah."

"I know. We lost our minds for a while. She forgave you for that, Tanner. Cut her some slack. Your comment obviously came out of nowhere. You probably surprised the crap out of her. You're reacting defensively right now because you can't imagine your life without Hannah anymore. I'm not sure you ever could, which is why you refused to talk about it when you broke up."

I'd actually closed off that part of my life until I was ready to deal with it.

Apparently, I'd never wanted to deal with the fact that Hannah was gone.

"If she wasn't trying to break up," I mused. "Then why was she crying?"

Devon shrugged. "I don't have that answer. You'll have to ask her. You obviously hurt her in some way, but she wasn't crying because she wants to break up. Were you honestly planning on just letting her walk away?"

"I was a little cold. It was a stupid, defensive reaction," I admitted. "But hell, no, I don't plan on letting her go. That's not possible unless she tells me to my face to fuck off."

After I had thought about it for a while, I would have sought Hannah out, tried to get answers from her.

Maybe I did get defensive because I'd been hurt by her reaction, but I'd always find Hannah because that was just what I did now.

I couldn't know that she was on the same planet with me without looking for her and finding her now.

If she didn't want to marry me right now, I'd fucking wait until she did.

I'd probably been waiting for years for her to come back into my life somehow.

I could just wait until she was ready to marry my sorry ass.

She hadn't really broken up with me.

Like an idiot, I'd just refused to let her talk because I wasn't ready to hear that she didn't want to get married.

"I was a prick," I admitted to Devon.

"I figured," he replied. "In all fairness, she did leave you once without a word. I think it makes sense that you're afraid it will happen again."

"Maybe subconsciously," I answered. "But realistically, that's not going to happen. Hannah is a different woman now, and she had her reasons back then. She'd force me to listen to her."

"And you're a different guy," Devon reminded me. "You would listen to her."

"I'll fix this," I vowed to Devon.

"Give her some time," he encouraged. "She looked pretty upset."

"Which is exactly why I'm going to find her," I told him.

I was over that ridiculous reaction I'd had just a short time ago.

I'd handle whatever Hannah had to say, and I'd work with it.

There was no way in hell I was going to let her go unless that was exactly what she wanted.

"Hello?" Devon said like I was a simpleton. "We have an important meeting shortly. Text her or call her. And then get your ass to the meeting. This acquisition is important to you. You know she's headed back to work right now anyway. You'll see her tonight."

Would I see her tonight?

I'd basically blown her off earlier.

Hell, yes, I'd see her.

I'd text as soon as I got my head on straight, but I'd *definitely* see her tonight.

Chapter 29

Hannah

"Are you okay, Hannah?" Reese queried quietly as she stopped at my open office door.

I looked up from my computer and plastered a smile on my face. "I'm good. Why?"

"You're really quiet," she said as she stepped into my office. "And when you got back from Billings, you looked like you'd been crying."

Reese and I were close, and I considered her my friend.

We spent at least eight hours a day together in the office, and we talked and hung out as friends. At first I'd done it because she was alone here in Crystal Fork. Now, I spent time with her because I honestly cared about her.

Luckily, Lauren and Anna adored Reese, too, so we all hung out together when we could.

Reese was easy to talk to, and she was so empathetic. I didn't really want to lie to her, and there wasn't much she didn't know about my life.

"Tanner told me that he wanted to marry me," I said.

"And that made you cry?" she asked, sounding confused.

"Everything makes me want to cry right now," I confessed. "I don't know what in the hell is wrong with me."

I could cry for no apparent reason these days.

"Are you still queasy?" she asked. "I know your stomach was bothering you this morning."

"I'm better," I shared. "Maybe I was just a little nervous about the meeting with the contractors."

"Hannah, this has been happening to you every morning for a few weeks now. I think you should see a doctor," Reese said gently. "Are you and Tanner getting married?"

"No," I said as my eyes welled up with tears. "I was so shocked when he mentioned getting married that I couldn't really respond to him right away. Reese, he's never even told me that he loved me, and I haven't said those words yet. The comment just happened out of the blue. By the time I was ready to talk, he'd already taken my lack of response wrong. I think we just broke up."

"Oh, Hannah," Reese answered in a soothing voice. "There's no way that man just broke up with you. He's crazy about you. Everyone can see that. I think it was just a misunderstanding. Do you want to marry him?"

I nodded and swallowed hard to get the lump out of my throat. "There's no one else for me *but* Tanner. I tried to date once or twice in Seattle, but it never felt right, and it went nowhere. Any guy I met would never be right for me because I was still in love with Tanner. I finally gave up on dating altogether."

"Then just tell him you want to marry him," Reese suggested.

"I tried. He blew me off," I said wistfully.

"He was defensive because you didn't immediately say *yes*," she concluded.

"I think so," I said thoughtfully. "But he was so nonchalant about the whole thing. It stung. That's why I was crying."

Tanner's reaction had hurt, and I'd been sure he was breaking up with me.

After I'd thought about it, I wasn't so sure.

Certainly, a guy couldn't say he wanted to get married one moment and then decide to blow me off a few moments later.

Tanner cared about me.

I *was* certain about that.

"He'll get over it," Reese said. "Men are idiots sometimes. I'm sure he was disappointed, but I have to say that wasn't the way to show it. He probably thought you were breaking up with him."

"How can he possibly not know that he's my entire life now," I said adamantly. "I love him. I've always loved him."

"Take my word for it," Reese replied. "Men can be incredibly dense when it comes to emotions sometimes. They react before they think. Everything will be okay, Hannah. That man loves you. He'll come to his senses. He's definitely a keeper, even if he does make mistakes sometimes. He spoils you, and he's always there to help with Glam Anywhere without intruding on your business. I've seen you two together a lot. He worships the ground you walk on. If I wasn't your friend, I'd probably be jealous. I have no idea what it's like to be with a guy like that."

I smiled at her. "You're young. You'll meet someone someday."

She shook her head, her eyes a little panicked. "Not interested. I'm not dating."

I knew that, but I wasn't sure why.

Reese was twenty-eight, not that much older than I'd been when Tanner and I had broken up.

She was certainly a lot more mature and together than I'd been at her age.

The woman was also gorgeous, and if not for her standoffish attitude with men, they'd be falling all over her.

"Do you want to hit The Mug And Jug with me after work?" I asked. "I could probably use a cocktail."

"I'm not sure that's a good idea," Reese said carefully.

My eyes widened. "Why?"

She let out a deep breath. "Hannah, has it ever occurred to you that you could be…pregnant? The signs are all there. The morning nausea. The emotional reactions because your hormones are raging. And you said you missed your period about ten days ago."

Stunned, I stared at Reese, my mind whirling. "That's not possible. I'm on birth control, Reese."

She nodded. "Yes, but you had that viral gastroenteritis not that long ago. You vomited almost everything you put into your system for at least two days. Is it possible you threw up more than one or two pills? You're usually safe if you miss one, but two is iffy, and three or more is usually a problem."

My mind flew back to that time that I'd had a short stomach flu.

I'd only been sick for two days, but the brief illness had started the night before, right after I'd taken my birth control pill.

For the next two days, I had thrown up most of what I'd put into my stomach. Once that virus had passed, I'd felt perfectly fine.

God, not once had I considered that I could be pregnant, and my mind still couldn't quite accept the possibility. "I'm really irregular sometimes even though I'm on birth control," I rationalized.

"I bought a pregnancy test when I went out for lunch because I suspected you could be pregnant," Reese replied. "There's only one way to find out. It's been ten days since your missed period. It will be accurate."

I nodded. "I guess I need to know."

Honestly, it probably *was* possible.

Unfortunately, I'd never even thought about it when I was sick.

Tanner and I probably should have used an alternate method of birth control.

"How is it that a woman who has never had to deal with pregnancy knows so much about it?" I asked Reese.

She shot me a smile. "I guess I'm a sponge when it comes to soaking in useless knowledge and facts."

With that, she went to retrieve the test from her purse. She watched with me a few minutes later as we waited for the results, both of us leaning over my desk, our eyes glued to that pregnancy test.

She took my hand, and I clung to it like it was my lifeline.

It wasn't that I didn't want to have a child someday with Tanner.

I just hadn't expected that to happen...now.

Not before things were settled for the two of us.

Not before we were married and ready to have a child.

God, I didn't even know if Tanner and I were still together right now.

And I had no idea if he still wanted the child or two we'd hypothetically talked about years ago.

My heart raced as the first line showed up, which Reese had explained was the control line.

When the second line started to appear and grew stronger until it was just as bright as the control line, tears filled my eyes.

"You're pregnant, Hannah," Reese said softly.

I felt a little lightheaded as I stared at the results like I expected them to change.

"Sit down," Reese ordered as she urged me into my chair. "You look like you're about to topple over. Are you happy?"

Tears flowed down my cheeks as I nodded and put a hand to my flat belly instinctively. "I'm just not sure what Tanner's reaction is going to be."

"He's going to be hovering over you, and worried about you," Reese said calmly. "And underneath all that worry, he's going to be ecstatic. Whatever little tiff you had is going to get worked out. I'm going to find you a good OB doctor in Billings and make an appointment for you. You need to get started on prenatal vitamins now. Trust me? I'll find you the best OB doctor in Billings. There's no one who specializes in OB here in Crystal Fork. I'd like to make that appointment today."

I nodded, still not over my shock, so I was happy to let Reese handle those arrangements for now since she seemed to know more about pregnancy than I did.

I briefly wondered if Reese had actually been pregnant before, but I knew she didn't have any children.

"I'll be back after I make that appointment," she told me as she walked toward the door. "Stay in that chair until you've processed the fact that you're pregnant."

I let out a deep breath when Reese left the room, grateful that she'd been here with me when I'd gotten those results.

"I'm pregnant," I said aloud, my hand on my belly, my voice filled with awe.

My business was still growing, and it was so new, but I'd work everything out.

There was no reason that I couldn't work through a healthy pregnancy, and Reese was so intelligent that she could already handle anything that came up.

My eyes flitted to my phone, and I realized that Tanner had texted me.

I looked at the clock and realized he was probably about to go into his meeting soon.

I picked up my phone and held my breath as I looked at his text.

Tanner: *I'm sorry I acted like an asshole. I should have heard you out instead of reacting like an idiot. I still want to marry you, Hannah, but I can wait if you're not ready for that. Can we talk at dinner? I'll get home as soon as I can after the meeting.*

Relief flooded through my body.

He didn't want to break up.

His reaction had been instinctive because he thought I didn't want to marry him.

I'd hurt him, and I hated that.

Part of me wanted to rush over to his house after work, but at the moment, I felt completely drained, and I wasn't sure I was ready to tell him about my pregnancy before I'd really absorbed that information myself.

I yawned, longing for my bed.

That exhaustion had been happening a lot for me lately. That was probably another thing I'd rationalized, telling myself that it was too many late nights burning up the sheets with Tanner.

Right now, all I wanted to do was sleep.

I wasn't sure I was emotionally ready to spring the news on Tanner tonight, and it was going to be a long day for him.

It was Friday, and we had all day tomorrow.

Hannah: *Just get some sleep, Tanner. We'll talk tomorrow. I think I'd like to get to sleep early. I'll come over for lunch.*

I sent the message and then realized that I hadn't said anything to let Tanner know that I wasn't upset about this afternoon.

Hannah: *P.S. If you had waited for my shock to wear off, I would have told you that I'd marry you tomorrow if that wasn't too soon.*

He didn't answer, which didn't surprise me.

It had been a while since he'd texted, and his meeting was about to start.

He probably didn't expect me to answer until I closed the office.

I put my phone into my purse, deciding to leave a little early since I didn't have anything urgent to attend to at the moment.

Reese shooed me out the door as soon as she saw me yawn, informing me before I left that I had a doctor's appointment on Monday.

I went back to my apartment, forced myself to eat something because I was eating for my baby, too, and went straight to bed.

Chapter 30

Tanner

I t was after seven by the time I left my offices.
I went straight home, grabbed a few things from my house, and
headed directly to Hannah's apartment.

I was elated when I saw her text message, but she hadn't answered
any of the messages I'd sent after the meeting, and she wasn't answering her phone.

Yeah, maybe she had wanted to get to bed early, but she'd never
gone to bed *this* early.

I needed to check on her to make sure that she wasn't sick.

The one and only time she'd told me she was going to stay home
and go to bed early, she'd been sick with a stomach virus.

I hadn't even known she was sick until the end of the following day.

That shit wasn't happening again.

I'd had a key to her place for weeks, and I was going to use it.

If Hannah was sick, I was going to fucking be there this time to
take care of her.

I thought about her message on the drive over to her apartment,
and I wanted to kick myself for being such an idiot.

Hannah wants to marry me.

Hell, I'd take her to Vegas tomorrow and seal the deal, but Hannah deserved better than a hasty marriage at some Elvis chapel.

That was the only thing that would keep me from dragging her onto my jet and getting it done as quickly as possible.

Honestly, Hannah and I rarely had disagreements or misunderstandings. But I supposed it was going to happen in the years ahead of us.

I doubted there were very many couples who didn't fight occasionally.

Hannah and I were both hardheaded at times.

Definitely me more than her. But I planned on being a lot quicker at resolving our issues in the future.

It had been hell sitting through that meeting, although it had ended up going well.

All I'd been able to think about was Hannah and her tear-streaked face when she'd hurried out of my office.

My gut had been urging me to go after her, but my damn pride had gotten in the way.

The conversation with Devon had helped me get my head on straight, but I would have come to my senses anyway.

I just wished that had happened *before* she'd gotten into that elevator.

I'd had flowers delivered to my office so I could take them to Hannah, and I planned to do some groveling if necessary.

I'd also made a quick stop at the market in Billings to get some deli food and soup in case she hadn't eaten or in case she was sick.

I'd bought her favorite ice cream because it was the first thing she'd wanted after her stomach virus, and she didn't keep it in the apartment very often.

I grinned because she'd mentioned that her butt wouldn't fit into her jeans if she kept it in her freezer all the time.

When I'd mentioned that she could just buy a bigger pair of jeans, she'd shot me a glorious smile and told me that I didn't understand women and their love/hate relationship with carbs.

After I'd read her text message, I'd devoured the rest of my Italian meal before I'd left the office, so I wasn't really hungry myself.

I just really wanted to see Hannah and make sure that she was okay.

I turned into an available spot near her apartment, unloaded the stuff from the cargo area, and let myself into her apartment.

The place was dark, and everything was quiet.

I dumped the stuff I was carrying on the kitchen counter and went to her bedroom immediately.

I turned on a bedside lamp, and found her sleeping in her bed.

Fuck! She *had* gone to bed incredibly early.

I put the back of my hand to her forehead, and she stirred.

She didn't feel like she had a temperature.

"Tanner?" she murmured, like she knew my touch.

"It's me," I confirmed immediately so I didn't scare her. "I wanted to check on you and make sure you weren't sick. You never crawl into bed this early. I didn't mean to wake you."

"I was just tired," she said sleepily as she sat up. "I hit the bed as soon as I came home from work. I feel a little better now. Maybe I just needed a nap. I missed you."

My gut had clenched tightly as she'd said those words.

Christ! I needed this woman, and I had no idea what I'd do if I didn't ever hear those words again.

She slid over to make room for me, and I quickly shucked off my clothes and climbed into the bed beside her.

She snuggled up to me and I put my arms around her, relieved that she wasn't sick.

Hannah usually slept naked when we were together, but she was wearing a thin pair of pajamas because she was sleeping alone.

"I missed you, too, sweetheart. Are you sure you're okay?"

"I'm fine," she reassured me. "How did the meeting go?"

I didn't really want to talk about the meeting, but I answered, "It went well. I think we're set for acquisition. Did you eat?"

"A little," she informed me. "I really was tired. Can I say something before we talk about anything else?"

"Shoot," I said, ready to listen to whatever she had to say.

"I love you, Tanner. I should have said it weeks ago, and I can't go another minute without saying it anymore. Maybe if I had said it, we wouldn't have had that misunderstanding today."

I hadn't realized how much I'd wanted to hear those words from her gorgeous lips again until this very moment.

It had been so damn long, and those words meant even more to me now than they had years ago.

I wrapped my arms around her even tighter. "I love you, too, Hannah. Always have. Always will. I could have said them, too, but I didn't want to move too fast. That statement about marriage was a stupid move. The words popped out of my mouth before I had the chance to think about them. That wasn't exactly a romantic way to propose, and I should have told you that I loved you first."

"I didn't mind," she said softly. "It was just a shock to hear you mention marriage. I planned my dream wedding once, and it never happened. I know we've moved on, but it was an instinctive hesitation because of what happened before. It didn't last long, but those thoughts crossed my mind for a split second. My brain froze for a moment. It wasn't that I didn't want to marry you. I just needed a minute to recover."

"You'll have that dream wedding," I promised hoarsely. "And I'll be involved every step of the way unless you kick me out of the planning."

"I've changed," she said thoughtfully. "I'm not sure I want to plan that dream wedding again. My business is busy, and I don't really want to wait that long."

Now she was telling me exactly what I wanted to hear.

"What do you want?"

"I'm not sure how to answer that because I have something else important to tell you."

She sounded nervous, and I hated that.

Nothing Hannah could ever tell me would change the way that I felt about her.

"Tell me," I urged. "There's nothing we can't talk about anymore."

"I'm pregnant, Tanner," she said in a rush, like she wanted to get that information out before she changed her mind. "I know the timing sucks, and it shouldn't have happened this way, but we're going to have a child."

"You're on birth control," I said, my mind still not quite able to process the fact that Hannah was going to have a child.

Our child.

"When I had that stomach virus, I must have thrown up a few of those pills," she explained. "I'm sorry. We probably should have used something else for a while. I was so busy with my business that I didn't stop to think about that. I took a pregnancy test today. It was positive."

"Christ, Hannah, don't apologize. We made this child together. I should have thought about that, too," I said hoarsely as I put a hand to her belly. "I'm not even sure what to say, but I'm happy. I feel like the luckiest guy in the world right now."

I meant that. Hannah and I had always wanted to have a child. We just hadn't planned exactly when that would happen.

She'd just given me everything I'd always wanted. She loved me. She wanted to marry me, and she was pregnant with my child.

"Are you okay with it?" I asked, concerned. "I know your business is just getting started, and it probably isn't an ideal time for you right now."

"I'm over the moon," she said breathlessly. "Maybe it isn't the ideal time, but I'm not getting any younger. I'll work everything out with Glam Anywhere. I can be a businesswoman and a wife and mother, too. Women do it every day, and they don't all have the support system that I do. I was just worried that you might not be ready to be a father."

"I'm ready, sweetheart," I assured her. "I'm not getting any younger, either. I'm still trying to wrap my head around the fact that I'm going to be a father, but I'm definitely ready. I want to get married as soon as possible if you don't have your mind set on that dream wedding you planned. I can arrange almost anything you want in a very short period of time."

"What are your thoughts about Vegas?" she asked hesitantly. "We could have an amazing wedding there if we have a little time to plan. Our entire family and our friends could all be there. I've never been there, but I had some friends who had extraordinary weddings there. No muss. No fuss. The wedding isn't important to me anymore, Tanner. I just want to be married to you. I'd rather focus on our life together and our child."

Hell, maybe we would be getting married in Vegas, which meant that wedding could happen soon.

"I'll still make sure it's something special," I promised her.

"Knowing you, I'm sure you will," Hannah said teasingly. "I'd really prefer not to be hugely pregnant at that wedding. I just want to be your wife."

"I'll make it happen so fast your head will spin," I warned her. "We've waited forever for this, Hannah. I'm fucking tired of waiting. I need you to be mine."

"Are you going to ask me again," she said sleepily.

"I'm going to ask you for the first time," I said as I sat us both up in bed, took her hands, and looked her directly in the eyes. "Will you marry me, Hannah? I'll never be perfect, but I'll try to make you happy every single day for as long as I live."

Tears streaming down her beautiful face, she nodded. "Yes, I'll marry you, Tanner Remington."

"I should have a ring," I grumbled. "But I don't want to pick it out without you approving the design. If I'm not giving you the wedding of your dreams, I'm sure as hell giving you the engagement ring of your dreams. I'll have a designer over at the house tomorrow."

"Just like that?" she said with a huge yawn.

I snapped my fingers. "Just like that. There are some advantages to marrying a man who is obscenely wealthy."

I gently pulled her back down to lay on the bed with me.

She needed sleep.

I was going to have to start reading up on pregnancy and what her needs would be, but it was obvious that she was exhausted.

She put her head on my shoulder and stroked her palm over my chest lovingly.

"There are a lot more advantages to marrying you than just your money," she told me. "I happen to be in love with you, not your money."

Fuck! I loved hearing those words.

"My body?" I teased hopefully.

She slapped me on the shoulder playfully. "Yes. But mostly your heart. You're an amazing man with a very big heart."

I reached up to turn off the light. "Don't tell anyone that you think that," I joked. "I like people to think I'm an asshole."

"I know better," she said sleepily.

"Sleep, Hannah," I said as I stroked a hand over her hair, feeling even more protective than usual because she was pregnant with my child. "We'll talk in the morning."

Right now, the only thing I wanted was to sleep next to the woman who had just turned my world upside down in the best of ways.

Chapter 31

Hannah

"What in the hell are you doing, woman?" Tanner growled a week later as he came through the door from work.

In the last week, he'd gotten me moved entirely into his home.

When I'd gotten home from work today, I'd decided to hang some of his paintings, my favorites that he'd saved and never given away.

He'd given them to me, along with everything he'd saved that I'd left when we'd broken up, including every gift he'd ever given me, and my old engagement ring.

I'd put most of that stuff away in a safe place because it was part of our history, and Tanner had insisted that I was not wearing my old engagement ring that had bad memories attached to it.

I'd agreed with him completely.

However, there was plenty of space in this home for more artwork, and I loved looking at Tanner's paintings.

"Hanging a picture," I informed him as I shot him a welcoming smile.

"Get the hell off that ladder right now!" he said dangerously.

I checked to make sure the painting was straight and stepped down. "It's not a ladder, Tanner. It's a step stool that has two tiny little steps."

I was getting used to the way Tanner treated me like I was made of fragile glass just because I was pregnant.

Part of me loved it because he was so protective of me and our child.

But it also drove me insane sometimes.

I couldn't stub my toe without him flipping out about it.

"You should be resting. You had a long day at work," he rumbled right before he wrapped an arm around my waist and kissed me.

"You think I had a long day sitting in my office on my computer?" I teased, trying to get him to lighten up.

I was pregnant.

I wasn't deathly ill.

"Hannah," he said in a warning voice.

"Relax," I insisted as I stroked my palm over his stubbled jaw. "I'm going to have a child. I'm perfectly healthy."

I'd seen the doctor in Billings.

The pregnancy looked perfectly normal.

I was still a little nauseated sometimes in the morning, but even that was getting better.

A few hours and a few crackers in the morning resolved the nausea.

I actually felt great most of the time.

When I felt fatigued, a short nap when I got home helped a lot.

"I'm going to make damn sure you stay healthy," Tanner informed me, holding me close to him like he was afraid to let me go. "We're getting married in two months. I'm finally getting exactly what I want. And I want you to be healthy enough to enjoy it."

"And then you're taking me to Australia," I said with a happy sigh.

"I'm still not sure that's a wise idea," he said grudgingly.

"You're not getting out of that honeymoon," I warned him. "Don't start second-guessing everything, Tanner. I'll be going into my second trimester. I won't be hugely pregnant, my morning sickness will be gone, the possibility of a miscarriage will be minimal, and the doctor said it should be perfectly safe. You have a private jet for

God's sake. You can have me home quickly, but that's not going to be necessary. It's not like I'm asking you to take me to an underdeveloped country. They do have good healthcare in Australia."

Tanner had offered the honeymoon without thinking about my pregnancy.

I'd jumped at the opportunity.

Not long after I'd enthusiastically agreed, Tanner had started to think about anything and everything that could go wrong with my pregnancy while we were out of the country.

Even though the doctor had assured him that travel, especially travel in a very posh private jet, would be perfectly fine at the beginning of my second trimester, Tanner had been worried about the trip.

"I don't care," he said stubbornly. "I think it would be better to have you at home. You're still nauseated in the morning, and you're still fatigued."

"I won't be," I assured him. "Just wait and see. Things are better during the second trimester, and we'll be too busy with a child to make that trip later. Maybe it's selfish, but I want you to myself for a few weeks in Australia."

"Fuck!" he cursed as his arms tightened around me. "I want that, too, Hannah. I want to give you everything you want, but the thought of anything bad happening is killing me."

He'd had those fears since the second day we'd learned that I was pregnant.

He'd been researching, and he'd been reading about everything bad that could happen to me during pregnancy, no matter how miniscule the chances were of any of those things actually happening.

"Nothing bad will happen," I said gently. "It'll be fabulous. I'll be your wife on our honeymoon. Nothing will make me happier than that."

It would probably take a while for Tanner to realize that my pregnancy was perfectly normal, and that nothing was going to happen to me.

Hopefully, things would be different in two months.

I wasn't going to convince myself that he wouldn't be protective, but he'd get used to the fact that being pregnant didn't mean I was fragile.

"I'll be overjoyed when you're officially mine," he rumbled possessively.

"I'm already yours," I teased. "But I'm really excited about the wedding, and I'm not doing much planning this time."

Tanner had gotten the ball rolling himself. We'd picked a tranquil, beautiful, and very exclusive location because Tanner had insisted on it. The wedding venue was outside of central Las Vegas, but the reception was happening in the city.

I'd asked him to limit the attendance to just close friends and family to keep it intimate and personal.

Everyone who mattered would be there, and that was all I really wanted.

Guests from here would be flown by private jet to and from Vegas.

His cousin, Shelby, and her husband, Wyatt, would be flying in from San Diego, so the guest list was complete in my mind.

What we were planning was actually my dream wedding now.

I hadn't picked a dress yet, but I was looking.

I was hoping I wouldn't be showing at three months, but I was trying to pick something that would work if I did have a little baby bump.

"I have something that will make me a little happier until we do get married," Tanner said as he released me and reached into the pocket of his suit.

My breath caught as he pulled out something that looked like a ring box from his suit pocket. "Tanner," I said breathlessly. "It's not possible that my ring is ready yet."

We'd just met with a jeweler less than a week ago, and it was a ring that was being custom made.

He shot me that devilish, cocky grin that I'd come to adore. "Sweetheart, when are you going to learn that your man can make almost anything happen?"

I let out a long, happy sigh.

When Tanner Remington wanted something, he got exactly what he wanted.

Although I'd come a long way in accepting his outrageous wealth, I was still getting used to that.

He lifted the lid of the box, and I stared at the beautiful ring with pure awe and amazement.

It was exactly what we'd asked for, and it was the most gorgeous ring I'd ever seen.

"It's beautiful," I said as my eyes welled up with tears.

Tanner and I had needed to compromise on the ring.

He'd wanted something big and prominent with a ton of carats.

I'd wanted something more delicate and subtle.

In the end, he'd let me have exactly what I wanted as long as the diamonds were excellent quality.

Nobody was going to be permanently blinded by the flashiness of my ring, but it was still extravagantly expensive.

There was a large center stone surrounded by small stones that looked like the petals of a flower, and those stones were entirely set in platinum.

Tanner took the ring from the box, and tossed the box aside. "I'm doing this right this time, with your ring. Marry me, Hannah?"

I looked into his eyes, and my heart skittered from the romantic gesture and the sincerity in his eyes.

I didn't say that I'd already said *yes*.

I didn't mention that we were already planning that wedding and the honeymoon.

I also didn't bother to remind him that we were already living together.

I fell into his heartfelt, beautiful gaze and whispered, "Yes. You're the only man I've ever wanted, Tanner."

After he put the ring on my finger, I threw myself into his arms, my damn emotions all over the place. "Thank you," I said before I kissed him.

The embrace was slow and thorough, a silent promise to spend the rest of our lives loving each other.

"Don't thank me," he insisted huskily after he'd released my lips. "I just got exactly what I wanted. My ring on your finger."

I nuzzled his neck as I answered, "Take me to bed, Tanner, and I'll get exactly what I want, too."

It had been a week since we'd had that hot sex in his office.

Tanner had been incredibly supportive about my pregnancy and uber protective, but he hadn't touched me sexually since he'd gotten the news that I was pregnant.

For some reason, he was afraid he'd hurt me if we had sex, even though the doctor had assured him that wasn't the case.

"You're sick and fatigued right now, Hannah," he said gruffly.

I nipped his ear. "I'm only a little nauseated in the morning, and I'm not that fatigued. My hormones are raging, and I want you, Tanner."

I reached down and stroked his rampant erection.

It wasn't the fact that Tanner didn't want me because I was pregnant.

He was afraid he'd somehow hurt me if he fucked me while I was pregnant, even though his rational mind knew better.

"Fuck!" he cursed as he gripped my ass. "Do you think I don't want you, too, Hannah? But I fucked you like a caveman in my office, and you were pregnant."

"And it was incredibly orgasmic," I told him softly. "I'd like a repeat performance please. I'm not going to break, Tanner. I'm exactly the same woman in the same condition I was a week ago, and I'm fine."

"I have zero control when it comes to you," he said hoarsely.

"And I love it when you lose control," I said seductively as I lowered the zipper of his pants.

I loved this man more than I could ever put into words, and I really needed him to take me to bed so I could show him just how much I loved him.

"Hannah," he said with a groan this time. "Are you going to make me crazy like this for the rest of our lives?"

"That's the plan," I said with a smile.

He scooped me up into his arms. "Just remember that you asked for it," he said as he carried me toward the stairs. "I'll try to keep things under control."

I let out a delighted laugh as he carried me up the stairs and to our bedroom.

His attempt to keep his control failed miserably.

And I loved every single moment of it.

Epilogue

Hannah

Two Months Later...

"**W**here do you think we are right now?" I asked Tanner excitedly.

Tanner grinned at me as he climbed into bed with me completely naked. "Probably the same place we were when you asked five minutes ago. Somewhere over the Pacific Ocean."

I sighed, my heart and soul so full of joy that I could barely contain it.

We were finally on our honeymoon.

And on our way to Australia.

We were in his private jet, getting ready for bed, winging our way across the world for the honeymoon I'd been dreaming about for years.

We'd left directly from Vegas after spending a few days there in the city after our wedding.

I sighed again as I thought about the beautiful wedding ceremony and the reception that had taken place just a few days ago.

It had been…perfect.

It was strange that I'd once envisioned anything different as my dream wedding.

Kaleb, Devon, and Wyatt had stood up for Tanner.

Anna, Lauren, and Reese had stood up for me.

We'd been married outdoors, and the grounds we'd been married on had been like something out of a fairytale.

Beautiful flowers everywhere…check.

A breathtaking gazebo that had been built custom just for our wedding…check.

The most handsome, thoughtful, and incredible groom on the planet…check.

Everyone I loved present to listen to Tanner and I say our vows…check.

Anna singing a song she'd written just for us…check.

Just thinking about that day almost brought tears to my eyes all over again.

In the end, I hadn't needed to pick out a wedding dress.

Tanner had commissioned a designer to do my dress because I hadn't been able to find anything that felt just right for a pregnant bride who might end up having a baby bump on her wedding day.

That baby bump had never shown, but I'd had the most beautiful wedding gown I'd ever seen.

Everything about that day had felt like it was always meant to be exactly the way it had happened.

"That's an awful lot of sighs coming from you, sweetheart. Everything okay?" Tanner asked as he pulled me close so I could rest my head on his shoulder.

We were both naked, and I savored the skin-on-skin contact.

I'd probably never take for granted just how good it felt to be this close to Tanner.

"I was just thinking about how perfect our wedding was," I told him honestly.

"As good as the one you planned years ago?" he questioned.

"Better," I said emphatically.

Tanner and I might never forget our past, and I'd decided I really didn't want to forget all of it.

We'd spent so many good years together.

But we had put the bad parts behind us now.

"Are you feeling okay?" he asked.

He'd asked that question more than once today.

He was still a little anxious about taking me far away when I was pregnant, but he wasn't quite as panicked as he'd been two months ago.

My morning sickness was gone.

My energy levels were just as good as they'd been before my pregnancy.

And I felt pretty fantastic compared to the beginning of my pregnancy.

I looked up and met his gaze. "I feel fabulous, and I've never been this happy in my entire life. We're married, we're on our way to a honeymoon in Australia, and we're going to have a child."

It was still hard to believe how much my life had changed in a pretty short period of time.

"I think you're almost as excited about this trip as you were about our wedding," Tanner said as he winked at me.

God, I loved this man.

I knew he still had his reservations about this honeymoon, but he was going to do everything possible not to spoil my excitement.

"We've wanted to take this trip for well over a decade," I explained. "It feels almost surreal that we're actually going now. Honestly, everything feels surreal to me right now, Tanner. We're actually married."

"Thank fuck!" he said emphatically. "I think this has been the longest two months of my entire life. It wasn't easy knowing that you were pregnant with my child and we weren't married yet."

"You wanted to be married because I was pregnant?" I teased, knowing full well exactly why Tanner had wanted to marry me.

"I wanted to be married because I wanted you to be mine," he corrected. "But you being pregnant made it even worse, which I didn't think was even possible."

I smiled. "I think I've been yours since the day we met. I couldn't imagine being married to anyone else."

Tanner adjusted our bodies until I was on my back, his warm body covering mine. "You've always been the only woman I've ever loved, Hannah," he said solemnly as he looked down at me. "Now that we're married, you're stuck with me. I'm never letting you go."

I wrapped my arms around his neck. "I've loved you almost my entire adult life, Tanner. You've always been my everything. Do you think I'm crazy enough to let you go? Did I tell you that you're the hottest man on the planet today?"

His solemn expression suddenly transformed into a wicked grin. "Yeah, but it doesn't hurt to hear it again."

I moved my body against his suggestively. "How about if I just show you how hot I think you are."

I could feel how hard he was, and my body was aching to be intimately connected to him.

"Hannah," he growled in that warning voice I adored. "It's been a long day for you. You need to rest."

He'd gotten over his hesitations about making love to me because I was pregnant, but he was still incredibly protective about my well-being.

"I'm not the least bit tired," I argued.

"I'm trying to be considerate," he said in a voice that told me his control was slipping.

"And I'm trying to seduce you," I answered, amused.

"You don't need to seduce me," he said in a self-mocking tone. "All you need to do is stand in the same room with me and I'm screwed."

"Make love to me, Tanner," I said, my voice heavy with desire. "We're on our honeymoon, and I need you."

"Fuck!" he cursed. "You know that hearing you say that makes me crazy."

I loved the way that Tanner always wanted to protect me and take care of me, but that wasn't what I wanted from him right now.

We were always honest with each other, and I *did* need him.

"I love you," I said, my heart so full of happiness that I couldn't hold those words back anymore.

"Now you know you're in trouble," he rumbled, his eyes blazing with heat as he held my gaze.

"God, I really hope so," I answered as I fell into his gorgeous blue eyes.

"You know I want you, Hannah," he said in a tormented voice. "But I also want to take care of you. You're pregnant with my child for fuck's sake, and we've been up since early this morning."

"Take care of me by making love to me," I suggested. "I'll sleep much better."

I could feel it the moment his control snapped and he capitulated.

"I love you, too, Hannah, but I'm not sure I'm going to make it through this pregnancy a sane man," he growled. "My protective instincts and my carnal instincts are constantly going to be at war with each other."

I let out a final sigh against his lips as they came down on mine.

I loved Tanner's fierce protectiveness, and he *would* make it through this pregnancy with his sanity intact because I loved him the same way that he loved me.

Eventually, he'd realize that he could have both of those instincts at the same time without them fighting against each other.

"I love you so much, Tanner," I told him when he finally released my mouth. "Just love me. That's all I need right now."

I'd make him happy and sleep...later.

"I'm going to love you for the rest of our lives, Hannah," he said hoarsely as he trailed his lips along my jawline. "That's who I am and what I do now."

My heart tripped because that heartfelt declaration meant everything to me.

I was going to love him for the rest of our lives, too, and I was going to savor every moment because it had taken us so long to get to our happy ending.

"We're taking this slow tonight, Hannah," Tanner said in a muffled voice because his mouth was pressed against my skin.

I smiled as I threaded my hands into his hair.

He said that almost every night, and he always tried, but Tanner and I usually didn't do slow and easy all that well.

Honestly, I didn't really care how it was going to happen.

As long as we were intimately connected, I was going to be ecstatically happy.

All I wanted was to be close to Tanner.

Moments later, Tanner passionately proceeded to give me *exactly* what I wanted.

~*The End*~

Please visit me at:
http://www.authorjsscott.com
http://www.facebook.com/authorjsscott

You can write to me at
jsscott_author@hotmail.com

You can also tweet
@AuthorJSScott

Please sign up for my Newsletter for updates,
new releases and exclusive excerpts.

Books by J. S. Scott:

Billionaire Obsession Series

The Billionaire's Obsession~Simon
Heart of the Billionaire
The Billionaire's Salvation
The Billionaire's Game
Billionaire Undone~Travis
Billionaire Unmasked~Jason
Billionaire Untamed~Tate
Billionaire Unbound~Chloe
Billionaire Undaunted~Zane
Billionaire Unknown~Blake
Billionaire Unveiled~Marcus
Billionaire Unloved~Jett
Billionaire Unwed~Zeke
Billionaire Unchallenged~Carter
Billionaire Unattainable~Mason
Billionaire Undercover~Hudson

Billionaire Unexpected~Jax
Billionaire Unnoticed~Cooper
Billionaire Unclaimed~Chase
Billionaire Unreachable~Wyatt
Billionaire Unexplained~Kaleb
Billionaire Unforgettable~Tanner
Billionaire Undeceived~Devon

British Billionaires Series

Tell Me You're Mine
Tell Me I'm Yours
Tell Me This Is Forever

Sinclair Series

The Billionaire's Christmas
No Ordinary Billionaire
The Forbidden Billionaire
The Billionaire's Touch
The Billionaire's Voice
The Billionaire Takes All
The Billionaire's Secret
Only A Millionaire

Accidental Billionaires

Ensnared
Entangled
Enamored
Enchanted
Endeared

Walker Brothers Series

Release
Player
Damaged

The Sentinel Demons

The Sentinel Demons: The Complete Collection
A Dangerous Bargain
A Dangerous Hunger
A Dangerous Fury
A Dangerous Demon King

The Vampire Coalition Series

The Vampire Coalition: The Complete Collection
The Rough Mating of a Vampire (Prelude)
Ethan's Mate
Rory's Mate
Nathan's Mate
Liam's Mate
Daric's Mate

Changeling Encounters Series

Changeling Encounters: The Complete Collection
Mate Of The Werewolf
The Dangers Of Adopting A Werewolf
All I Want For Christmas Is A Werewolf

The Pleasures of His Punishment

The Pleasures of His Punishment: The Complete Collection
The Billionaire Next Door
The Millionaire and the Librarian
Riding with the Cop
Secret Desires of the Counselor
In Trouble with the Boss
Rough Ride with a Cowboy
Rough Day for the Teacher
A Forfeit for a Cowboy
Just what the Doctor Ordered
Wicked Romance of a Vampire

The Curve Collection: Big Girls and Bad Boys Series

The Curve Collection: The Complete Collection
The Curve Ball
The Beast Loves Curves
Curves by Design

Writing as Lane Parker

Dearest Stalker
Dearest Protector
A Christmas Dream
A Valentine's Dream
Lost: A Mountain Man Rescue Romance

A Dark Horse Novel w/ Cali MacKay

Bound
Hacked

Taken By A Trillionaire Series

Virgin for the Trillionaire by Ruth Cardello
Virgin for the Prince by J.S. Scott
Virgin to Conquer by Melody Anne
Prince Bryan: Taken By A Trillionaire

Other Titles

Well Played w/Ruth Cardello

Printed in Great Britain
by Amazon

54303439R00137